It Goes Like This

It Goes Like This

MIEL MORELAND

FEIWEL AND FRIENDS
NEW YORK

A Feiwel and Friends Book
An imprint of Macmillan Publishing Group, LLC
120 Broadway, New York, NY 10271
fiercereads.com

Our books may be purchased in bulk for promotional, educational, or business
use. Please contact your local bookseller or the Macmillan Corporate and
Premium Sales Department at (800) 221-7945 ext. 5442 or by email at
MacmillanSpecialMarkets@macmillan.com.

Library of Congress Cataloging-in-Publication Data
Names: Moreland, Miel, author.
Title: It goes like this / Miel Moreland.
Description: First edition. | New York : Feiwel & Friends, 2021. |
    Audience: Ages 13-18. | Audience: Grades 10-12. | Summary: "Eva,
    Celeste, Gina, and Steph used to think their friendship was unbreakable.
    After all, they've been through a lot together, including the
    astronomical rise of Moonlight Overthrow, the world-famous queer pop
    band they formed in middle school. But after a sudden falling out leads
    to the dissolution of the teens' band, their friendship, and Eva and
    Celeste's starry-eyed romance, nothing is the same"— Provided by
    publisher.
Identifiers: LCCN 2020038386 | ISBN 9781250767486 (hardcover)
Subjects: CYAC: Best friends—Fiction. | Friendship—Fiction. | Bands
    (Music)—Fiction. | Lesbians—Fiction.
Classification: LCC PZ7.1.M6693 It 2021 | DDC [Fic]—dc23

LC record available at https://lccn.loc.gov/2020038386

Emojis © by Denis Gorelkin / Shutterstock

First edition, 2021
Book design by Trisha Previte
Feiwel and Friends logo designed by Filomena Tuosto

Printed in the United States of America

ISBN 978-1-250-76748-6 (hardcover)
10 9 8 7 6 5 4 3 2 1

To everyone who has ever fallen in love with a song,
and to all those who believed in mine

JUNE 2021

moonlite-babe:

Cosmic Queers, gather round! If you missed every article this morning, here's what we know:

Celeste and Gina went to the same club last night (birthday party for celebrity I am not even naming because I don't want to deal with the irrelevant anons)

Gina was SMOKING HOT as per usual

Celeste also very, very nice, no complaints from my gay heart here

They look friendly in pics, so ::cue potential reunion headlines::

Look, babes. Obviously I'm not their managers or PR folks, and obviously if Moonlight Overthrow was going to get back together, this would be a nice little golden seeding opportunity. But. It's been a year and a half. Gina and Celeste both have ongoing contracts and upcoming projects. So, a reunion? Nawt. Happening.

#moonlight overthrow #business as usual #reunion rumors #celeste rogers #gina wright #look I'm sorry I'm trying to be profesh but Gina's entire makeup game was on FIRE last night

maybeitsmoonlight:

I'd give my first child for a Moonlight Overthrow reunion tour (lbr) and I sooooo appreciate the opportunity to see 2/4 (!!!) looking fierce and friendly, but yeah if there's any PR angle here it's gotta be because they're looking to get some headlines for their current stuff.

OT4 might be over, but we've still got some of our iconic queer band giving us quality queer content you know?

Celeste is doing her thing.

Gina is doing her thing.

Eva. Her thing.

Steph . . .

#MO updates #CR #GW

EVA

Seeing the pictures is like someone pouring a bucket of ice water over her head. The kind of shock where you can't even breathe.

"Eva," her mom says, still in her ear, because she's still clutching her phone.

Eva tries to reply, but sound is beyond her.

Her other hand rests, shaking, on her tablet. She scrolls. Another photo, another, each a discordant note because *this wasn't supposed to happen*. Gina, Celeste, a party. The two of them, together, in public. Without her. (Without Steph, either, for that matter.)

Eva wants to throw the tablet across the room.

She wants to dive into it, insert herself into the picture, be laughing and close, for the world to see.

"Eva?" her mom says again, more worried than the first time. "I wanted to make sure that you didn't find out from Twitter."

Sometimes Eva regrets teaching her mom about Twitter.

Sometimes Eva tries to pretend she regrets Moonlight Overthrow.

"Yeah," Eva manages. "Yes, okay. Thanks." If hurt is sadness overlaid with anger, Eva bumps the anger way up. "I mean, I'm in L.A. too, it's not like they don't know that. We have a freaking group chat, technically."

They all still change phone numbers a lot—even Steph—and keeping the current number in the chat is all the direct contact they've had after those final meetings a year and a half ago.

After that final breakup.

At least, that's what Eva thought. Maybe Celeste and Gina have stayed friends, quietly, without her.

"Evie, you've had other opportunities too," her mom chides gently.

She means opportunities to reach out. To reconnect.

But her mom also knows why Eva wouldn't contribute to the soundtrack for one of Gina's movies. She knows why Eva didn't bother to return the call from Celeste's label—their old label—asking if Eva would write a song for what she, along with the rest of the fandom, was still thinking of as CR2. Celeste's second album turned into the probably-going-platinum *Silhouette*, no thanks to Eva.

To her credit, the rep called back the next day and left Eva a second awkward voice mail, this one apologizing for intruding. She assured Eva this was all her idea, all the label's idea, nothing to do with Celeste. As if Eva hadn't known all that. With Hayley Kiyoko and Ariana Grande featured on separate *Silhouette* songs, it wasn't like Celeste was hurting for collaborators.

"*Work* isn't the same," says Eva, keeping her voice harsh so it doesn't wobble. "They went to a party."

She continues to scroll through one of the tabloid articles, each additional photo accompanied by some new tidbit: attendance numbers at Celeste's latest concert, the expected release month of Gina's new Netflix series, what they're both wearing. Gina's natural curls are longer than they were in the spring, when she'd had a short Afro while filming, and she's working with a new stylist: bright, bold colors, shades that wouldn't work on her pasty-white ex-bandmates.

Former bandmates, Eva means. That's what the press always

writes. She doesn't know how their publicist got them all on board, but they were, they are. That's what Eva said in interviews, back when she was still giving interviews. There's something very bitter about that "ex" prefix, and they couldn't have that.

And Celeste?

Celeste is . . .

Well.

In one picture, her hand is on Gina's arm. She has a fresh, silvery manicure—nothing new there—and there are blue highlights in her hair, which are.

Gorgeous.

The word lodges in Eva's throat.

"Try not to get too caught up in this, okay?" her mom says.

Fifty percent of her ex (former) band went to the hottest party in town last night. The last time they'd gone to a party as a foursome, Steph was the only one who could vote.

Getting *caught up in this* isn't a choice.

Her mom clears her throat. "Any plans for the day?"

"Homework."

"It's just the one summer class, right?"

Eva's nineteen years old, a chart-topping songwriter, and a former member of a two-time Grammy Award–winning band—and her mom is still asking about her schoolwork. Eva wants to be annoyed about it—the worrying, the insistence that she not dwell for more than thirty seconds on people who used to shine so brightly in her life—but there's a little tendril of gratitude, too. It loosens her shoulders. She flips her tablet facedown on her bed.

"Hope you're okay with whatever weird December graduation speaker they get two years from now," Eva says.

Her mom's right: it's just the one summer class this year, but Eva's planning on taking a full load the next two summers so she can graduate two quarters early.

"You know I will be," her mom says.

"And hey, you'll get to see me onstage again, how about that?" Eva tries to keep her voice light. After the years of media training, you'd think she'd be able to do it, but even ex (former) pop stars can't lie to their moms.

"I'll be just as proud for this one as I was for all the others," her mom says.

She really will be, is the thing. Eva's not sure she's there yet. Most days, she thinks she is. Today is an exception to all her new rules.

They hang up, and Eva conducts a quick self-survey about whether it's worth getting dressed before breakfast. No class today, no studio sessions, so she's free to never change, if she doesn't want to. Most of the time, she still goes through the motions. It was freeing, those first couple of months, to be able to pick out her own clothes. It was the only good thing, really. Eva clung hard.

She's kept a stylist on retainer—for the interviews she did right after, for that awful awards show in which she was the only one on hand to not accept the Grammy they didn't win—but dresses herself, for the most part. She hasn't lost the habit of getting most of her clothes tailored, though. It really does make a difference.

Eva wanders downstairs in her pajamas, opening the curtains as she goes. The midmorning Hollywood Hills sun streams in. She flops onto one of the couches, turning the pictures over in her mind, one element at a time, like if she can focus on just one thing—Gina's hoop earrings, Celeste's wedges—the whole will hurt less.

It doesn't.

They can't do this without me, Eva thinks. *They're not supposed to do* anything *without me.*

The four of them scattered to the four winds: fine. But cutting Eva out like this? With no warning?

Stop, she tries to tell herself. *Don't go there.*

But she sinks into it, falls under it, the feeling weighing her down stronger than gravity. Around her, the house seems to pulsate with emptiness, a silent, remonstrative echo.

Nineteen is too young to have a house this big, except in L.A., and she couldn't leave L.A., after. She wanted to stay stateside, a music city, and Celeste had already claimed New York. Where else was Eva going to go? Nashville?

So it was L.A. and a six-bedroom house for Eva.

Besides, she also had to think about where she was going to go to college. She's the only one of them who has, properly, at least. Gina did an acting intensive last summer, or something, whatever they're called. She's had some training, Eva means. They're not casting her just for the publicity boost, and Eva will face down anyone who insinuates that they are.

Privately, that is. Anonymously. Eva doesn't do those kinds of interviews anymore.

But there are limited options for a child star who wants to get a four-year degree without being a total freak on campus: Harvard, Brown, NYU, Stanford. And UCLA.

She had to meet with an academic adviser before her first quarter, who'd been surprised when Eva said she didn't plan on adding a minor in music industry (a real option, who knew?) to her comparative literature major.

Eva's already put in three years full-time in the industry, thanks to the band, and she's coming up on two years part-time, thanks to the breakup. Luckily, she's in the part of the business that will substitute experience for education. Thirty-plus songwriting credits and counting, four number one singles (and counting, probably). It's not usually a hard sell.

Eva leverages herself off the couch and wanders into the kitchen. She puts Halsey on her speakers as she makes a smoothie for breakfast. It's been that kind of morning. You need a voice like hers when you see your ex looking beautiful on the arm of another girl.

Even though Eva knows it's never been like that between Celeste and Gina.

Even so.

MAY 2021
CELESTE

"Celeste, what a journey you've been on since you were last here. *Landlocked*, of course, debuted at number two last year, and then *Silhouette* just two weeks ago at number one—what a feat. Congratulations."

"Thanks, Jane. I'm so grateful to all my fans who have stuck with me from my Moonlight Overthrow days, and to all the new fans who have joined me since *Landlocked*, who trust me enough as an artist to give me that number one spot. It's an amazing feeling, and I'm so thankful."

(*The Just Late Enough Show Starring Jane Leigh*)

INTERVIEWER: Now, Celeste, I've got to ask, the girl you sing about in this new album—is she the same one you sang about in *Landlocked*?

CR: I think what's important to keep in mind about music, about musicians, is that we're artists. We're storytellers. Of course, I work hard to keep the emotion in my music genuine, but the particulars of a story aren't necessarily real, or maybe they are, but not to me. So these songs are a collection of stories, some mine, some not. Sometimes they're not really about a girl, but a feeling, a place. Sometimes *I'm* the girl. But ultimately, it doesn't matter who or what I was thinking of when I wrote the song. It matters what my fans are thinking of when they're listening, who or what the song is about for *them*. That's the magic of it.

(Transcript of *Rolling Stone* interview)

"Celeste, thanks for taking the time to talk to us today."

"Of course, thanks for having me."

"So, your second solo album is out now, amazing success—congratulations, by the way."

"Thank you."

"Are you hoping this will finally put reunion rumors to rest?"

"I'm so humbled that Moonlight Overthrow continues to have fans who are rooting for the band. I hope they keep loving the three albums we did as a group—I'm very proud of how hard we worked on them—and that they'll join all of us on our new, individual journeys."

(Apple Music interview)

"Celeste, in the run-up to your first album release, you refused to answer almost any questions about Moonlight Overthrow. Is the new approach just for promo?"

"Celeste, can you confirm you're doing a collab with Hailee Steinfeld?"

"Celeste, the girl your album is about—has she listened to it?"

"Celeste, who is your album about?"

"Celeste!"

EVA

Eva does some of her reading for class, then heads online.

Presumably some Tumblr fans are inventing feuds or reunions or anything else chaotic or dramatic, but she doesn't know it. She cultivated her secret Tumblr carefully: no drama, no hate, OT4 'til the moon crashes into the sea.

They all had secret Tumblrs, at the beginning when they were their own PR, and then in the middle, when they wanted to be able to check in on the fandom without PR censorship. Eva's the only one who's kept hers.

There's a message waiting for her when she logs on.

kaystar: Assuming you've seen the pictures already? Our girls ::heart eyes:: so gorg

Eva's reply is instinctive.

celestial-vision: Stellar, as per usual ::heart eyes::

Before the band broke up, she didn't reblog anything, much less make original posts or talk to anyone. But after . . .

Right after, there were so many gifsets and photosets and edits and testimonials, so much love for who they'd been for all these strangers, and she couldn't walk away from that. She couldn't keep her bandmates, but she was desperate to be able to keep this love, if only in Tumblr archive format. Somewhere along the line, Eva started adding corrections or clarifications to other people's posts, if they were getting the name of Gina's PA wrong or mixing up the terms of Celeste's solo deal. Business stuff. Nothing you'd have to be an insider to know, just a committed, research-savvy fan who could understand and explain.

Thanks to the not-insider insider info, Eva started collecting followers. She tried not to talk to them individually, privately— she drew the line at lying in a DM—but Kay sent good questions, off anon, and Eva liked her tags.

> **kaystar**: Do you think Eva's jealous they got together without her? The party was in LA, after all

> **kaystar**: (I know you don't really follow Eva. Indulge me this once?)

Eva tries to limit her narcissism here. It's a delicate balance— she can't be too obvious about ignoring herself, or she'll get called out on it, accused of not being a true OT4 stan.

(*Honey*, she sometimes thinks when this happens, *I'm the original*.)

> **celestial-vision**: I don't know. I don't think she would know the bday boy. So why would she be there?

> **kaystar**: But it's LA! And famous people! You don't actually have to know people to go to their party, right? It didn't seem like super intimate or anything. It's not like C's ever worked with him

celestial-vision: Point. But C's still doing the public celebrity thing

Eva has spent most of her teenage years with her body being evaluated from every angle, in every time zone, by stylists and photographers and so many fans. So many not-fans. Every puberty-born curve immediately accessible for scrutiny. It's nice to no longer be required to go to flashy parties—and really nice to have a space where people only know her as her double rainbow icon.

kaystar: Ooh, you think maybe Eva went but there just aren't pics?? They didn't want to stir up real reunion rumors?

kaystar: WHAT IF THEY'RE ALL HANGING OUT. (The three of them I mean.)

Eva's stomach twists, as it always does at the implication that Steph is no longer part of even their post-band "all." It was what Steph wanted, but Eva still aches every day that she can come online and see Gina and Celeste laughing with talk show hosts and stunning on red carpets with new clothes and new haircuts, while Steph is frozen in 2019.

celestial-vision: I feel like we would have heard if Eva was there

kaystar: You're probably right

kaystar: She might not have even been in LA last night. She could be visiting her parents or something. She hasn't updated any of her sm in almost a week

Eva could be visiting her parents. Since her summer class meets only once a week, it's not like she wouldn't have time to visit Chicago for a few days. She doesn't want to worry her fans. Or her parents.

celestial-vision: You know I don't follow any of them on social media

kaystar: I know, girl. I know. You follow me instead

celestial-vision: 😙

celestial-vision: Eva or no Eva, they looked happy. And together. I'll take that every day of the week

Around three, Eva changes into her workout clothes and texts Lydia. (So today is not quite an all-day-pajama day. It's eight a.m. somewhere.)

Eva
About to leave for jazz . . . invitation's still on the table

Lydia
lol I love how you never give up on this

Go to your pop star dance class

Former pop star, Eva thinks, even as she replies with a stuck-out-tongue emoji, followed by the rolling-eyes one.

Maybe at first she took the classes with a *just in case* propelling every turn and combination, but she's not waiting on that kind of phone call anymore. Dancing just feels like *hers* now, something from her old life that she gets to take with her, but privately. Something nobody else owns. Every other part of her is still so wrapped up in words—writing songs, writing essays—it's a relief to move and nothing else.

> **Lydia**
> Hang out Tuesday or Wednesday?

> **Eva**
> Can't do Wednesday, but tomorrow yes!

> **Lydia**
> I'll text you when I'm leaving work

Lydia was a sophomore when they met during winter quarter, but she's planning to take the fall off to work. Eva offered to let Lydia live with her, rent-free, or at least rent-seriously-reduced. In her mind, it made perfect sense: Eva had empty bedrooms that were never going to be filled by reconciled bandmates; Lydia was strapped for cash. They might as well have been in an Amy Winehouse song, though: *no, no, no.*

During winter registration, Eva thought about taking some 101 version of astronomy, astrophysics—*space*, essentially—before she decided somebody would leak that to the press. Coming from a band named Moonlight Overthrow, there would be a story there the way there wouldn't be if she took an environmental class for her science requirement instead. She's long since gotten over her initial disappointment, since if she'd taken astronomy, she wouldn't have met Lydia. Lydia had the same eyes-on-the-prize, no-nonsense drive that had made the band work so well. And Lydia's goals now aligned with Eva's: no drama, just a degree. They mocked couples on every kind of *House Hunters* while devouring the snacks left by Eva's part-time chef, and TMZ didn't report on her class schedule.

A single Eva had written for a rising pop phenom debuted at number one the day of their midterm; Gina's first day of filming for her Netflix series was the day of their first lab; Celeste was getting ready to release *Silhouette*. Steph . . . So at first, there was a deliberate conversational no-fly zone around Moonlight Overthrow, her former friends, and Eva's solo songwriting career. By the end of spring quarter, though, it wasn't so much a no-fly zone as . . . irrelevant. Sometimes Eva got second (and third, fourth, and fifth) glances when they went out. Sometimes a Moonlight Overthrow song came on the radio in her car. Sometimes a song of Celeste's came on instead.

But what did that have to do with *them*, with ice cream after a morning at Manhattan Beach, with poring over the online course catalog when it came time for Eva to register for the fall? Their friendship didn't revolve around not talking about the other part of Eva's life; it revolved around this one.

This is how the week goes: Monday, homework and jazz class. Tuesday, homework and Lydia, at Eva's house because Lydia's got student loans and, thus, three roommates. Wednesday, hip-hop, then actual class, then a late meeting with her accountant. Thursday, Eva makes herself sit down at her piano (a Baldwin, and her Christmas present to herself after the second tour) until she's written two shitty songs as a warm-up and manages a hook and a workable opening verse for a song with real potential. When she *knows* a line is going to make the final cut, something about it lodges between her ribs, vibrating at just the right frequency, a perfect fit. She doesn't have her band or a whole group of friends, but she has this.

On Friday, there's core followed by ballet, followed by another shift at the piano. In a few weeks, Eva will go into the studio with a producer to refine lyrics and replace her acoustic draft with a demo for something meant for radio. Maybe one day she'll get better about songwriting with the performers themselves, like the co-writers she worked with in her early MO days, but she can't make herself do that quite yet. If they want her words, that's what they'll get.

Eva has to schedule her life like this, something productive every day, so she feels like she's working. So the emptiness of the bandless days doesn't overwhelm her. She laughs a little when she thinks about it. Three years of overwork, long tours, late recording sessions, and endless press, and now she doesn't know what to do with all the time she has to rest?

On Saturday, there's a party.

Eva chooses a sleeveless blue dress that hits halfway down her thighs, with a high boat neckline in front that scoops down in the back. She likes to think there's a shade of *likely queer*, too, but that's probably just her imagination. Not that Eva needs the help: she's been out to her parents since she was twelve and to the world since she was fourteen and it became relevant for the world to know.

All the world isn't going to be at this party. Just a little entertainment industry slice of it.

Olivia, the host, was a producer on their second and third albums, and Eva has worked with her since. Unless they're an asshole or you're switching genres, you don't stop working with someone who got you three top-ten singles, two albums in a row, and Eva's too far removed from the industry now to bother to go to assholes' parties.

She takes a selfie for Instagram—updated social media, check—and grabs her keys. Lydia's babysitting her cousins tonight, or Eva would have invited her. Lydia might not have accepted anyway: she's more into pizza and *Parks and Rec* than parties she'll have to get glammed up for. Eva can respect that.

When Eva walks in, Olivia greets her with a hug and presses a gin and tonic into her hands.

"Deja and Sylvie are here, too!" Olivia tells her. "They're around here somewhere—check out back by the pool, maybe?"

"Thanks," Eva says, her voice rising to compensate for a sudden influx of people in the entryway. Neither Deja, Olivia's producing protégée, nor Sylvie, a sound engineer, knew Eva in her Moonlight Overthrow days, and it's always a relief to talk to people who only know her as herself, not as someone to be pitied for losing her band.

Olivia waves her toward the patio doors, and Eva slips out.

It's nearly the end of June. When Eva first moved to L.A.— when they all first moved to L.A., at the beginning of high school, at the beginning of everything—she was startled by how much the temperature would drop in the evenings. She kept forgetting to bring sweaters. Celeste wouldn't give Eva hers, but she'd tuck Eva into her side and wrap her arms around her. They didn't start dating for another year, but you'd better believe Eva was already falling. Every touch was already sparks, skidding across her skin.

Eva spots Deja and Sylvie on the far side of the pool, talking with a couple of other people whose faces are in deep shadow. Chances are she'll know them; the music industry might be Big Business, but it's not really a *big* business.

She makes her way around the pool, pausing now and then to exchange hellos with anyone who's more than a passing acquaintance. She coughs a little as she passes a loose cluster of smokers. There's music playing from outdoor speakers; whenever the patio doors open, a different tune spills out from inside, random song ft. random other song. She wants to get caught up in it, to sink into the ebb and flow of this kind of party, but—even a party where she's a little known and a little loved would be easier with a real friend.

She holds her glass close to her chest, shielding it with her arm so she doesn't spill it on increasingly tipsy people's designer clothing. (It's only quarter past eleven, people. Have some self-respect.) She breaks out from the last bunch standing between her and Deja and Sylvie. Sylvie hasn't seen her yet, but she shifts, and so does the person standing next to her, and it's—she's—

Celeste.

EVA

Eva drops her gin and tonic.

Shit.

She was still holding it close, and it splashes all down her front. She's expecting the glass to smash spectacularly, to shatter next to her foot and spread its jagged seeds, but it must be that unbreakable kind. It clatters onto the concrete and rolls into the pool, where it bobs on the surface for a heart-clenching moment before sinking into the chlorinated water.

The night wind pushes the wet fabric against her skin. She shivers.

Celeste stares at Eva, her mouth open slightly, maybe in a gasp Eva lost beneath the party noise, maybe an aborted hello. Eva doesn't think anyone outside of their little group has noticed; it's all shadows and smoke back here, literally. She feels like shouting, *Don't you know how bad smoking is for your voice?*

For *hers*, not that it matters much these days.

For Celeste's, which does. That's a multimillion-dollar voice right there, and Eva's lungs are filling with all this secondhand smoke and she is staring, staring, staring.

Celeste.

Here.

Oh my god.

"Let's get you inside," Deja says, breaking the frozen scene. "C'mon. Olivia will have something you can change into."

"I think I'll just go," Eva says, her words somehow coming out numb, automatic, even as her mind is spinning out in total panic.

She's still staring at Celeste, who hasn't said a word. Hasn't moved at all.

Celeste is wearing a light green dress that hugs her in all the right places, which is to say, all the places: boobs, hips, ass. Statement earrings, simple necklace. The backyard lighting makes her look like she's onstage, only her makeup's wrong for that.

"We should at least pat that down a bit," Sylvie says, appraising the wet stain.

A year and a half ago, they would have gone back to wherever they were staying—the hotel, if they were on tour, which was most of the time, an apartment if they weren't, which was almost never—and Celeste would have unzipped her. Slowly. Eased the dress off her shoulders. Stayed behind her while she ran a finger over the cold that had seeped from the drink through Eva's dress and onto her skin.

The middle of a party, standing in front of Celeste after Eva dropped her drink in shock, is probably not the time to start fantasizing about Celeste's hands skimming along her stomach, between her breasts. Definitely not.

"Gerry will have a sweatshirt for you in the car," Celeste says briskly. It's the first thing she's said directly to Eva since the breakup—the breakups.

"He's working for a Jenner now," Eva says.

It's like she's separated from her body, watching this scene at a distance. There are words, calm words, coming out of her mouth. But inside? Her brain is still filled with that jumbled static, surprise and curiosity and so much hurt, and against her will, a little hope—

"Oh," says Celeste.

"I drove myself."

A beat of silence. Another. The silence between them now is more devastating than anything Celeste could say. Because this silence says there's nothing left *to* say.

After everything, to be nothing?

"Let's get you inside," Sylvie says, echoing Deja. A hand on Eva's arm, this time, and suddenly she's thinking about the picture of Gina and Celeste, the two of them at a wilder party than this.

Eva thinks about saying something more to Celeste. Something bland: *It was good to see you.* Something defensive: *No one told me you'd be here.* Something angry: *Why the fuck haven't you called?* Something sad: *I miss you.*

A perfect four-part harmony.

She lets Sylvie tug her away.

The front of her dress has already started to dry, but Eva stands still while Sylvie pats it with a towel she unearths from a kitchen drawer.

"How awkward," Sylvie's saying, on repeat. "I had no idea you'd both be here. I thought . . ."

People who actually knew them invited one of them, or the other. Clearly, in the wake of the party last weekend, order has broken down. As if Celeste and Gina at a huge birthday bash is comparable to Celeste and Eva at a truly private party. Still, Olivia's never been shy about demanding that people get over their own egos for the sake of a larger goal.

"It's fine," Eva tries to tell her, even though it's obviously not. The dampness of her dress is evidence, and if she cries on the way home, at least her tears will blend right in.

The kitchen is crowded, people jostling for drinks and food and other people, and she's not sure Sylvie can hear her. Eva adds, "It was bound to happen."

It worked, when Eva was going to class and Celeste was making her albums in New York, and then going on tour. But—her mind catches on the calendar—Celeste's at the Staples Center on Monday night, and of course Olivia and all the rest wanted to see her. Of course she wanted to see them. Why hadn't Eva thought of that?

Sylvie walks Eva to the front door. "You're sure you want to go? You're sure you're okay?"

"I definitely need to go," Eva says. "I will be. I mean, I am. I just can't be here. It's fine."

"You're sober enough to drive?" Sylvie asks.

"Olivia sent me toward you guys as soon as I came in. I only had time to drink whatever didn't end up on my dress," Eva says. She adds, wryly, "So as you can tell, not much."

Sylvie laughs. "All right, then. Drive safe."

"Thanks for the assistance," Eva says. In her old life, Celeste would have teased her for pulling out too-formal words when she was uncomfortable. "Good night."

She drives home. It's not a long drive, but it's enough time to think about silence, and all the things she almost said to Celeste.

EVA

Eva wakes up on Sunday to more texts than she's used to these days, but the only message she cares about is in the never-used group chat.

> **Gina**
> I guess it's your turn next, Steph.

What?
She's still trying to parse the message when a new one comes in.

> **Celeste**
> I'm so sorry, Eva

Celeste must have told Gina they ran into each other last night.

> **Eva**
> The dress will survive, it's fine

It's not fine. Nothing about this is fine. Celeste is her ex—her only real ex, because she's never managed to get past "a first date" and into "definite relationship" since—and Celeste is . . . apologizing because Eva spilled a drink on herself last night. When Eva wasn't even drunk. When Celeste hasn't even apologized for any of the rest of it.

> **Gina**
> You're rocking that dress, babe.

Eva presses a hand against her mouth. She squeezes her eyes shut. Didn't she give them all her goddamn tears a year and a half ago? Didn't they take them all already? They can't come waltzing in now and demand more.

> **Celeste**
> Oh shit

> Not about the dress, though I'm sorry about that too

> You haven't seen . . .

Eva's stomach drops. Seen what? What is there to see?

Are Celeste and Gina forming a duo? Is Celeste . . . dating someone else? Eva's thoughts trip over each other, each worse than the last, each in a hurry to shore Eva up against some imminent, terrible news. Is Celeste engaged? Is she *married*? (But then: What about Steph? And why is Gina talking about the stupid dress?)

> **Celeste**
> Somebody put a picture on Insta

> Of us at Olivia's

Oh shit is right.

Eva tosses her phone on the duvet and scrambles for her laptop. If she's going to be flipping through Tumblr and Twitter and a half-dozen shitty celebrity websites on top of that, she wants a fifteen-inch screen and full keyboard.

She examines the picture before she reads any of the articles, which aren't hard to find: they're trending on Twitter. The picture is after Eva dropped the glass, which has already fallen out of frame. Even through the weird lighting, you can tell Eva's dress is stained. Her face is pale, her eyes wide; across from her is Celeste, her mirror image; Sylvie and Deja hesitating between them.

Which explains why the headlines are like this: DARK NIGHT FOR MOONLIGHT? FORMER GIRL BAND MEMBERS FEUD AT HOLLYWOOD PARTY and CATFIGHT! CELESTE ROGERS THROWS A DRINK AT FORMER BANDMATE EVA BELL and ROCKY REUNION: REUNION TALKS ON HOLD AFTER LATE-NIGHT FIGHT BETWEEN CELESTE ROGERS AND EVA BELL.

It's a shit storm, that's for sure. (For fuck's sake, there are no reunion talks. Much less stalled ones.)

Eva should probably be grateful they never officially came out as a couple, or it would definitely be worse. Of course, they were all *out*. Celeste and Eva just weren't publicly together. They weren't private either, exactly, but girls are touchy-feely, and girl groups even more so. They'd been friends before, anyway, so of course they held hands on red carpets and vacationed together. And they were all still so young . . . At least, that was the angle their publicist encouraged the press to take.

So unified, these gal pals!

Eva picks up her phone from where she dropped it near a pillow and backtracks to scroll through the rest of her messages: her manager, her publicist. Her mom, her dad, Lydia. Olivia, Deja, Sylvie. A handful of other people who mean well. A handful of other people who pretend they mean well.

Eva
I'm clumsy af, alert the media

Gina
When not onstage, you mean.

It's such an obvious lie, it's not believable without the caveat.

Fuck you too, Gina, she thinks. *Whose fault is it that I'm not onstage anymore?*

Celeste
So . . . my publicist will call yours, we'll work out a statement?

Eva
The good old-fashioned way. Yeah

Eva's fingers fly across the screen. Even though her anger feels cold and precise, autocorrect indicates otherwise.

Eva
Pip's still got Isabelle's number?

Celeste

Eva
No hard feelings all around, we're all shocked because I spilled that drink on myself, everybody wishes everybody else well, no reunion. That about cover it?

Eva's jaw clenches. She hates this. She hates that she went to the stupid party last night. She hates that they have to create a public narrative so they can forget this happened without being asked about it at every turn for the next month. She hates that once upon a time, not so very long ago at all, the thought of this whole situation would have been inconceivable.

Gina
Something to preempt any coverage that tries to say you've become an alcoholic.

Technically, you're still underage.

Eva
I had maybe three sips of that stupid drink

Gina
Hey, I believe you. Trying to help.

Eva
I know. Going to call Isabelle, hang on

Before she can pull up Isabelle's number, though, another message comes through.

Celeste
Wait

Or we could do this ourselves

Mostly ourselves, anyway. Obviously there will need to be a statement

Obviously.

> **Eva**
> You still have control over your
> Twitter?

Eva does, of course, but she's been going to college, not on tour. She doesn't want people showing up in her classrooms the way she wanted them to show up to her shows.

> **Celeste**
> You bet I do

The old Celeste—Eva's Celeste—would have said something like, *You bet your cute butt I do. Get over here, angel.*
Eva doesn't call Isabelle.

> **Eva**
> Pip might not let you after today . . .

> **Celeste**
> Follow me back?

And just like that, two new notifications: Celeste Rogers is now following her on Twitter and Instagram.
Again.
In the span of two clicks, Eva's following her back.
Again.

@celesterogers: *Note to future self: next time you want to surprise your girl @evabellofficial make sure she's not holding a drink first? #moonlitmistakes*

Not your girl, Eva thinks. *Not in any way, not anymore.*
Celeste made that very clear.

Celeste
Ok?

@evabellofficial: *@celesterogers lol at least this washes out! I can remember some middle school set-painting adventures that didn't end so well.*

It's a response that will be Isabelle-approved, Eva's sure: light-hearted, reminds people they were genuinely friends before the band became popular, so it shouldn't come as a surprise that they're still friends after the breakup. (Shouldn't. Does. For Eva, anyway.)

Celeste and Gina like the tweet; Gina follows Eva, and Eva follows her back, and suddenly they're one perfect triangle. It's no diamond without Steph to balance them out, but it's something. If Eva knew back then that all it would take was a spilled drink, she'd have sacrificed so many dresses.

But it's not then, it's now, and for a hole this deep to be papered over by an accident? Another spark of anger flashes through her. Shouldn't it take more? Given the wounds that they left her with, she deserves more than a Twitter follow. There's a riptide of sadness she's been trying hard to avoid, and it turns out it doesn't take much to knock Eva off course.

JUNE 2021
CELESTE

"Could you at least have pretended it was water?" Pip's exasperation is clear, even by way of video call.

"Pick your battles," Celeste says. She props her phone against the hotel's bathroom mirror and splashes her face. Pip would normally be good enough to let her have a post-workout shower before calling, but minor PR crises wait for no woman.

Pip sighs. "I'm just saying, for a girl you're so adamant about protecting, setting her up as an underage alcoholic was not a great move."

"Pip—"

"Who's your album about, Celeste? Are *Landlocked* and *Silhouette* about the same girl? Has she listened to the songs? What does she think?"

"Message received, thanks." Celeste picks up her phone and moves into the living room area of the executive suite, sinking into one of the couches. "Anyway, none of that can touch her. She's in college now, haven't you heard? She's usurping Gina's place as the smart one."

"She won't be in college forever," Pip says.

Even though three, four years is a long time in their industry. Enough for a rise and a peak, even the fall. Enough for four teenagers to churn out three albums and three solo tours. Enough time for them to squeeze in homeschool high school between interviews, between shows, between studio sessions. Steph's the only one who even went to a prom, with a neighborhood boy, a childhood crush that had grown into a friendship fame couldn't shake. At the time, Celeste wasn't jealous: she had Eva.

"If she wanted a solo career, she'd have it by now," Celeste says. She reaches for her water bottle, taking deep gulps to avoid looking at Pip.

Eva didn't want a solo career.

That was the whole damn point.

The whole damn problem.

EVA

It's not like that first month after the breakups, when she stayed in a room in her parents' house in Chicago that was technically hers but that she'd never been in long enough to give it the "childhood bedroom" vibe that movies liked to emphasize. She hated to leave the house, back then. She hated to leave the *bed*. What was the point, when her three best friends had not only dumped her from their band but weren't talking to her at all? Who even was Eva, without Moonlight Overthrow?

To be fair, she didn't actually want to hear from Celeste unless it was a heartfelt acoustic apology. But continuing not to hear from Gina and Steph meant that every day her heart broke a little more. When they first signed their contract, Eva hadn't paid attention to the leaving member clause. By Christmas, she practically had it memorized. They'd decided to leave, and now all she was left with was a reminder that the terms of an early escape hatch had been built in from the start. Plus Spotify, to provide her with the raging, classic comforts of Adele tracks and early, angsty Kelly Clarkson.

Eva hasn't fled to Chicago, and she's not in bed, but it hurts that now that the PR dust has settled, she hasn't heard anything else. They're still so ready to drop her when they don't need her anymore. Yet unlike last time, they're not the only people she has in her life, and if she's pretty comfortable stretched out on the floor of her living room, phone in hand as she scrolls through Tumblr, there's no one around to call her out.

> **kaystar**: Where you been, lady?

Eva grimaces. She didn't mean to disappear on Kay for a few days.

> **celestial-vision**: Some high school friends are in town, so they brought the old usual drama with them

> **kaystar**: ::hugs::

> **kaystar**: A hs friend is going to apply to my grad program this round, for next fall, and if she gets in we'll probably be roommates

> **kaystar**: But I get that not everybody has my hs friend experience <3

> **celestial-vision**: Kinda already tried the roommate thing with these ones. Anyway! What's up?

The fandom was big on alliterative epithets—Her High Holiness of Harmonies, Marquess of Melodies, Baroness of Beats—but so far no one had noticed that Eva was the Royal of Redirection. If Kay noticed that about Eva's fandom persona, she doesn't seem to care.

> **kaystar**: QUEEN C TONIGHT @ STAPLES

> **kaystar**: I can't believe you're not going, how could you do this to us

kaystar: (I'm kidding, I know tickets were stupidly expensive)

kaystar: Two of my mutuals are going to do livestreams for sure, if you want the links later

Eva could get to the Staples Center before the opening act even started, if she left now. Isabelle could call Pip along the way to arrange it. She aches from the possibility. She could get into the car. She *could*. But she's not stupid. She has no intention of getting her heart stomped on all over again, the way it would if she went in person.

celestial-vision: Not sure if I'll have time, but I'd love the links just in case!

Eva didn't mean to watch concert footage that first year, Celeste's first tour. At least, she told her parents she wasn't going to. But the gifs were just *there*, all over her dash, and the videos, too, and there was her girl. Owning that stage. Alone.

It's easier to be a fan through the screen. If she were there, whatever space or crowd separated her from the stage and Celeste would be unbearable.

kaystar: np, always here for sharing the glory of Celeste ;)

kaystar: speaking of Celeste . . . I'm assuming you saw the picture of her and Eva?

Seen it, lived it, sent the dress to the dry cleaners via my PA, Eva thinks.

celestial-vision: I tried not to. But even on a dash as well cultivated as mine . . . blacklist never manages to get all the tabloid crap

kaystar: tag that shit, I know :/ only reputable sources and formal interviews for our CV!

kaystar: But like, seriously. They both just look sooo shocked, this was clearly not like the Gina-Celeste thing, there's no way in hell this was planned

Eva flinches. At least someone understands the truth. Her fingers hesitate over the screen as she strategizes an exit.

celestial-vision: No disagreement from me on that

kaystar: I just want to bundle them up with like, tea and fuzzy blankets and probably a trained therapist so they can work through this and go back to being besties like they both clearly want to

Is Eva that pathetic? Is she that obvious? She is *fine* without Celeste. She doesn't want Celeste back if it's just going to result in a mess, which it will. And Celeste definitely doesn't want to be besties with her again.

Celeste could have fucking called. She could have sent a pass for the concert tonight.

Eva takes a deep breath, in-out, the way she thinks maybe a therapist would have advised, if she'd ever gone to one. She's not Eva Bell, former star and current hit maker, when she's chatting with Kay. She's celestial-vision, IRL drama-avoider extraordinaire.

celestial-vision: But they both tweeted? So there could be/is probably stuff going on bts that we don't know about . . .

kaystar: Yeah, you're right. Maybe they did talk Saturday night

kaystar: AND THEY'RE ALL FOLLOWING EACH
OTHER AGAIN ::swoon:: I'm so happy for them. They
were obviously so close, and they were all sad after the
breakup

Panic claws at Eva's throat. Can't they stick to their usual topics, like Celeste's set list? Kay's two cats, Marvin and Florence? That banana cake recipe Kay sent Eva a while back, and are there any more easy recipes where that came from?

Even though Eva's happy for the three of them, too.

Maybe.

Even though it'd been a way to shut down dramatic fight rumors, not a genuine rekindling of friendship.

kaystar: Even though I'm LOVING what they're all doing
now, I just want them to be happy, and I think that means
being friends with each other

kaystar: I hope that's what it means, anyway

Eva knows what to say to this.

celestial-vision: OT4 'til the moon crashes into the sea

CELESTE

Sound check was hours ago; Celeste has left her opener to their vocal warm-ups. She fiddles with her phone while makeup and hair work their magic.

She likes the blue streaks; that was a good choice on her part.

"Waiting on somebody?" Anna asks, tilting Celeste's chin for a better angle.

"Mmm."

Yes, always, although she shouldn't be, so—no.

"I'm still expecting the full recap of the birthday party, by the way," Anna says.

The birthday party. The staged pictures of her and Gina feel like a million years ago already. Celebrity time. What's a planned pap shoot compared to seeing *Eva*?

Thank god for Gina breaking the group chat moratorium.

"Actually," says Celeste, crossing from hesitancy to excitement in the span of a single word. "Can I have five?"

Anna glances around the crowded dressing room, then at her watch. "If it really is five, go for it."

Gina answers on the second ring. "Celeste? Is everything okay?"

Celeste's heart skips. It's just—so good to know that Gina will still pick up when Celeste calls.

"Are you still in L.A.? Are you doing anything tonight?" Celeste blurts. The words come out too fast, too wobbly. *Dammit.* She wants to sound collected, confident, *casual.* Not the messy little kid Gina met all those years ago, not someone pathetically trying to regrow a friendship that has lain mutually dormant.

"Still in L.A., so doing the usual orgy, babe," Gina says. After a beat, she adds, "Going over some contracts. But don't you . . ."

"Have a concert. Staples Center. Wanna come?"

This is—okay, objectively, asking Gina to come to her show isn't making her more nervous than when Celeste first asked Eva out. Probably because Eva had kissed her first. Eva tried to make things easy on her like that. But an ex–best friend is still an *ex.*

"*Yes*, but are you sure?"

Celeste is done missing them. They're all *here.*

L.A. again.

(Except for Steph.)

"Absolutely. You can stay backstage the whole time, no pictures, no narrative—"

"No reunion?"

Celeste swallows. "Right. Just us. I mean—there's no—it's whatever you want it to be, Gi." She pauses. *Get it together, C.* "But I wouldn't be doing this without you, and I want you here."

She honestly meant to keep in touch with Gina after the band broke up, something casual while Celeste hand-stitched her heart back together. Something private, so their professional narratives could grow firmly apart. But it was just *hard*, okay? It felt wrong to message her separately when there wasn't another conversation happening in their group chat at the same time. She didn't know how to push past the awkwardness, and before she knew it, it'd been weeks, then months. They only exchanged small talk at the birthday party, since Gina was on her way somewhere else. A scheduled photo with Celeste had been nothing more than a pit stop on her way to some production party. That stung, Celeste admits.

"Is Eva coming?" Gina asks.

And hadn't *that* been every fantasy for the past month, ever since the tour started—Eva shouting the lyrics Celeste wrote for her from the VIP section, Eva kissing her backstage, on the bus, in their bed. Then she actually saw Eva, and she fucked it up, trying to cover shock with cool.

"Nope."

"I'll be there."

Gina doesn't make it before she has to go on—damned L.A. traffic—but Celeste can't delay the show. She makes her entrance cue, her grin a little wider than usual.

The Staples Center—twenty thousand seats—erupts.

For her.

JUNE 2021
GINA

Celeste's PA ushers Gina to a spot in the wings, but it doesn't count as a pop concert if you're not surrounded by cheers, screams, off-key melodies, and sweating, euphoric, dancing bodies. Their publicists will fix it in the morning, she decides, turning away. She has to be here for real.

There are a handful of other celebrities in the VIP section, chatting as best they can over the noise of the crowd as they sip their drinks, carefully bouncing along to the music. Gina slips inside, but she straightens her posture before making her way to an empty space. She's not some kid sneaking in late to class. She's Gina motherfucking Wright, an Oscar-nominated actress and Grammy Award–winning singer. She's a Moonlight Overthrow alumna. She's been here since Celeste's first shitty chords.

She outranks all these people.

She accepts and returns greetings, but she stays focused on her goal: making it to the front of the section, for the best view of the stage. Celeste is wearing high-waisted shorts and a crop top, which is an outfit that would not have flown back in their Moonlight Overthrow days, but she looks comfortable as she jokes with the crowd between songs. She starts strumming the opening chords to a song Gina doesn't recognize. Gina listened to both albums all the way through when they were released, of course, but she admits she doesn't have them memorized.

"Called my sister, you know which one,
trilingual and married young,
so we could talk that love lifelong
and all the lessons I'd learned wrong."

"Do you know which song this is?" Gina asks her neighbor, who was on the cover of the March issue of a foreign edition of *Vogue*.

"'Before,'" the model shouts into her ear. "Bonus song on *Silhouette*."

Gina turns back to the stage, tuning out her companions' commentary and focusing on Celeste. On the lyrics. Which . . .

"There's a white flag inside my head,
but in front of you I'm waving red."

Holy shit.

And not just the lyrics, but the emotion. There's a rawness to Celeste's voice, and Gina *knows* her: she knows when the emotion's an act, or if not exactly an act, a shadow, a memory pulled out for the spotlight.

"I can't just act
like we were meant to be and I was meant to stay,
but when I'm driving your streets,
I'm looking for the road from before to someday."

This is no shadow.

Holy shit.

Celeste—solo-act Celeste, who was just as adamant as Steph, just as adamant as Gina about not continuing—Celeste, who must have been back in the studio, writing for her first solo album almost as soon as they finished their final show as a group—is still in love with Eva.

Holy *shit*.

JUNE 2021
CELESTE

Celeste can't actually see Gina, but during a quick-change, her assistant told her Gina moved from backstage to the VIP section. Which means she doesn't care if people take pictures of her and post them online. She's really here.

Celeste is used to multitasking during shows: sing, dance, don't think about Moonlight Overthrow, definitely don't think about Eva. In her defense, Celeste is mostly successful at the last two points. She loves her fans and her music and performing and— yeah. Okay. Still Eva, in a tucked-away corner of her heart that creeps toward the center every time she stands in front of a crowd and sings. It takes all night for the retreat. Celeste has come to think of it as tidal: in, out, in, out.

She's supposed to start playing the intro for her penultimate song, but she signals to the band that the change of plans she'd told them was a possibility before the show is now a sure thing. She'd purposely picked a song she wouldn't have to trade out her guitar for.

"So, I don't know how many of you have looked at the set lists for my previous shows, but we're going to do things a little bit differently tonight," Celeste says.

Screams greet her announcement.

Just wait, she thinks.

"I have a very special guest in the audience tonight." (Pause for more screaming.) "It's her first time at one of my shows and—hey, I bet that's true for a lot of you, too. Let's give all these first-timers a round of applause." (Applause, cheers.) "So, because this friend of mine is here, I thought I'd do a cover of a song she really likes, but before I start, I'd love it if everybody could wave and say hi to her. So on three, we're going to wave over there"—Celeste turns so she's facing the VIP section—"and say, 'Hi, Gina!'"

There is an absolute explosion of sound within the arena.

Celeste is grinning too widely to start the countdown, so she lets herself laugh and duck her head instead. The excitement pours off the crowd, washing over her by way of ecstatic screams and sobs, tumbling over the stage and toward Gina.

"I know," she tells the crowd. "I know. Full same. Okay, so, ready? One, two, three—"

"HI, GINA!"

The crowd's not totally in sync, and some people are clearly saying it more than once. The word repeats around the arena: *Gina, Gina, Gina.*

"That was great, everybody, thanks," Celeste says. "So, I've never sung this song by myself before—you know, outside of the shower, the car, whatever—so I might need some help. Can you do that for me?" (Affirmative screams.) "Awesome. Okay. Let's go."

The audience quiets a little as she starts to play. It takes less than a single measure for the screaming to start again, and the sound makes Celeste's eyes prick with tears. They know where she's heading. They know what she's playing.

The crowd fills in the harmonies of Moonlight Overthrow's first number one single, and part of Celeste wants to close her eyes, live in the sound, but the other part of her needs to keep looking, beyond the lights, to all the people singing "This Afternoon" with her. They still love it—and so does she.

EVA

"Gina's going to kill us if we keep flirting during shows," Eva says. Her back is pressed against the wall of their dressing room. Her nerves are humming with excess energy, like she's ready to sprint back on for a second encore, now that the venue is empty except for them and the crew.

Celeste's left hand is resting on Eva's waist; her right is tangled with Eva's left. Their bodies are so close, Eva can almost feel Celeste's heartbeat, fluttering, just like hers. It's tantalizing, the sliver of space left between them. Eva's tempted to pull her forward, be held in place by the firm, physical reality of Celeste's body, instead of just the idea of it. The heat of it.

"She's not," Celeste says.

Eva has almost forgotten who they're talking about, or what. *Surely* the only relevant fact in this moment is the two of them, alone, adrenaline-high bodies poised on the edge, ready to touch.

"Mm-hmm," Eva manages. "Online . . . there's all this stuff about how scandalized their baby Gi is. Too much blatant flirting for her. Allegedly."

"*Allegedly* flirting or she's allegedly scandalized? Because, baby, we're definitely flirting." Celeste's fingers find their way beneath Eva's shirt.

"There are . . . gifsets. Of her reactions. Eye rolling, um . . ." Eva trails off. She never lets herself get quite this distracted during shows, but backstage is fair game.

"She's *sixteen*, and she's not scandalized," Celeste murmurs, right in Eva's ear.

"I keep telling her . . . our engagement numbers go up when we flirt."

"Appealing to her professional instincts. Smart." Celeste presses a kiss to her pulse point. "I like it."

"Cel*este*."

"Something you want, sweetheart?"

Eva shifts, and Celeste's knee slips between her open legs. "Ten minutes until they start looking for us. Kiss me."

Celeste takes her time, like she always does, kissing along her neck, beneath her jaw, before finally sliding her mouth against Eva's. Eva wraps her right arm around Celeste's waist, pulling Celeste's body flush against her own.

"Do you know how gorgeous you are onstage?" Celeste asks, breaking away from her mouth to breathe.

"So you keep telling me."

"Gonna keep telling you, love," Celeste says.

When Eva laughs, Celeste adds, as Eva knew she would, "Gonna keep calling you 'love,' too."

Eva shakes her head, but she plays with the hem of Celeste's shirt as she does so. "Kiss me," she says.

JUNE 2021
GINA

Gina waits in Celeste's dressing room while Celeste meets fans. She's almost forgotten what that's like, the crowded backstage rooms for post-concert autographs and pictures. Somehow, in less than two years, she's gotten used to the press of red carpet walks, and nothing more. No stage door for film actresses.

Honestly, it kind of sucks.

Back in her Moonlight Overthrow days, if one of them tripped onstage or told a new joke, within half an hour they could meet a fan who knew exactly what made *her* show different from all the others. Gina would fly offstage, dab on perfume, and vault into the waiting arms, smiles, cameras of people who had been there for every moment.

She doesn't have that anymore, but she's glad Celeste does.

Gina plays with her phone, replying to a dozen or two fans out of the thousands squealing about her concert attendance on Twitter: *Celeste was so sweet to have the audience greet me, I feel so lucky to call her my friend, a brilliant show for a brilliant album for a brilliant artist, she killed that cover, I was crying too no shame babe.*

How's *that* for feeding the fire of some reunion rumors?

Gina wipes away a lingering tear. Yes, she's crying over Twitter, not just the show. *So what*, she argues with a nonexistent witness.

Every tweet feels like an apology, even though she's technically replying to fans, strangers, not Celeste. Like if Gina can pour out enough support tonight, it will make up for her silence for two album releases, for Celeste's first solo tour—for birthdays and holidays and just because. That's what friends do: show up just because.

And yet . . . It didn't feel possible to stay friends with both Celeste and Eva simultaneously, and reaching out to one would have felt like picking sides. How do you choose which third of your heart to follow?

It's been easy, over the past year and a half, to get caught up in Hollywood: auditions, character research, people telling her she's going to be a movie star. It's a relief to realize that she's not the only one who walked away and still cares for what she left behind.

"Well?" Celeste says, entering the dressing room. She's changed into a flowing halter-top dress, fashioned out of burgundy layers of almost see-through material, and her dark hair has been twisted into a loose bun.

"Congratulations, babe." Gina pulls her into a tight hug.

"Yeah?" says Celeste, releasing her. "You had a good time?"

Gina puts a hand on her hip. "You were amazing, and you know it." She hesitates, then continues, "I'm so glad one of us is still singing. And—you've been doing it so well."

It hurts a little, she can admit. It stings that *she's* not singing anymore. There's still something jarring about Celeste doing music on her own—but there's enough pride mixed in for Gina not to feel ashamed of her hurt. She knew Celeste *back when*, and look at her now.

Celeste laughs and shakes her head.

"Yes, yes," Gina insists. She takes Celeste by the hand and tugs her onto the small couch pushed against one wall. "Okay, serious talk time. Between the two of us, is there anything we can't do?"

"Stay in a band with our best friends for more than a few years?"

Gina winces. Her heart is still beating in time with Celeste's bonus song. "C . . ."

"I'm assuming the right answer to that question is no."

"Gold star for the Grammy winner," Gina says. "So you know what we're going to do now?"

Celeste shakes her head.

"We could start by talking about 'Before.'"

Celeste flushes, and Gina knows she's right. "I think—I hope—you're the only person in the audience tonight who . . . got it."

"Yeah," says Gina, keeping her voice gentle. "Have you ever thought about . . . ?"

"I couldn't. I'm too scared, for one. If, when, she says no . . ." Celeste looks away. "Well, eventually my fans are going to want me to stop writing sad breakup songs, you know?"

Gina considers Celeste for a long moment. She's believed in Eva-and-Celeste for a long time, well before their first kiss. Gina likes to think her instincts are pretty good.

"Listen to me," she says.

Celeste meets her gaze, her face open, confused, still heartbroken.

"This thing where you sing your sad breakup songs to sold-out arenas? It's working for your career, but it's not working for your *life*. If you still love Eva, you need to tell *her*. Directly. Or else, yeah, you need to try writing different songs."

"They're not *all* about Eva," Celeste tries weakly.

It's true, but not nearly true enough for Gina to pretend they don't need to have this conversation. Celeste's solo records have the general girl-power, queer-power songs, the "I'm in the Big City but love my hometown" songs, the "media needs to sit down" songs. But the love songs are all Eva.

"You want me to make a pie chart?"

"I get it," says Celeste. "Now what?"

"We're going to get her back."

JUNE 2021

mooningoverthrow:

So for over a year and a half we've had NO band interactions (unless we're counting those early Eva interviews that make me cry every time because, baby), and we've been sustaining ourselves getting excited about all their individual projects, but now IT IS ALL HAPPENING SO MUCH. Gina/Celeste sighting! Eva/Celeste sighting! OT3 Twitter! GINA AT CELESTE'S CONCERT BE STILL MY MOONLIT HEART. I don't know what happened behind the scenes to make this happen (~~bets on Eva, anybody?~~), but I am LOVING IT.

#OT4 #er #OT3 #brb smiling through my tears #too happy for tags

ginestebest:

Whoa. According to my inbox, there are like . . . a lot of you who are new and don't know where to start. I'm just going to throw out a bunch of links to masterposts here and delete all my asks, and if you have more questions, send another. (After you do the reading, though, please. Seriously. I HATE TO SOUND LIKE MY ECON TEACHER, BUT: if the answer can be found in one of the links below or is the first result on Google, I don't have time for that.)

There are maybe a dozen of us who will tell you the truth, so listen up: the truth is that nobody has a fucking clue who is or was together in that band. I've been here basically since the beginning, and, for real, it could be anything/everything (for the babies: I mean, not just a fun fantasy for fic or video edits or whatever, although HELL YES for all that).

Obviously I've got my own opinions, but everybody new here needs to figure it out for themselves. We've all gotten super burned on PR narratives in the past, so . . . let's not do that to each other, okay? You can't ignore evidence just because you can't find a way to fit it into your pet theory.

Gina/Celeste masterposts: here, here, and here are my favorites. (Plus mine, here.) Ciara also has some really good thoughts about the band breakup/them post-MO here and here.

Gina/Steph masterposts: here and here. The first link has more gifs and video clips, but the second really gets into a lot of industry nitty-gritty, so READ BOTH.

Eva/Celeste masterposts: the best are here, here, and here. Semi-related, there's really good analysis about who their songs are about here and here. (Note: The second one gives equal time to the idea that some of the songs are about Gina.)

There's not as much for Gina/Eva and Celeste/Steph, but WHO KNOWS, maybe that means one of them is the real deal, so check it out <u>here</u> and <u>here</u>. If you're sitting here like YOU FORGOT ONE, nobody* has ever thought Eva/Steph is a thing, and people can be pretty good at hiding relationships when they want to be, but nobody is this good. Not that they're not adorable friends, but there is just zero romantic chemistry IRL. If you need fic recs, on the other hand, <u>ephorever</u> has your back.

. . . Whew. I will see you all A VERY LONG TIME FROM NOW AFTER YOU'VE DONE THE READING.

#*nobody serious nobody you should actually pay attention to ok? #I only link to people who actually put thought into their work #relationships masterpost #MO masterpost #mine #key takeaway: sit back relax enjoy the ride #4 beautiful stars what's not to love? #if anybody tries to tell you they KNOW they're lying

JULY 2021

EVA

Eva watches fireworks with Lydia on the Fourth of July. They're at a beach, and the sand is cool beneath her skin. Beneath the crackle and boom of the fireworks, her heart pounds, steady, but in that hard, firm way it does right before it starts accelerating. Right before it decides to launch into action, or panic. A hook crawls its way inside her, and despite the noise, it lingers in her ears.

Remember this, she tells herself.

She has a pen, somewhere, in her bag, which is—somewhere. Being used as a pillow for Lydia, actually. But if she can't remember it by herself, then it's not that good, anyway. The very first person to have the song stuck in her head needs to be Eva, and if it's not Eva, it won't make it to a second (or a second millionth).

She wonders what song Celeste is on now, up in Seattle. If she's going to cover another Moonlight Overthrow song, or if that was a one-off, just because Gina was there. The group chat has stayed quiet. Nobody seems sure what to do with it, now that the silence has been broken.

No sooner has the finale exploded above them in a *boom-boom-boom* of color than someone with an unfortunately good speaker set turns on Demi Lovato's "Made in the USA."

"Hey, you—2013 called," Lydia shouts at the speaker owners. "It wants its song back."

Eva thinks about where she was in 2013: barely in middle school, already writing shitty rip-offs of her favorite songs. Trying to do her own harmonies. Having a blast.

Me too, she thinks.

STEPH

The storm rages most of the night.

The storm wakes and wakes and wakes Mari, who screams along with the thunder.

"Shh, shh, it's okay," says Meghan, over and over again into her daughter's ears, even though Steph would like to point out, *maybe not*.

There is the crash and the roll and Steph knows if they were to go outside, the lightning would be long and bright and close.

"It's just rain," says their mom.

It's been raining for twenty hours, though, and it's not just rain anymore.

"If it's just rain, then you wouldn't have made Steph wake me up," their grandma says, as Mari continues to wail.

Steph had coaxed Grandma Marit into the basement, where she then deigned to sit in an armchair they dragged into the storage room—the most secure spot in the house. A year ago, she would have been pacing the length of the room with Mari in her arms, but now there's a stubborn weakness in her left arm, lingering tingles and spasms that make her reluctant to hold Mari unless she's sitting down.

"You don't know what the wind sounds like, when it's really

going," Grandma Marit continues, addressing the room at large. "You can't really understand until you've lived on the plains. Somewhere rural."

"I've been on the plains," Steph says, almost surprised as the memory jolts through them with the latest clap of thunder. "I tried to make recordings of it. The whistling was *so* loud, I remember. Gina had to sleep with earplugs in."

"Bet you wish you were in L.A. now," says Matt. He's stretched out on a sleeping bag, all gangly adolescent limbs, squinting at his niece, who is still screaming with the full power of her fourteen-month-old lungs. Which is to say: loudly.

"Shut up," says Steph. They made their choice more than two years ago, even though it'd taken a while longer to actually get home. Duluth, not Los Angeles.

"Can you tell that to the thunder?"

"Let's be quiet to help Mari settle down. That would be helpful, wouldn't it, Meghan?" says Steph's mom.

"That would be a big help, thank you," says Meghan. She sticks her tongue out at her younger brother.

"Well, of course, babies need their rest," says Grandma Marit. Primly, she tilts her head back to lean against the armchair.

Steph flashes Matt two fingers, then one. Quiet means no more Grandma grumbles *and* (hopefully) an eventually sleeping baby. Birds, stone, check. Matt leans toward Steph for a silent fist bump. For a sixteen-year-old boy, their brother is gratifyingly fluent in Steph's gestures. And has adjusted pretty well to the middle Miles sibling adding a baby to their household.

When Mari falls into a fitful doze, sometime after four in the morning, Steph gently lifts her from Meghan's arms and places her in the playpen they'd set up earlier, after the severe weather alarms had gone off. By the time Mari is settled, Meghan is already asleep in her chair.

Steph stays awake and keeps watch.

* * *

After the storm, there are the electrical fires.

Steph stays frozen in the basement, unable to tear away from the local news. National is on the scene before long, but fuck CNN, Steph thinks. They'll get to pack up and leave whenever their producer says the story's "over."

The fires aren't close, not to the nice house Steph bought them all three years ago, but. They know those apartment buildings. Meghan and Matt used to play with kids who lived there, back when they were in public school, before Steph's money got them into private school. For all the good that did them.

Fuck.

Eight dead, then nine.

Thirty missing. No, sixty-three. No, fifty-nine.

Somewhere upstairs, Steph's mom and grandma are going through the freezer and refrigerator, deciding what to keep and what to throw away. Their power's back now, but it was out for thirteen hours. Steph's just grateful Meghan's no longer pumping. And that it wouldn't matter if they had to throw out the entire contents of both the kitchen and basement refrigerators and freezers. Before the band, it would have mattered. After—well, Steph's investments are good for that much. Still, there's an old anxiety there that Steph can't logic away.

Twelve dead, then thirteen.

Forty-five still missing.

The newscasters are throwing around phrases like "hundreds left homeless" and "scene of total devastation" and "millions of dollars' worth of damage." It's too soon to know anything other than the names of the buildings on fire. There are too many intersections washed out and too many cars nose-dived into sinkholes to count right now, much less estimate the cost of repair.

Steph knows the news's "millions" is really "hundreds of millions." The last fall they were on tour was pretty bad, one of those "two-hundred-year storms" that keep becoming more common. But after the last bad flood Steph was home for, way back in 2012, the damage crested $100 million. And that was without any electrical fires.

There's a number running along the bottom of the screen for people to text to donate. One reporter mentions a GoFundMe page for medical bills and the replacement of . . . everything, really. The few hotels that escaped significant damage are opening rooms for the displaced, if anyone can actually get there. Steph stares at the number until their eyes blur. They could text that number. They could dig up that GoFundMe page. But this is Duluth. This is the city that raised them, the city that let them go and then let them come back.

"Hey, Matt," they shout, angling their voice in the direction of the stairs without actually looking away from the TV screen.

"What?" The shout comes from the top of the stairs.

"Print the permission slip for Mom to sign and then get ready to go," Steph says.

"Go . . . ?"

Steph stands up from the couch. "The O negative train is leaving in five minutes."

The basement door shuts, hopefully because Matt is actually finding the permission slip that will let Steph escort their underage brother to the Red Cross donation site.

Steph takes a last look at the TV screen: eighteen dead.

JULY 2021
EVA

Eva is woken up by a phone call.

From Celeste.

According to her phone, it's seven in the morning. She and Lydia went to bed around four, so her brain is a sticky, sleepy haze of *what the fuck*, even though her heart is already tripping into overdrive, because Celeste still, somehow, has that power.

Eva wishes she didn't. Celeste kicked her out of orbit, and Eva has tried so damn hard to start circling her own star. It's not fair that Celeste can give her one look, one word, one call, and send Eva hurtling back across all that space and so much time.

Mindful of Lydia in the guest bedroom across the hall, Eva snatches her phone from the bedside table. "Celeste?" She shoves aside the tangled blankets, struggling into an upright position. Ideally, she'd be wearing something other than pajamas for this conversation, but if she's going to talk with Celeste—in pajamas, in bed—she can at least be sitting up.

"Have you heard from Steph?" Celeste's voice is urgent.

"What?"

"*Steph*. Have you heard from Steph?"

"No," Eva says, confused. "I haven't talked to Steph since—you know. Anything in the group chat? Sorry, you woke me up, let me—"

"Just turn on the news," Celeste interrupts.

"*What?*"

Would Steph really do that? Announce a comeback, a solo album, whatever, without telling them first? At least with Gina's and Celeste's projects, Eva knew *something* was coming.

"There was a storm in Duluth," Celeste says.

"A storm," Eva repeats.

She fumbles for her laptop one-handed, opens it, and loads CNN.

A large picture takes up most of the main page: an apartment building on fire, in a once-familiar skyline. She scrolls down, eyes darting between more photos and large headlines, bullet points summarizing the little there is to know. A muted newscast starts to play, even though Eva hasn't clicked anything. The camera pans to Lakewalk Trail along Canal Park, presumably because it's the part of Duluth most recognizable by tourists. Boulders have been pushed into hotel parking lots by the storm surge, benches overturned. The water still hasn't fully retreated from whatever high it reached in the night, Lake Superior asserting its name.

"I haven't heard from Steph," Celeste says. "As far as I can tell, that neighborhood wasn't one of the worst hit, but—what if Meghan wasn't home last night? Or Matt, or . . ."

Or.

What if.

Eva takes a shaky breath.

It's just a storm, she tries to tell herself. *Happens all the time, I'm sure Steph is fine, I'm sure everybody is fine, this isn't Hurricane Maria, for fuck's sake, this is Duluth and a bad storm and mostly people survive bad storms . . .*

But.

What if.

Fear scrambles up through her stomach, clawing at her heart, her throat. Eva hasn't spoken to Steph in over a year and a half, not so much as a text—if Steph's not okay—if something's happened—

Eva lowers her phone, quickly scrolling through her new messages. Most of them are Celeste in the group chat, asking Steph to check in.

Eva brings the phone back up to her ear. "I haven't heard anything. Did you—"

"Gina hasn't, either," Celeste says.

Of course she's already talked to Gina, Eva thinks, and then winces. She doesn't even know if Steph's *alive* and somehow that panic isn't enough to eradicate her jealousy?

She takes a deep breath. "Okay. Do you still have Ms. Miles's number? How do you want to do this?" Already she feels like she's back in middle school, calling Steph's mom to confirm Sims-marathon sleepovers before Steph got a cell phone.

Celeste lets out a frustrated huff. "She changed it, right after, probably, and Steph never gave us the new one. I called Pip, asked her to put out some feelers, contact other people we all worked with."

"Steph doesn't work with anyone anymore," Eva says.

She clicks on the main article, scrolls through more pictures, skims the text. As the home page already hinted, it's not just a bad storm. It's electrical fires, a flood, a dozen zoo animals drowned and another dozen swimming in the floodwaters that carried them out of their enclosures.

"What's your idea? I'm not going to send a freaking reporter to the house," Celeste snaps.

"No, god, of course not," says Eva. "I'll go."

"What?"

"You've got—" Eva stops herself. Celeste doesn't need to know Eva knows *exactly* when and where her next concert is. "Another concert coming up, right? You can't be flying all over the place. I was supposed to have a meeting with my professor today, but that doesn't matter. I'll go."

After years on the road—even with assistants—Eva knows how to pack, and fast. She can be out the door in thirty minutes.

Fifteen, if she doesn't shower and leaves Lydia a note instead of waking her up.

"You shouldn't skip that," Celeste says. "Sending one of us is a good idea, though. I'll ask Gina."

"I can do it," Eva insists.

"You'd have to skip your meeting."

Eva isn't sure what to do about this, a Celeste who calls her and needs her and at least pretends to care about her college work. Back when Eva was sure they'd be doing this through the typical college years and hopefully beyond, she thought they were somehow childish, compared to all the kids who would get to roll their eyes through freshman orientation and discuss Allende over dining hall food.

Now, she feels like the childish one for going back to school, retreating into a mostly ordinary life, while Gina and Celeste went on to steal scenes and sell out arenas. She doesn't get why Celeste doesn't tell her to skip. It's not even class; it's just a meeting.

"Let me know, I guess," Eva says.

"Yeah," says Celeste. "Keep your phone on ring? I'll let you know if we need you to go. Or Gina will, or—sorry for calling so early. I wouldn't have, but . . ."

"It's Steph," Eva finishes.

Celeste is silent for a moment. Finally, she says, "Thanks for picking up."

Eva swallows. She doesn't say *of course* or *always* or anything dumb and sappy about all those years and ties that bind. She says, "Thanks for calling."

MAY 2019
GINA

"Thanks for agreeing to switch meeting days with Steph." Kayla, their manager, gives Gina a hug before waving her to a seat at the large conference table.

It's the kind of conference table that's meant for bigger meetings: the four of them, plus label reps, plus publicists, plus lawyers. Plus . . .

"It's no trouble. Steph's on vocal rest, and besides, I'm ready." Gina pulls out a black leather portfolio, but she doesn't open it. Not yet.

"Well, then." Kayla hitches a smile onto her face. "Let's hear your thoughts."

"I won't be doing the additional albums."

Kayla is too much of a professional to let the shock show, but Gina knows her too well by now to be fooled. Didn't every girl dream of her label supporting her band for more albums, more tours?

Gina has other plans.

Plans that don't involve her being one of four, being "that girl from the gay band" or even "Gina from Moonlight Overthrow." Gina is done with having to turn down invitations to collaborate—on songs, music videos, more besides—that are extended only to her, not the band. She's tired of trying to mold herself to the Brand, this image that's in theory some impossible amalgamation of the four of them that in reality is Celeste mixed with Eva. Gina's not going to get to where she's going while stuck in a band. MO put her on the map, and now she's going to take herself the rest of the way.

"Celeste and Eva, once Celeste convinces her, will become solo acts," Gina says. "That'll keep the label happy enough, and there's not room for all of us to go solo—"

"But you have to consider—" Kayla interrupts.

"That I'm the Black one?" Gina raises her eyebrows. "I think we can stop that line of thought right there. I'm not interested."

Destiny's Child was great; *Beyoncé* is the greatest. But Gina's not looking to be the ex-girl-group heir to Beyoncé's still-occupied throne. She's aiming for this next stage of her career to be more *Dreamgirls* and less Jay-Z.

Kayla rests her hands, palms down, on the smooth surface of the table. Her thumbs and index fingers touch, leaving an empty triangle between them. Someone, not Kayla, will have to polish her fingerprints away, later that night, or maybe early the next morning.

"Why don't you tell me what you are interested in, then?"

Gina lets the words hang in the air between them. She contemplates Kayla calmly. Coolly. In a way she wasn't quite capable of when Kayla had signed her before she was even fourteen. For so long, she's been dancing to Kayla's tune.

It's time to flip the script.

"I'm going to become an actress," she says, and opens her leather portfolio.

She knows Kayla understands what she's leaving unsaid: *And you can either help me get there and get part of the take, or you can get the hell out of my way.*

OCTOBER 2019
CELESTE

Eva is sleeping beside her, her body curled away from Celeste. She's always been the little spoon. Celeste brushes a stray curl away from Eva's face. She won't stir, not from these little adjustments, little caresses. You can't survive as a touring artist if you're a light sleeper. Too many bus nights, across the vast darkness of the United States, then Europe, if you're lucky. Overnight flights on private jets across Asia and Australia, if you're the luckiest. Which they are.

Tonight, though, is a hotel night. A real bed, a room to themselves.

Celeste sits propped against the headboard. She tips her head back until it connects with the wood with a soft, satisfying *thump*. She lets an idle hand drift over Eva's hair, her shoulder, come to rest on her arm where the blanket has fallen away. It's pitch-dark in the room, thanks to the blackout shades. Celeste knows Eva's body so well by now, though. She knows its curves and divots, its bumps and angles.

I'm going to break up with you, she thinks.

She has to.

There is no other option, not really, because. Well.

Gina's leaving. She and Gina haven't talked about it so much as honestly answered *who are you emailing* or *who was that on the phone* when Eva and Steph aren't around.

Steph is a spiral, obviously with no interest in continuing to record, nor the energy to pretend. A spiral, but not stupid.

And then there were two.

Celeste can't stay with her. You don't stay with your teenage girlfriend, you know? First loves don't get a happy ending. Especially not in Hollywood.

First loves crash. First loves burn *out*.

Celeste knows this, okay? She knows it intimately. The sticky, long-fingered shadow of her parents' relationship was the only proof she ever needed. Her own existence was a last-ditch attempt to save their marriage, and the world has provided plenty of other examples along the way. Sometimes the universe is explicit about things like that. *First love: do not pass go, do not collect a happy ending.*

Being with Eva—it's too easy.

Celeste can't breathe sometimes with how easy it is, how much she loves Eva, how much every part of her life is twisted up in her. It's too much. It's especially too much when she knows it can't last. She needs to know she can make music without Eva. And if she can't have Eva for music, she can't have Eva any other way, either.

Celeste is never going to be anyone other than exactly who she is, right now, if she stays with Eva. Eva is never going to be anyone else if she stays with Celeste.

Celeste is doing this *for them*.

For *her*.

Eva's going to be a star, she knows it.

STEPH

As a rule, Steph does not answer phone calls from numbers they don't recognize, but the storm seems to have upended other safe harbors, so they answer. Maybe it's one of their Trans Youth Alliance friends, calling from a neighbor's cell.

"Steph speaking," they say.

"Steph, thank god," says whoever is on the other end of the line. "Celeste said you weren't responding to any of them, and they were worried."

Celeste.

Steph still doesn't know who they're talking to, but this person knows Celeste—knows all of them, apparently. And they're worried.

Steph couldn't bring themself to answer the messages or return the calls. There's no space in their head today for the mess that is MO. They'd know if Steph were dead; Steph is pretty sure that would still make the news. They told themself they'd answer later, only now later showed up all on its own.

Steph ducks out of the living room, where Mari is admiring Matt's Band-Aid, and heads upstairs to their bedroom. "Who . . ." Steph's voice comes out as a croak.

"This is Pip. Sorry," says Pip, a publicist who worked with them during their last year, and then for Celeste, after the split. It's been just long enough for Steph to forget her voice.

A flash of annoyance runs through Steph: They really had to get Pip involved?

"Well, I'm fine," says Steph.

"They'll be very glad to hear it," says Pip. A beat. "*I'm* very glad to hear it. And your family?"

Grumpy and exhausted, but what else is new, Steph thinks.

"Everyone's fine," they say.

"That's great, that's so good to know."

"Is that everything?"

There are a bunch of tree branches down in the yard, and Steph needs to commandeer Matt to help them before their grandma gets it into her head to start taking care of the mess herself. Branch removal is not exactly on her list of approved post-stroke activities, and the last thing today needs is a trip to the hospital.

A new knot of grief pulses in their throat. It's been over a decade since they sat in a hospital waiting room while their mom told them what Steph had already predicted. That was just how Dad had raised them: to be practical and realistic. That lesson stuck, even when it came to his own death. Now, it's days like this that make Steph miss their dad more acutely. What wouldn't they give for him to hold them while they try to track down Grandma's sewing club members? What wouldn't they give to be able to look out the window and see him teaching Meghan how to use a chain saw?

Fucking storms.

Fucking drunk drivers.

"Actually, not quite," says Pip, drawing Steph firmly back into the present reality.

Steph sits down on the edge of their bed. Apparently they're going to be here for a little bit longer.

"I received, well . . . an unexpected call earlier today. About you. About you and the group, in fact, because this person didn't know who to contact, since the band doesn't have a publicist or a manager anymore."

"We're not a band anymore," Steph reminds her. They start to draw arcs in the carpet with their toes.

It didn't hurt to say that, they tell themself. *It didn't hurt. This doesn't hurt.*

They haven't had to remind someone of that in . . . a while, really. After the first few months back, people here stopped making concerned faces and asking nosy, Midwestern-polite questions. It helped that Steph didn't go out much. There was plenty to keep them busy at home.

Fewer people forcing them to justify, again and again, that they'd done the right thing.

This is not allowed to hurt.

"Of course not," says Pip. "But I wanted to share the offer with you first, before I bring it up to the rest of them."

Not just a call, an *offer*.

"Celeste doesn't know?"

"No. I thought I should start with you."

Steph has all the answers on the tip of their tongue: *We're not doing a joint red carpet appearance, we're not doing a documentary, we're not reuniting to finish the extra albums.*

Steph's not, anyway. The rest of them . . .

"I'm listening," says Steph. They're actually listening for Mari to start crying from tiredness, but Pip doesn't need to know that.

"A benefit concert." Pip's voice is even, very professional, no hint of wheedling or incredulousness at the offer or anything.

Steph freezes, their toes pointed at the top of the arc.

"And I would . . . we would be involved how, exactly?" Steph asks.

"You'd headline it. The four of you. The organizer is thinking of bringing on a bunch of local acts for the opener, but—you're all from there. You still live there. It would—"

"I don't sing anymore." Steph forces the words out. They wish they hadn't answered the phone.

Unfamiliar numbers are *always* trouble.

"You could use prerecorded vocals," Pip says.

"While everybody else sings live? I don't think so." Their words are edged with scorn.

Steph left—they all left—and Steph left for *this*, for Mari and Meghan and Matt and *Duluth*, and the whole point of not being in the band anymore was so they could be with their family, here. And *now* Pip wants to bring the band back? *Here?* After all this?

"Have you really not been singing?"

Crap. Steph closes their eyes.

"You know it's not the same. I don't have a vocal coach anymore. My basement when the kids are out isn't the same as Celeste's two albums and tours."

It's not even close. Steph stands in front of the big windows sometimes, angled just right, so that they can see their reflection and pretend that on the other side of the glass is a producer. Steph isn't fifteen anymore, though; they know better than to let pretend things become real.

"Gina and Eva don't have solo albums, either," Pip says.

"As if Eva doesn't sing the demos for the songs she writes," Steph says. "As if Gina doesn't still do vocal warm-ups for her acting. Her agent has probably told her to keep her voice strong so she has the option to do musicals, if she ends up wanting to."

Steph's expecting that Gina will, at some point. Gina starred in all their middle school musicals, back when they had real lives and went to real schools.

"Okay," says Pip. "I hear you, Steph. But this would be a charity gig at a small venue. A one-time thing for Duluth. Nobody's going to judge—"

"Everybody's going to judge. It'll be this pitiful, awful thing instead of amazing, which is what Duluth deserves," says Steph, letting anger into their voice.

Pip doesn't get it. It wasn't Pip's band, even though it was her job.

And she's never lived in Duluth.

"I think I've been approaching this from the wrong angle," says Pip.

There is no right angle to ask me this, Steph thinks.

"Do you want to do it?"

"That has nothing to do with it," says Steph.

But beneath everything, they want it. To sing with their girls again, the C-major triad that lent them pitch and direction for those nonstop, fleeting, pop-star years? To stand in front of a crowd—a small one, a hometown one—singing back at them? To do this for Duluth?

"That's everything to do with it," says Pip. "If you want to do this, we'll make it happen."

"The rest of them . . ."

"I know Celeste will be in. Gina, too. Gina was ready to get on a plane if you didn't pick up," Pip says.

Gina didn't know about the show yet, which meant—she was ready to get on a plane just for Steph. No other motive.

Fuck, Steph misses them.

"Eva?"

She chose to step away from the spotlight too, even if she hasn't really left the industry.

"We'll get Eva on board. Don't worry about it. Do you want this?" Pip asks.

Steph sighs. They tip their head back, eyes open, to stare at their ceiling fan.

It's that time again, they think. Their heart rate picks up, as it always does.

"I can't be in a girl band anymore," they say.

"Nobody is saying you're getting back together. It's one concert, for a city you all love, for a city you *live* in. It's a show of support. Ignore the journalists; I promise you, nobody at the concert is going to care if you're rusty—"

"Not all that," Steph interrupts.

Sometimes people just make it *so hard*. They think they know where you're going, but except for their mom, no one ever gets this particular direction right.

"Help me out here, Steph. Let me find a way to make this work for all of you," Pip says.

"I can't be in a *girl* band anymore," Steph says. "I'm not a girl. Not that I was back then, but I won't do it anymore."

And there.

They've said it.

"That's fine," says Pip, who, to her credit, doesn't miss a beat. "We can slip it into the concert press release. What pronouns . . . ?"

"They/them/theirs," says Steph.

Their heart is pounding, despite their relief. They've never come out to anybody in the industry, not for this. Steph had been out as pan since their first MO rehearsal outside of school, but by the time they realized there might be a *reason* why they were using their band Tumblr to read about gender identity and follow anyone they could find who didn't feel like the cis girl everyone thought they were, it was too late. Kayla was delighted to offer representation to the next big "girl" group. Steph tried to . . . not forget about it entirely, but set it to the side. For later. A secret they got or had to keep while everything else about them was made loud for the world. It seemed easier for the band that way.

Getting a record deal was hard on its own, especially as they'd all been clear about all being queer from the start. Their parents wouldn't let them sign until it was written into their contracts that everybody could be out. *Their* kids were going to escape addiction and eating disorders and rampant homophobia from their own team, goddamn it, or at least the adults would go to hell trying. And by hell, their parents meant the one their kids were going to put them through, if they made them wait until they were eighteen to sign away their lives. The band would still have been screwed if Eva's dad wasn't a lawyer, probably. Or maybe not the band, as such. Maybe just the four of them.

After the contract but before the breakup, Steph didn't like to think about what the online reaction would be, if they started correcting the people who misgendered them (which was everyone). Some of it was awful already. Plenty of condescending comments addressed to Eva and Celeste (*you haven't met the right boy yet*) and to Gina (*girls only say they're bi for the shock value—you'll grow out of it, wait and see*). The grossest comments were always the ones that said the band could get with girls if they wanted to, as long as the commenters could watch. Even before any of them were old enough for a driver's license. The worst comments were all rape threats.

And so Steph ended up back here, trying to determine without all the industry noise if they were really *not* a girl or if it was normal to hate the merchandisable image that was constructed around a California conference room, especially when everyone assumed the image was genuinely synonymous with your identity. Well, Steph's realized it's both, and now California's come calling.

"Consider it done," says Pip. "One-time reunion concert by Grammy Award–winning pop group Moonlight Overthrow, featuring four renowned singers."

It sounds . . . official.

Oh my god, Steph thinks, then: *Oh fuck*.

It's a better mantra than *this doesn't hurt*.

Normally, Steph holds their MO life at a distance, done by someone else. Now, that other self comes crashing back into their body. *Grammy* Awards—they did that. For real. But Steph has spent so long trying not to have any feelings about music, it's an uneasy fit. Every time an emotion tries to rise—excitement for singing, for seeing the girls, for being the beat driving the audience's dancing bodies, or nervousness about all those things—Steph is already squashing it down. It's an instinct now: *this doesn't hurt*.

It's okay, they try to tell themself. But won't it be harder to shove it all away, after, if Steph lets themself fall too deep into it now?

"Outlets that use your pronouns without being transphobic will get exclusives with Celeste later this summer; outlets that don't will go on my blacklist."

"Thanks," says Steph, feeling a smile sweep across their face.

"It's my job."

"It's really not." Steph doesn't have a publicist anymore, or a stylist, or a vocal coach, or anyone. A live wire of panic starts to coil in their stomach.

"It involves Celeste, so I'll take it on as part of that. Assuming the organizer is able to work a few more things out, and you're still on board then, there will be some basic contracts for all of you to sign, to keep everything clear," Pip says.

Steph was anticipating that, so they say, "I'll text you my new email after we hang up."

"Great. Do you want me to ask the others about the benefit concert, or do you want to? Your call."

Right.

The rest of them, whose calls Steph has been ignoring. What if the others don't sound the same? What if they do? Steph knows nothing about their new lives beyond grocery store magazine headlines.

What if Eva hates Steph? What if Celeste and Gina think their quiet life is . . . lesser? But Pip said they'd all say yes. Steph clings to that. And if they do say no—Steph's asking for Duluth. Steph's not asking for themself.

It won't be personal.

It won't hurt.

It will, and they want it anyway. Because when it comes to this band and these girls, Steph has a history of doing the naive, hopeful thing.

"I need to talk to my family first. And then I'll call. I'll let you know after I've talked to everyone."

"Of course," says Pip. She pauses. "It really was a pleasure working with you before. I'm hoping that we're able to work together again on this."

"Thanks," Steph manages, swallowing the lump in their throat.

"I'll talk to you soon, then," says Pip.

"Yes," says Steph, as much to themself as to Pip.

Yes, they'll talk to Pip soon.

Yes, they want to do this.

EVA

The four of them are gathered in the living room area of Eva and Celeste's hotel suite: Eva and Celeste on the sofa, Steph and Gina in the two armchairs. It's long past midnight, and Eva's already changed into her pajamas: light purple cotton pants and an over-sized T-shirt that originally belonged to Celeste.

"Let's get this show on the road," Eva says, yawning and tucking herself closer to Celeste.

"Been there, done that," says Steph.

Celeste straightens up, although she doesn't dislodge Eva. "Okay. So . . . we need to decide what we're doing, as a band. No managers, no publicists, just us."

Gina nods.

Eva frowns. "What's there to decide? The label is calling their options—we owe them three more albums. I thought we all just wanted a lighter summer before we actually start fulfilling it. That's why we didn't record an album this year, right? Because we need a little break."

The other three exchange glances.

There's a beat of silence, then two, then three.

Eva's long since come down from the post-show adrenaline, and her head feels foggy, her blinks too slow, and she can already feel the meeting slipping somewhere beyond her comprehension and out of her grasp.

"Right?" she presses.

It's Celeste who says it, looking straight ahead to some empty middle distance. "No."

Eva pushes away from Celeste.

"What do you mean, 'no'?"

"I'm leaving," Gina says, her tone even, as if she is not pulling the rug out from under Eva's feet with that deceptively simple sentence, as if she is not taking a jackhammer to the foundation on which Eva's entire life is based.

"No," Eva says.

"I talked to Kayla about it months ago," Gina says, still in that calm, steady voice. "The announcement will go out in December, after we're done here."

"We're not done," Eva says.

"I'm done," says Gina.

"The *fuck*?" Eva says. "And you've been planning this for months, and you didn't even bother to *tell* us?"

"I haven't made a secret of the fact that I was in no hurry to start recording again."

"What are you—what are you even going to do? So you're throwing this all away, this band, your best friends, for what? It had better be pretty goddamn good, Gina," Eva snaps.

Beside her, Celeste is still. Steph is staring at the carpet.

Why is Eva the only one reacting? Why is she the only one who seems to care?

"I want to act," says Gina. "I don't have time to try that now, not with our schedule. I've always wanted to—you know this, Eva. I've always been honest about that. And the whole band thing is starting to feel stifling, and we'll be done with this tour soon, so . . . yes. Now's the time for me."

"*Stifling?*" It comes out as a screech. Thank god the whole floor belongs to them and their tour team tonight.

Gina sighs. "I want to do something else right now, okay?"

"No, not okay. What the hell, *not okay*," says Eva.

"Don't you want to try other things, too?" Gina asks. "Write music without having to think about balancing all our voices, without taking into account all of our ranges? Don't you want to—"

"No," says Eva. "I love writing for us. I love that challenge. I never wanted to do any of this without you."

"You'll be an amazing solo artist, babe," Gina says, the words sounding more sincere and earnest than anything else she's said since Celeste called their meeting to order.

"Just because you're leaving—" Eva starts, but Steph interrupts her.

"Stop giving Gina a hard time. The second the last concert is over, I'm on a plane home."

"We . . . all are, I guess," says Eva.

"For good," says Steph, voice shaking. "I'm out. No more band, no more L.A."

Worn out as they all are, on their ninth month of touring, Steph looks exhausted without makeup on: T-shirt hanging loose; hair, still damp from the shower, limp and tangled.

"We can fix this," Eva pleads.

"We are the problem." Steph's voice catches, drops, until it's a growl. "Us, this band"—Steph waves a hand to encompass the room, the whole damn life they've *all* been working to build— "this is the problem. I barely made it to my grandfather's funeral because of this tour, and I sure as hell didn't get a chance to say goodbye, because I wasn't fucking home." Eva winces, but Steph barrels on. "My sister, my little sister, is four months pregnant. Don't tell me that doesn't have to do with the fact that I haven't been home in ages, that my mom flew out to *so* many shows and photo shoots our first two years and left Meghan and Matt with our *grandparents*. Speaking of Matt, he's one suspension away from getting kicked out of that private school I was so happy to pay for, because he keeps getting into fights, and do you know how hard I have to work to keep all this shit off social media? Away from the press?" Steph is staring straight at Eva now. "None of you have younger siblings. You don't get it. I need to be home. I'm done letting this band ruin my family."

A memory of Meghan, pre-band—or at least, pre–first tour—flames through Eva's mind: thirteen years old, braces, adjusting the strap of her first real bra as she listens to them rehearse in Ms. Miles's basement. Young, above all else.

"She's only sixteen," Eva whispers.

"Yeah," says Steph, accusatory.

"But . . ." Eva shakes herself, sits up straighter. "That's what the break is for, right? You could go home. We don't need to start working on an album until next fall, next winter even. That's enough—"

"No, it's not enough. I'm done putting them second, which, in this industry, might as well mean dead last. I'm sick of having fucking time limits there. They need to know I'm going to be there, that I'm going to stay." Steph's arms are crossed, and Eva can see the goose bumps.

"It's—and I know I'm an only child, I know, but—they're not your responsibility, not really. I know that you love them, but there's your mom, and your grandma," Eva starts.

"You don't get it," Steph repeats. "Just stop trying."

"I want to understand . . ."

So she can fix it.

So she can stop Steph from leaving.

So she can make sure Steph will come back.

"The only thing you have to understand is that I'm not doing this again. I'm done," says Steph.

The words feel hollow, hanging across the coffee table between them.

They're—incomprehensible. Inconceivable.

Steph can't just leave. Steph can't be done.

Moonlight Overthrow isn't supposed to be something that ends.

"Isn't there anything—"

"Eva," says Celeste.

And that's all it takes for her to know.

NOVEMBER 2019
EVA

Steph and Gina depart for their own rooms.

Eva is still frozen on the couch. Celeste doesn't move either, but Eva knows it's not because she's stuck: Celeste is waiting.

Finally, in a low voice, Eva says, "What are you talking about?"

"I'm going solo," says Celeste. "And you should, too."

Celeste is still dressed—skinny jeans and a loose top, something made out of flimsy, high-end material, ethically sourced. If Eva went online right now, she'd see pictures of Celeste wearing the same clothes with fans after the concert.

"When did you decide?" Eva rests her forearms on her thighs, clasps her hands together. She stares down at her fingers.

"This summer, I guess. I knew Gina was leaving . . ."

Eva jerks upright. "You knew."

Celeste meets her gaze. "You could have known, too."

"Nobody told me!"

"Because you were going to react like this. I thought—I thought with a little more time, if I waited a little longer, you'd come around to it on your own . . . you'd see that this is really the best plan, for all of us."

"So you waited until the very end? We have *seven more concerts*. Two weeks left to *plan*. Does that sound like fair fucking warning to you?" Eva stands up and moves behind the chair recently vacated by Gina. Anger is roiling through her, her skin burning with it.

"I really thought you'd want this too, eventually," Celeste says. A faint note of pleading makes its way into her voice, and an irrational hope of victory sweeps through Eva.

"How could you ever think I'd want the band to break up? I thought we were all in it for the long haul. I planned for that. Just like us."

"Like us," Celeste repeats. Eva can't read her tone.

She sits down in the chair. "Yeah, like us. Did you . . . did you even think about how leaving the band was going to affect the two of us?"

"I did, actually," says Celeste.

"I just don't get why you didn't talk to me about this. I could have figured it out for you, found a way for you to get what you wanted without leaving—"

"Leaving is what I want. I didn't want you to figure it out for me. I figured it out for myself."

"And your solo stuff? When are you going to tell me those details? Are you going to make the album in L.A., or somewhere else? Have you even had somebody look at apartments for us in this mystery city yet? All of that affects me, too. I can't believe—"

"No, it doesn't," says Celeste.

"I'm your girlfriend. If I'm expected to learn Swedish or something in the next two months, I need to know that." Eva wonders how many people on their team—how many people on all these new teams that started forming behind her back—knew before she did. Thank god the press hasn't found out yet, or at least has been bribed to keep it under wraps. That would have been humiliating.

Celeste sighs. "What's your plan here?"

"What?"

"There's no more band. I'm going solo. What's your plan? Because it can't be to follow me around," Celeste says.

That anger, lying dormant for a moment as simple exasperation reigned, surges up again. "I don't have a fucking plan, because nobody around here—including you—bothered to tell me I was going to need one." She takes a deep breath. "And I don't see why not."

"Why not . . . ?"

"Why I can't 'follow you around.' Which, by the way, is a shitty way to say that. I'm your girlfriend, I don't 'follow you around,' I *stay* with you," Eva says, glaring.

"And what are you going to do while I'm in the studio? While I'm on tour?" Celeste glares back at her.

"Write for you? Take some online college classes? Be backstage every night so you're not on this stupid solo tour by yourself?" Eva is seething. How dare Celeste ask her that? An hour ago, she didn't know any of this. And now she needs some twelve-point plan?

Celeste sinks back into the couch. "You're just going to let me have this."

"I'm sorry, is getting everything you want a problem for you?"

"I didn't want it like this," Celeste says.

"Fine, tell me how you did want it, and I—"

"You can't come." Celeste closes her eyes for a second, and when she opens them, she looks away from Eva. Doesn't look back.

"Excuse me?"

"You can't come with me. Not on tour, not . . . not for any of it."

Eva can't speak. She can't *think*. She can barely breathe. The others are her eyes, her limbs, her lungs, nothing happens without them, and beneath the band, one level deeper, there's Celeste, always Celeste.

"Go to college like you want to. For real," says Celeste. "Go solo."

"What about us?" She means to ask it calmly, confidently, but it comes out as a whisper. She doesn't have enough air for anything stronger.

Celeste shakes her head. Still not looking at Eva. "I can't," she says.

There's a roaring in Eva's ears, a mess of noise in her head, but it's not like a cheering crowd, not like that at all. It's like ten thousand discordant harmonies all playing at once, desperate to be the loudest, and the only thought that can slip through this tangle is *no*.

"I *love* you," Eva says. "You love me."

They've been together for over two years. They've said "I love you" so many times, Eva has almost forgotten the first.

Celeste doesn't deny it, but all she says is, "First loves don't last."

"That's a *lyric*. This is real life."

"Please, Eva . . ."

As if Eva is the one being difficult here. As if Eva is the problem.

"You're the one—" Eva swallows. She can't say it. She can't say *breaking up with me*. The words won't come.

"I need to do this," says Celeste. "It's—" Her voice catches, and any other time, Eva would be by her side in an instant, holding her, whispering songs in her ear.

Eva stays where she is.

"It's better this way. For both of us, in the long run," Celeste finishes.

"You're wrong," says Eva.

Celeste stands up. For a single, burning millisecond, Eva thinks she's going to cross toward her. Touch her, cry, apologize, something. But Celeste heads for the door.

"I'm going to stay in Alix's room tonight," Celeste says. How nice of her to have warned their stylist and not Eva. "And I guess . . . we'll rearrange a little, for the rest of the tour."

"I guess."

"And—we should take 'Girl Says Yes' off the set list."

Eva chokes back a sob. More than anything else, she knows that's the point of no return. If Celeste won't sing their song anymore—the one they wrote together, about all the ways they say *yes* to each other already, and all the ways they want to say *yes* in the future . . .

Eva wants to rip the song up into a hundred shattered chords.

How could you have sung this song with me tonight, she wonders, *if you knew you were going to tell me no?*

"You're brilliant." Celeste is at the door now. "You're so, so brilliant. You're going to be amazing on your own."

I'm amazing with you, Eva thinks. *I don't want to be on my own.*

Celeste leaves.

Eva curls up in the chair, tucking her knees against her chest. Celeste's T-shirt is soft against her skin, and if she weren't already shivering, she'd rip it off. It's not like there's anyone in the room to see her. One night—mere minutes—and everything's swept from beneath her feet: the band, her friends, Celeste, her future.

This is supposed to happen to other people. Other bands. Other friend groups, other couples. Not to her.

She feels a damp patch grow on the knee of her pajama pants, and she realizes she's crying.

'Til the moon crashes into the sea, she thinks.

Crash.

EVA

The first message from Steph in over a year and a half reads like this:

> **Steph**
> Hi. Pip called earlier. There's something we should talk about. Video call at 6pm pacific?

Eva reads it at least ten times. Steph. Wanting to talk. She's relieved that Steph messaged, but that relief isn't free from trepidation. What's gone wrong now?

Gina is the first to answer:

> **Gina**
> I'm so glad to hear from you, babe. See you then.

I have to leave by 7 for dance, Eva types, then feels like an asshole. She hasn't talked to Steph in ages, and that's what she opens with?

That's fine, Steph replies at once. We can always talk more later.

Can we? Eva thinks.

That's news to her.

A few minutes later, Celeste agrees to the call, and Eva is left to wait alone for the appointed hour. It's a good thing Lydia had to work late today. Eva wouldn't be very good company right now.

Her phone buzzes with a Twitter notification: It's Celeste, expressing her sympathy for the victims of the storm, with a link to one of the fundraising pages.

Eva's dad was already mostly working out of Chicago by the time they went on tour as a support act, the spring she was fifteen. He and her mom moved permanently after their four-month solo tour that summer. Eva's never really felt at home in Chicago—home base for her has been L.A. for years now—and it's been a long time since she's been back to Duluth for anything other than a concert.

Celeste's mom left for Des Moines that same summer, to be closer to her first grandchild and far enough away from the city in which her marriage to her childhood sweetheart fell apart. It's probably been a long time since Celeste's been back, too.

Eva lies down beneath her piano, staring up at its silent underbelly. Whatever happens with this call, with her former friends—she has her own life now. After the call ends, she'll have dance class. She'll have Lydia and Kay and the songs she's working on right now. This is a weird, wild, random blip on the post-band radar.

When six o'clock approaches, though, she makes herself set up in the main living room. She doesn't want to look like the kind of person who hangs out on the floor beneath her piano.

At six precisely, there's an incoming video call from Steph Miles. And then they're all there.

Eva chokes back a gasp. She thought Gina and Celeste might spend the rest of their careers making sure they never crossed her path at industry events. She thought she might go for the rest of her life without ever seeing Steph again—in whose arms she'd cried when she was homesick, who always had an extra tampon, who kept Eva steady when every outside force would push her to arrogance, despair, chemical disequilibrium.

"Hey," says Steph, and Eva almost bursts into tears at Steph's voice. A few messages are one thing, but seeing them all . . . well, not in person, but almost, is surreal.

Steph has an undercut now; Celeste is looking expectant from a hotel room desk chair; Gina's wrapped up in a Howard sweatshirt one of her cousins gave her years ago.

It's been a year and a half since the four of them have had a conversation. Eva never could have predicted that, not at twelve, not at seventeen. And at eighteen—well. By her birthday, two months after the breakups, two months of silence, she stopped thinking *this* was ever going to happen again. Her heart is heavy with all that lost time, swollen with sorrow but contracting each time she remembers her anger. *She* isn't the one who cut off contact. The lost time isn't her fault.

Steph continues, "Before we really start, there's something I want to say. I'm non-binary, so if and when you talk about us in the press, I'd appreciate it if you didn't call Moonlight Overthrow a girl band, and you don't say things like 'the girls.'"

"Of course. We love you," says Gina quickly, and Celeste echoes her.

Eva can't help but feel relieved at the undercurrent of surprise in their voices.

"We've got your back," says Eva, even as she thinks, *Shit*.

Another thing she didn't know about the people she once thought she knew like the back of her hand—like the back of Celeste's hand, anyway. Had she been as willfully ignorant about this as she had been about Steph's family, Gina's movie star dreams, that year leading up to the breakup?

"And . . . your name? Have you kept . . . ?" Gina asks.

"Still Steph—*just* Steph. I've been thinking a lot about a new middle name, but I haven't decided yet." Steph shrugs, in a move Eva knows is calculated to look casual while being anything but. "My pronouns are they/them/theirs."

"Thanks for trusting us." Eva tries to make her voice as warm as possible.

"Okay," says Steph. "The thing Pip called me about."

"Hang on," says Gina. "You're okay? Your family's okay? The house?"

Steph runs a hand through their hair, and the video freezes, blurs, focuses again as it tries to keep up. "Nobody's hurt. Some downed branches, but no real damage. Mari thinks hail is like, the next best thing, though."

"Mari?" Gina asks.

"Meghan's girl. Meghan's baby."

Before the band breakup, Meghan and Matt weren't allowed public social media profiles, and Eva is sure that after—after the pregnancy, the breakup—the rules became even tighter. There was no public birth announcement, no easy way for stalkers and paps and fans to know—no way for Eva, either. She'd never gotten around to following their accounts. She'd assumed she could get updates from Steph.

"I'd love to see pictures," Eva says softly. "If that's something you and Meghan would be okay with."

"I can do better than that, if you're all interested," Steph says. "Which brings us back to Pip. I'm just going to say it, and then we can talk, or we can hang up and everybody can take some time to think it over, talk with your teams, whatever. But someone's setting up a benefit concert, and they want us to headline. As Moonlight Overthrow."

Eva stares at her screen. She's not used to hearing "Moonlight Overthrow" said aloud anymore. She reads it all the time on Tumblr, but online like that, it doesn't feel as real. It doesn't feel connected to this thing that was once *hers*. That was once her.

Steph saying it out loud is dragging it into being all over again, like the past year and a half has all been a dream, but they're finally waking up.

"Well," says Celeste, after a long, long moment. "That's . . . not what I was expecting to hear." She clears her throat. "Steph? It's—pretty much your town now. And you've been the most . . ."

"Out of the industry?" Steph supplies.

"That," says Celeste. "So . . . I'm going to follow your lead on this one. I've got a short break coming up, I can squeeze in a benefit concert if that's what you want. And if you want to pretend Pip never told you about this offer, I'll let her know, and we won't talk about this again."

Eva feels frozen. She wants to slam down her computer screen, stand up and scream, something, but her muscles stay locked in place. Making her hear Celeste out.

Celeste, who wanted out. Who is now willing to go back in.

Following Steph's lead.

So if they want—but when Eva wanted—

"I want to do it," says Steph.

"Are you sure?" Eva asks. "If you're not comfortable with it but want us to do something as . . . a group, to show support, I'm sure we've all still got some old merch. We could all sign some stuff, auction it off." She thinks that sounds reasonably neutral, mature.

"That's a good idea, and we should do that, too, but I want to do this," Steph says again. "It feels right."

Right?! Eva thinks.

She's been okay with the breakup now, she has. She likes studying comparative literature, likes the way it bleeds into and reconstructs her songwriting. She likes going to class, a bit of normalcy that still leaves her enough flexibility to write a chart-topping hit here and there.

That all feels right to her.

But, unlike for Steph, the band felt right to her, too, back then.

"I'm in," says Gina. "I agree with Steph. This is the right thing to do."

"Eva?" It's Celeste who asks, of course, but she doesn't wait for an answer before she looks away from her camera. She fiddles with her Star of David necklace instead, running her fingers along the chain.

"I don't know," says Eva.

She *doesn't*.

She feels like a selfish asshole, being the one holdout—this is for Steph, for Duluth, for charity—but it's not like the plan is for them all to come on separately, sing a song, leave. They're supposed to get on that stage as *Moonlight Overthrow*. It's something she doesn't let herself want anymore, hasn't let herself want for well over a year.

Back then, all of them thought she'd follow their lead. That she could be talked into going solo. She's made her peace, and now they want to drag her back. Temporarily.

It doesn't fucking work like that.

"What will it take?" Steph asks. "We can find a way to make this work for you."

It sounds like they're repeating something someone said to them, probably recently, probably Pip, but Eva can only think of That Night. Eva trying to cling to all of them, only it turned out she was grasping at shadows, at ghosts, and they were all already long gone.

"I won't do it without you," Gina says.

She means well, Eva knows, but, "I can't believe you're saying that now. And I can't believe you let me give all those interviews that winter, all those stupid interviews where I was *saving your asses* from negative breakup press, and nobody backed me up, nobody thanked me, nobody's PR people thanked me, and now you're—like that didn't even happen, or it didn't even matter, and now you're pretending . . ." Eva cuts herself off, before her voice can break or she starts to cry or any other embarrassing evidence that she still cares.

"Thank you," Gina says. "You're right. Thank you."

Celeste clears her throat. "I think we should do this. We didn't . . . we didn't do things right at the end," she admits, her voice growing softer. "We didn't. We were—at least, I was dumb and seventeen, and I didn't do it right. So let's do it right. Let's have a last concert, all of us, for a really good cause."

Weirdly, Eva thinks of Kay. How happy she'd be if Eva agreed. How disappointed she'd be if she knew Eva was the holdout. She thinks about all the time she spends reblogging Celeste's and Gina's latest accomplishments and magazine covers and premiere appearances. Being a fan means supporting the artists' projects, right? And she might not be their friend anymore, but she's always been a fan.

Let yourself have this, she thinks.

Her favorite band, back together again, and only she can make it happen. Just for one show. To help Duluth. To make up for *not* helping Steph that last year in the band, or any time since. This time around, she won't be tricked into thinking she needs them all. She can be gracious, and then she'll come home.

"Okay," Eva says. "Let's do this."

STEPH

"They'll stay here, of course," Steph's grandma says, setting her knife down.

They're chopping vegetables for dinner. Steph's mom is still at work, and the kids are in the backyard, which Matt and Steph started clearing yesterday. There's a lot of work left to be done, but at least all the larger branches are out of the way. They're lucky they didn't buy a waterfront house. It's the structures at the bottom of the hillside that got the worst of it, all that water and debris speeding down the steep slope Duluth is built on. At least the fires by the harbor are all out now. Nineteen dead, at final count.

"A date hasn't even been decided," Steph says. They know the general time frame—it has to work with Celeste's tour schedule—but they're still working things out with the venue. Any other time Duluth's convention center would have been the natural choice, but right now it's serving as a base of operations for the relief effort.

"There's no reason for them to take up hotel rooms when we have space for them here. The people who lost their homes need those rooms," says Grandma Marit, as if Steph didn't personally call the two hotels hosting the most and pay for the rooms.

Steph frowns down at the cucumber in front of them. "I don't know if that's a good idea, Grandma."

"Of course it is," Grandma Marit insists. Her fingers curl around the knife, still a little clumsy all these months later. "You're all best friends, and in your band together. Of course they'll want to stay here."

"I'm not in the band anymore," Steph says. "Nobody is."

They don't bother to correct the "best friends" part. It's too depressing to argue with your grandma about that kind of thing.

"But you have a show together here."

Steph sighs and pulls their grandma's cutting board toward themself. "Just one show."

"I remember when those girls would all come over, and . . ." Grandma Marit trails off as she lowers herself into a kitchen chair.

She can't remember them coming over, is the thing. Steph's grandma didn't move in with them until after her husband died, and she'd lived a little outside Duluth, anyway. The band never practiced at her house. She must be thinking of some other group of teens, maybe Steph's mom's friends, when they were young. It's not like her memory was absolutely flawless before the stroke—usual signs of aging, her doctors had said, nothing that's making her unsafe, nothing to worry about—but now it's hard to tell what's because of the stroke and what's the normal progression. In practice, maybe it doesn't even matter.

"I can ask if they want to stay here," Steph offers, "but it might be too much. It might be awkward."

Awkward might even be the best of all the realistic options. Steph doesn't know how Eva got through those last shows, except—yes, they do. Eva was a professional, and, Steph thinks, she might have thought that if she could just hold it together for a few weeks, everyone would come to their senses. Or at least, Celeste would.

Grandma Marit gives them a Look.

Steph tries again. "It's—we're not a band anymore. We don't talk."

"I didn't realize those things had to go together," she says, adjusting her glasses.

Steph flinches, almost dropping the knife.

Their grandma nods, tapping a finger to her nose. "You talked before the band, didn't you?"

"It's different now." Steph sweeps the second sliced cucumber to the side, making room for the carrots.

They don't know why they're arguing about this. It *is* different. They hope . . . maybe . . . it doesn't have to be. That it could be different again. Not quite a one-eighty from their one-eighty, but back to texting and talking and comfortable familiarity instead of the awkwardness of lost intimacy, even if it's not exactly the same place as before.

It might be a lot of hope to place on a slapdash reunion concert.

"Steph, come sit with me a minute."

They step away from the counter and take the seat next to their grandma, who places a bony hand over Steph's.

"Invite them here," Grandma Marit says. "You can want lifelong friends even if you don't want lifelong colleagues. Gina, Celeste, Eva—they're going to dance at your wedding someday."

Will they sing at it, though? Steph wonders.

Could Steph sing at theirs?

Get married so we can sing again, they imagine saying. *Hold a recommitment ceremony. And another.*

Steph had felt so honored, watching Celeste at her bat mitzvah. It hurts to think about all the milestones they're going to miss out on, ones that have nothing to do with music awards. But Steph had chosen that hurt over others.

"It's not that simple."

"Maybe you're overcomplicating it," their grandma says.

Steph pulls away. "When did you decide to be so wise?"

"June eleventh, 2001."

Steph's birthday.

Steph stands up, intending to return to the counter to finish the veggies, but they kiss their grandma on the cheek along the way.

JULY 2021
EVA

They arrange for another group call on Thursday, but Steph is running late, so it starts out just the three of them. With the concert set for the following Thursday, things are moving dizzyingly fast. Eva guesses they have to be, so the money can get to the community as quickly as possible.

Eva spent most of Wednesday with a vocal coach. She stuck around after comp lit to tell her professor she'd miss next week's class for vague, personal reasons. Back at home, she worked on a few old Moonlight Overthrow songs by herself, ones she doesn't remember as well as the others but thinks might make it onto the set list. Her lung capacity has diminished somewhat, and her pitch control isn't what it used to be, but she still won't be the worst pop artist to ever sing live. She only stopped to cry three times, which she frankly thinks is an accomplishment.

"How are you getting there?" Celeste asks. Eva can tell she's on her tour bus, but she makes herself focus on Celeste, and not on trying to catalog the differences between Celeste's bus and the ones they used to use.

"Well, a flight," Eva says. Obviously. The angle of the sun through her kitchen windows is making a weird slash of light across her screen, so she shifts the tablet until the light evens out.

"Burbank?" Celeste says, and Eva nods.

LAX is where you fly into or out of if you want to be seen; Burbank is where you go to keep a low profile. Eva is all about the low profile these days.

Steph's icon pops up on the screen, then Steph themself. Today they're wearing a maroon UMD hockey T-shirt, oversized even on their stocky frame.

"Hey," they say, then "Good news or bad news first?"

"Good news," says Celeste.

Eva would have said the opposite.

"The good news is that all the local acts are confirmed, and the Ticketmaster page is almost all ready to go. It will launch tomorrow morning, right after we're announced as headlining," Steph says.

"We really appreciate you running point on the ground, Steph. We'll be there soon to help," says Gina.

Steph nods.

"And the bad news?" Eva prompts.

They grimace. "The bad news—well, maybe bad news—is that Grandma insists that you all stay here."

"That's fine," says Celeste. "Save the hotel rooms for other people."

"Anyway, I like your grandma," says Gina.

Eva does, too. All of her own grandparents had died by the time her family moved to Duluth, and Steph's grandma insisted they call her "Grandma Marit" from the first time she met them. It was nice to have more family than expected.

"So . . . ," says Steph, clearly waiting for Eva to get on board.

"It's not a big deal," Eva makes herself say. "We'll be there, as long as it won't cause too much disruption for the rest of your family."

Privately, she's half hoping Steph will come back and say, no, with the baby, it'll be too much, even though Eva *knows* this is the most logical plan, Grandma Marit's feelings aside.

"Thank you," says Steph. "Honestly, Grandma will fuss the whole week if you don't, so like, Matt and Meghan can deal."

Damn.

A week, living in each other's pockets again, and not in some neutral hotel, but Steph's home, with their whole family, the family who was there for them when Eva and the others weren't. Eva's surprised Grandma Marit doesn't hate them all.

A week living with Celeste again, probably looking rumpled in the mornings and loose and tired in the evenings, after a long day's rehearsal, not at all camera ready, but like a girl you could sit next to in choir class.

Eva's so screwed.

Her entire post-band mental stability rests on not having to interact with any of them. It's one thing to forgive—or at least forget—when you don't have to see the people involved anymore. It's a different tune entirely when you have to work *and* live with them. Hopefully she'll at least be able to retreat to Tumblr for a few minutes each night to remind herself who she's doing this for—other than all of Duluth, of course.

"Tell your mom thanks," Celeste says.

"Actually—" Steph sighs. Their eyes focus on something off-screen. "Yeah, it's not fair not to give you fair warning."

Eva suppresses a snort. Been there, done fucking that.

"About?" Celeste asks.

"Grandma had a stroke. In February."

Could Eva *get* any more selfish?

"Oh my god, babe," says Gina. "You didn't say anything on Monday."

"How is she?" says Celeste.

"She's okay. The stroke was mild; she's had great doctors." Steph sounds like they're reciting talking points at a press conference. "She's still going to PT. She won't be standing up the whole show."

"*I* don't even stand for my whole show," Celeste jokes.

On Eva's screen, Steph doesn't crack a smile.

"It's not just that. Sometimes she gets upset about what she can't do anymore. I would, too, if one day I were doing 5K charity snowshoe walks on Lake Superior and then I have a stroke and five months later everyone around me is still watching for seizures."

"Seizures, shit," says Celeste.

Eva can't even imagine . . . Grandma Marit was always one of those younger, active grandparents, at least compared to some of their classmates'. Eva has lost track of her birthdays, but she can't be much past seventy. It's disconcerting to think of her as fragile.

"It's not super likely at this point, but I know Mom's still worried. We're just, like—trying to keep things calm, mostly." Steph shrugs, a show of nonchalance that they clearly don't feel.

"With a former pop star, two teenagers, and a baby?" says Gina, raising her eyebrows.

"And the three of us," says Eva.

"It's not *glamorous*, PAs running everything, it's—but she really wants you to come."

"Then we'll be there," says Gina.

"It'll be easier to coordinate everything if we're all staying in the same place, anyway," says Celeste.

"Thanks for telling us all this," Eva adds. She still has to get through the rest of this conversation, but she has an instinctual need to talk to her parents, immediately. She needs to know they're as okay as they were yesterday, when they talked about this charity concert until past midnight Chicago time. She needs to know she's still so lucky.

Gina chimes in about how she's looking forward to seeing everyone, and then the conversation moves on. Eva and Gina decide to fly out tomorrow morning, on separate flights, as Gina's PA informs them there isn't a flight with two first class seats still available. Neither of them is about to fly economy the day of the concert announcement.

After they hang up, Eva heads for her piano. She plays through the hook she came up with on the Fourth of July a few times, then slips in between the bench and the piano, resting a hand along one of the pedals. It's smooth and cool in her palm. Steady. It won't move until she makes it.

Think about staying with Steph like the benefit concert, she tells herself. *One last hurrah, for a good cause.*

If she looks at it as a way to end on a good note, finally, maybe it'll be okay.

JANUARY 2020
EVA

Eva stands in front of the hotel suite's full-length mirror as her stylist checks the fit of her dress one last time.

"You look gorgeous, Evie," her mom says from a nearby chair.

Her dress *is* gorgeous, with its cascade of dark blue silk and delicate silver beading. It has an off-the-shoulder sweetheart neckline, a style Eva has never worn before to an awards show.

"Isabelle?" Eva says, blinking furiously. Her hair and makeup are done. There's precious little time to fix either if she has a breakdown now.

Isabelle steps into her line of vision, dark tablet case in contrast against her pink gown. "They're not coming. I'm sorry."

Eva tilts her head back so her tears can't escape her eyes. "Not even Gina?"

"No. She's definitely in London."

Eva takes a few long, shaking breaths. The others apparently hate her and everything they did as a band enough to skip the most prestigious awards ceremony of the year. Their pre-band selves would be furious. Eva's furious. Don't they have an obligation to their fans? To all those queer kids out there, to say, *Yes, I'm not doing it anymore, but I'm still proud of it, I'm still proud of you?*

"Well." Eva clears her throat. "One of us has to be there, obviously. It'd be rude, otherwise. It's the Grammys."

Eva's mom stands to press a featherlight kiss to Eva's hair. "Honey, I'm so sorry."

"It's fine. I shouldn't have expected otherwise."

Eva has been *perfect* on social media, in interviews. Surely in all of pop music history, there's never been so gracious a band breakup. And still, no one's contacted her.

She understands why Steph doesn't. It felt like a second stab to the heart when Steph deleted all social media accounts—secret, private, and otherwise—after the announcement went out. Never mind the fans: Eva understands very clearly that Steph doesn't want Eva or the others to know anything going forward. Eva hates it, but she can respect that.

But Gina, who usually handles most of the tricky media questions? Celeste, who surely someday wants to end up at the Grammy Awards again herself?

Eva has been a confirmed attendee for weeks now. Three years in the band, and years of friendship before that, and no one has bothered to message her at all. Radio silence was in none of Eva's five-year plans.

"I'll walk, but I'm not doing any interviews," she reminds Isabelle.

"That's all arranged. They'll shout things, of course, but just smile, switch your angle for the cameras, keep moving. It will be over before you know it."

"I'll be waiting for you just inside," her mom says. "You'll get through this."

Unlike the last two years Moonlight Overthrow was nominated, nobody's talking now about a potential win. Everyone's focused on making sure Eva doesn't start sobbing in front of a thousand hungry camera flashes.

She hasn't practiced a speech, not even in her mind. It seems inevitable that, with the others' notable absences, they won't win.

If they do—Eva's had enough media training to stumble through, probably, if she keeps it short. Surprise, sparse thank-yous, a reference to her speechlessness, the end.

All too soon, it's time to leave the hotel suite.

"You don't have to do this," her mom says as the car pulls up in front of the Staples Center.

"I do," Eva says. "I really do."

"I'll be with you the whole time," says Isabelle.

It's not quite true. Isabelle can only hover on the edges, stepping forward when Eva needs to move along. She can't share the spotlight.

Eva tries to keep her mind as empty as possible as she poses for the cameras. It's so noisy, it's easy to let the reporters' questions blur into incomprehensibility. Once Isabelle has guided her inside, Eva floats through interactions with the other nominees. She's excited for them, it's an honor to be nominated, will you excuse her, she has to see to her mother.

"You're doing so well," her mom whispers as they take their seats.

As the show begins, Eva can't focus on the host or the performers. Every time someone passes by—celebrity or seat filler—her heart jumps. She can't help but want the eleventh-hour appearance. Wouldn't that make for a good song? She thinks she's alone, and then someone shows up, a ready explanation on her tongue, a hand to hold when they win.

The show drags on.

No one comes.

A hot wave of humiliation burns through her. She's so pathetic, actually showing up. Giving all those placid interviews none of them cares about.

Her category is introduced, and she manages a smile, automatically, knowing the cameras are watching her closely, and every fan will be scrutinizing her for any hint of troubled waters. In turn, she watches the envelope more fiercely than she's ever watched one before. She's watched with a naive sort of desire, with seat-bouncing hope, with total awe.

This is different. This is pure need.

Over the last two years, they won two out of their three nominations. Who's to say they can't do it again? The feeling of pride, of joy, catches her by surprise, turning her smile more genuine. She did this; she was part of music so good, she got to hear her band name read amid all these other greats.

All of a sudden winning feels like a foregone conclusion. Eva will give a viral speech on queer love and friendship. Celeste will be on the first plane out of New York.

They are *inevitable*.

Fated.

Written in the stars.

And then—

They don't win.

JULY 2021

@people: *Moonlight Overthrow to reunite at benefit concert for victims of Duluth storm*

@hellogiggles: *Moonlight Overthrow is back! (Temporarily, and for a good cause!)*

@outmagazine: *Moonlight Overthrow alum are sending more than thoughts & prayers to Duluth—they're sending themselves*

@celesterogers: *Proud to announce that Moonlight Overthrow will be headlining the #DuluthBenefitConcert next Thursday!!! I can't think of a better reason to perform with them again. Link to tickets and donation site in my description. xoxo*

@ginawright: *Heading back to the start to prep for #DuluthBenefitConcert. Please join Moonlight Overthrow in supporting rebuilding efforts!*

@evabellofficial: *Haven't performed for going on two years. Hoping to do Duluth proud. For more info/to support, see pinned tweet! #DuluthBenefitConcert*

maybeitsmoonlight:

OH MY GOD.

OH

MY

GOD

#that's all I've got #sjdflskjflksjdflksjf #I HAVE BEEN CRYING SINCE I SAW THE NEWS

mooningoverthrow:

I may have just screamed from the check-in desk. Don't mind me, yoga moms, nothing to see here. ~~Lies. EVERYTHING TO SEE HERE.~~

In honor of this most holy day of (anticipated) OT4 reunion, please enjoy some of my favorite performance videos of them. Bask in their talent. Bow down in the face of their queer power. THEN <u>DONATE</u>.

1. Their <u>performance</u> at the 2019 Grammys, shortly before they won their second Grammy.

2. This <u>performance of "Girl Says Yes" at the O2</u>. This is my go-to whenever I'm happy, whenever I'm in love, whenever I want to be happy and in love.

3. <u>This hidden gem</u> of their karaoke performance of "I'm a Believer" at someone's birthday party in 2018. So young. So precious. This is peak mid-MO in terms of group dynamic, just them doing what feels fun to them. (Also, if you've never thought of this song as gay before . . . watch MO sing it to each other. You're welcome.)

4. <u>The Tonight Show in February 2019</u>. Who had an album debut at no. 1 the week before? THIS BAND.

5. Their cover of Mary Lambert's "Heart on My Sleeve" for <u>Radio 1's Live Lounge</u>. RIP me. RIP you.

#OT4 #MORE SMILES MORE TEARS

moonlite-babe:

Wow. I think I can safely say this was unexpected news. I'm so proud to call myself a fan of this band! I'm not going to be able to attend the concert, but of course I'll be posting here all the other ways to support it—<u>promoting it on Twitter</u>, <u>donating to the official charity page</u>, etc. Our band is rallying behind their hometown and the people who were affected by this storm: let's rally behind them.

#duluth benefit concert

cylic-ally:

If you got a ticket to the benefit concert, I am a teeny bit jealous (okay, a lot), but mostly excited for you, they're amazing, you're going to have a great time. Some reminders . . .

Obviously we are all thrilled they're doing a show together, but let's please remember (whether you're attending or not) that this is a benefit concert. More than a dozen people died. Hundreds lost their homes. This was a really devastating storm, and people in that community are really hurting. Be respectful. This isn't just another concert: it's a time and place for the community to come together, in both joy and grief.

On that note, I'd really like us to spotlight the local openers! I'm going to dig in to their backlists later today and promote my favorites. They deserve some love.

Last thing. As I think we've all noticed, MO is no longer calling itself a girl band, presumably out of respect for Steph. I'm sure there will be lots of discussion in the days ahead about whether we should go back and change our fics, past tumblr posts, etc., but DEFINITELY in all future things from today on out, use their correct pronouns.

#Ally speaks #moonlit loves #duluth benefit concert

JANUARY 2018
GINA

Press conferences should go on Moonlight Overthrow's list of banned interview formats, Gina thinks. Press conferences are for professional sports teams and ensemble casts at Comic-Con. Their publicity team disagrees, hence the long, linen-covered table and the branded backdrop behind them. At least the press conference is for something good: their second album, *Bright*, will be released next month; the lead single, "This Afternoon," keeps climbing up the charts.

"What's different about the new album?" a reporter calls out.

"With *Supernova*, we were still finding our feet," Celeste answers, leaning into the mic in front of her. "We're more confident in our voices now."

"Our singing voices, and also in our artistic vision," Eva adds, from her spot next to Celeste. "Our sound's a little different this time around, and we're really happy with it and excited to share it with our fans next month."

Gina thinks it slows down the process if they all answer each question, but let it be known: she's thrilled. She contributed more substantially to the music and lyrics, and her range has expanded, giving her solos an extra edge they didn't have before.

"Happy sweet sixteen, by the way," the reporter says to Eva, whose birthday was the week before.

Eva thanks the reporter before calling on another.

"Your single is a love song," the journalist begins. "Who's in a relationship?"

Gina clears her throat instead of rolling her eyes. If someone out there isn't tracking the music-to-personal-life questions ratio, she's going to start. "Let's be clear. 'This Afternoon' isn't just a love song. It's a crush song, an I-really-like-you song, a daydream song. I was fourteen when we wrote it, and I'm fifteen now. I love the song, and I've never been in love with someone."

"All right. Anybody with a crush, then?"

"No relationships to speak of here," Steph says, even though Gina knows Steph kissed a boy on New Year's.

Without turning her head, Gina glances sideways at Eva and Celeste. Celeste is watching Steph with too-wide, too-innocent eyes; Eva is biting the inside of her cheek to keep from laughing. Adorable, but so very hopeless.

"Next?" Gina prompts, nodding at someone in the front row.

"There's a rumor that you're going to break up and cancel your tour."

Gina would bet a lot of money that the reporter created that rumor in saying it, but she'll do her due diligence later to check.

"That's a complete lie," says Celeste, her eyes narrowing. "We worked really hard on the album. We're excited for tour to start soon."

"Your source doesn't know anything," says Steph. "We're solid."

"I'm not going to break out *Grease* here, but we go together, the four of us." Eva lifts her chin. "Until we can't sing anymore. Until not a single queer girl out there wants us to sing anymore. Until the next extinction-size asteroid, the sun exploding, the reverse

Big Bang. We're it, we're—'til the moon crashes into the sea, you know?"

"Practically speaking, forever," Gina translates. She pushes her braids over her shoulder. "Next?"

EVA

The first thing Eva sees when she turns off airplane mode after landing at the Minneapolis–Saint Paul International Airport is a message from Celeste. Scratch that, three messages from Celeste. And they're not even in the group chat: they're just for Eva.

Celeste
We don't have to stay with them if you don't want to. If it's too uncomfortable, don't worry about it. I'll handle it with Steph and their grandma

Safe flight/hope you had a good flight, depending on when you read this

See you soon

Eva is ushered out of first class before she can decide how to respond.

She should feel happy that Celeste reached out, that she's trying to be friendly and thoughtful. Except it feels more like Celeste is reminding her that Eva didn't want to break up in the first place (not with Celeste, not with the band). She doesn't need Celeste's condescension. For fuck's sake, it's been a year and a half. She can't really expect Eva not to be over it.

Even though . . . yeah. She's not.

Eva's led into a private lounge, and suddenly Gina's arms are tight around her. She breathes in the familiar scent of Chanel perfume and squeezes back.

"Hey, babe," Gina says, releasing her.

"Hey, Gi." Eva grins back.

There's a moment where neither of them says anything else: they just look at each other, smiling so wide their breaths turn into laughter. All the rest of it—Gina leaving, never calling, hanging out with Celeste without her this summer—is for now inconsequential in the face of Gina's obvious joy. Eva knows everything else still matters, still hurts. But for a few seconds, only at this temporary beginning? They're just two old friends who haven't seen each other in a while.

"Well?" Gina says. "What do you think? Duluth?"

"Let's do it," says Eva.

Gina offers her arm, and together they head back into the terminal.

The next half hour is a blur: someone collecting their luggage from baggage claim, the rental car company trying to give them an upgrade Eva doesn't want. They're going to *Duluth*, for god's sake.

"You know you're driving, right?" Gina says as they approach a car that had finally satisfied everyone.

"Yeah, I assumed," says Eva. "Do you even have your license?"

"I got it this winter, after I finished filming," says Gina, referring to her second post–Moonlight Overthrow film, which, like her first the year before, is scheduled for a December release.

"Nice," says Eva.

"It's mostly theoretical," says Gina. "Even the idea of driving in

L.A. makes me hella nervous, and they always send a car to drive me to set anyway."

"Still."

They fall silent as Eva finds her way out of the airport complex and onto MN-5.

It's only once they've merged onto I-35 that Gina says, "I haven't actually asked yet, and you don't have to tell me, but—how are you? I love the writing you've been doing, but how's everything? How's *college*?"

Eva starts laughing. She can't help it: they've been in contact now, in fits and bursts, for two weeks, they're about to do a *concert* together, nobody really knows if anyone but Celeste can still sing—and they haven't asked each other that. She laughs so hard, shoulders shaking, she almost pulls over, but she manages one deep gulp of air, then another, then another.

"I'm sorry," she says. "We were never very good about asking each other that, were we?"

"No," says Gina.

"It might have helped," says Eva.

She doesn't mean it would have stopped the band from breaking up. But it might have made those last months easier on all of them.

"It might have," Gina agrees.

"Hmm," Eva says. "College is . . . I'm so glad I'm there. Going to class, half the time I still feel like I'm in a brochure, this can't be real, but it *is*. I have *midterms*. How wild is that?"

This time, it's Gina who laughs.

"I always thought it was going to be you who went, if any of us did," Eva says. "You're the one who skipped a grade."

"But I wanted to be Whitney Houston. Rihanna. Janelle Monáe."

"Wanted?" Eva asks.

"We'll see." Gina turns her head to look out the window.

Eva wonders how long it's been since Gina's been back to Duluth. Her parents own a real estate business in Minneapolis now, and Gina bought them a house in Kenwood after MO's second album debuted at number three. Gina's spent the year and a half since the end in Vancouver, New York, and London, with pockets of time in Los Angeles that Eva pretended to ignore.

"We've got almost three hours. You know what we should do?" One-handed, Eva fishes out a cord from her bag and passes it to Gina.

"Moonlight Overthrow marathon?"

"Just like old times." Eva winks.

At the very beginning, it wasn't anything formal or dramatic. It was Celeste and Gina messing around in the choir room over lunch, until they realized Gina shared a voice teacher with the soprano Celeste kept having to compete with for solos. It became Celeste, Gina, and Eva over lunch, then in Eva's basement with Steph, who kept walking through the choir room on their way to band and, as it turned out, had a lot of suggestions.

When they said, *Let's be a band, we should have a name*, it felt more like copying old teen movies, playacting, just fun, than anything momentous. But even when they did something for pretend, they wanted to do it *right*, and at some point, there is no difference between doing the real things for pretend reasons and doing the real things for real.

Fifty-three minutes later, listening to *Supernova* has taken them north to the outskirts of Rush City. Partway through *Bright*, Gina says, "We should do a quick video for Insta."

"Cue a Cosmic Queers heart-eye explosion," Eva says. "Go ahead."

"Full disclosure, 'A Little More' is also Georgia's favorite song, so this is not exactly accidental timing."

Georgia. Eva's seen the pictures on Tumblr, reposts fans make of Gina's posts elsewhere. There's shipping speculation, as there always is when someone their age shows up in Gina's photos, but Eva couldn't be sure. Gina never dated anyone before the band breakup—publicist-arranged patio dinners with up-and-coming actors didn't count—so Eva doesn't know Gina's genuine tells. Plus, Eva tried to avoid the analysis posts, even though she couldn't avoid the pictures. She didn't want to be convinced of a secret relationship via fandom; she wanted Gina to suggest they all meet for frozen yogurt.

"Georgia?"

"We met while filming for Netflix. You'd like her—it was a film school placement thing."

"Nice. Well, we can definitely make her day. Take it back to the chorus?"

"Good call," says Gina. She fiddles with the music, then holds up her phone. "Okay, eyes on the road, but sing along."

Eva keeps singing even after Gina's stopped recording. She wishes she weren't driving—it's hard to properly jam out when you've got to keep at least one hand steady on the steering wheel. The other, well. In the video, it may be on her heart.

They're only a few songs into *Lunar* when Eva pulls off the highway and turns down the volume so she can properly listen to Google Maps. She's never been to Steph's house here before. Her mind settles a little when they pass a park she used to go to with her dad after piano lessons. Steph isn't too far off her own mental map after all.

Except there's a thick branch blocking the slide like a giant, splintery seat belt, and the divots in the wood chips beneath the swings are filled with standing water. No one's going to play there today.

"Have you and Celeste talked at all? About how you're going to manage to . . . cohabitate this week?" Gina asks.

Eva comes to a complete stop at a stop sign, then turns left, trading one tree-lined street for another. "This band brought

Steph's family a lot of grief, or at least didn't make certain things easier on them. If pretending I'm still on good terms with my ex for two minutes a day is going to make this whole thing easier for everyone, I can't say no to that."

"Have you dated anyone since?"

"Not . . . really," says Eva.

A date here, no date there. Some dancing at some clubs. Nothing as intimate as a single shared look with Celeste had been, once upon a time.

"She hasn't either."

Right, now that you guys talk all the time without me, Eva thinks.

"She's been busy," Eva says. "Two albums, now in the middle of her second tour . . ."

"Have you listened to them?"

Eva could lie and say no, but then Gina will probably drag her off for a midnight listening session tonight, and she'll have to listen to Celeste sing about love while under Gina's all-seeing scrutiny.

Also, Gina could always tell when Eva was lying.

"Yes," she says.

She glances over at Gina. Her expression can best be categorized as *I rest my case.*

Both of their phones chime at once; Gina checks hers, then announces, "Pip dropped Celeste off at Steph's."

"She beat us?" Eva takes another left, pulling onto Steph's street.

"She was in Denver last night. Flew straight into Duluth this morning," Gina adds, after their phones let off another simultaneous chime. "Steph's house is the brick one, third on the right."

Eva pulls into the driveway, her shaking hand clutching the gear stick a little harder than usual as she shifts into park.

"Shall we?" Gina says.

Shall we? Eva wonders. *Shall we pretend to be Moonlight Over-throw for one more week?*

"Once more unto the breach," Eva says.

She turns off the car, unplugs her phone, and follows Gina.

EVA

As soon as they've wrangled their luggage inside, Gina starts hugging everybody, which means Eva has no choice and has to hug everybody, too. Everyone is there, except for Steph's mom: Matt and Meghan and Mari, all of them blond and blue-eyed and just a little wary.

Steph's grandma.

Steph.

Celeste, who Eva dodges by pretending she has to carefully take off her ankle boots the moment their eyes meet.

"We're so happy to be hosting all of you," Grandma Marit says. "It's good to have friends all back in one place."

"We really appreciate it," says Gina.

Eva smiles and fiddles with the handle of her suitcase. She knew seeing them all in person was going to be hard, but it's worse with the audience of Steph's entire family, spread out in the big kitchen, the colorful high chair prominent amid the light wood of the other kitchen chairs. Eva thought she could be . . . okay with having to interact with Celeste. She's a big girl. She signs contracts, she's met important politicians, she does hospital visits. She can be mature about seeing her ex. Now that Celeste is in front of her, though, she's not so sure.

Steph and Gina are watching her closely. As if she would make a scene in front of Steph's family. Celeste sends a tentative smile her way. Eva turns a little more pointedly toward Grandma Marit. Eva's plan for the week is to let herself love their old MO songs and performing enough to let them go for good once it's over. No part of that requires soothing Celeste's feelings until the uncertainty leaves her eyes.

"Steph can show you where you'll be staying, and I'm sure you'll want to freshen up a little after your drive." Grandma Marit sends Matt a Look, and before Eva can worry about whether she was obviously rude, they're all being ushered upstairs, Matt with a suitcase in each hand.

Steph stops outside the first door on the left. "Meghan is going to stay in Mari's and I'm going to take her room, so one of you can stay in mine here, and the other two can share the guest bedroom."

"Who knew a seven-bedroom house could feel squeezed for space?" Matt jokes.

"I already put my stuff in the guest room—" Celeste says.

"Then I guess I'm taking your room," says Eva, smiling at Steph.

Steph glances between Eva and Celeste. "Look . . . Is this going to be okay?"

"Of course," says Celeste. "We're not here to stir up trouble."

Fuck you, Eva thinks. Since when does Celeste get to speak for her?

The snarky part of her has a ready answer: *Since Celeste oh-so-wisely decided breaking up with me was in* my *best interest, remember?*

Before Eva can say anything, though, Steph jumps in. "Grandma's really into this whole friends reunion thing, but if that's not going to work—"

You owe me, Eva almost says, but she doesn't, because maybe it's Eva who owes Steph. Maybe they're all one big mess of owing each other, and who can tell, at this point, where one more favor will fall on the ledger? If there still is one anymore, she should probably throw it out.

"You've got enough on your plate. We can handle this," says Celeste.

"Enough with the 'we,'" Eva snaps.

It's true that she doesn't want to add to Steph's list of problems. But telling Steph—*for Eva*—that they can just ignore the fact that Celeste broke up with Eva romantically and musically, all in one night, seems a little extreme.

"Oh," says Celeste. "I just—"

"I don't care. *Just* stop," says Eva.

Celeste looks away.

"Maybe you two should talk this out on your own," Gina suggests.

Eva flinches. She can't imagine anything she wants *less* than to be left alone with Celeste.

Matt, standing awkwardly a little ways down the hall, clears his throat. "So can someone tell me which suitcase I'm supposed to put in the guest room?"

"Let's just put them all there for now. We can decide who gets Steph's room tonight," says Gina.

Me or Celeste, Eva thinks, but she follows Matt down the hall.

The room they enter is very obviously a guest room: minimal decorations and personal touches, inoffensive color scheme. A large window overlooks the backyard, and a half-open door leads into a bathroom. The bed is queen-size, wrought iron, with a cream duvet and a light blue throw blanket spread across the end. There's a suitcase open on the floor at the foot of the bed. Specifically, at the foot of the left side of the bed, which is Celeste's side. Was. Whatever.

"Oh," says Celeste, looking at her suitcase.

Matt flees the scene.

Eva keeps staring at Celeste's suitcase. And the bed. It doesn't even matter that she and Celeste won't be sharing it. It's all still right here, taunting her.

This is fine, she tells herself. *This is all going to end on a good note.*

As justifiable as her anger is, she's never going to get through this week if she can't stay calm. She'll never be able to give Duluth what it deserves. Never mind a Moonlight Overthrow music marathon—Eva knows what she and Gina really should have done on the drive up. Until Eva can claw her way toward genuine civility, she could use some acting tips.

CELESTE

The four of them settle into a well-appointed entertainment room in the basement: Steph and Eva on one couch, Celeste and Gina on another. Eva changed before coming down; now she's wearing yoga capris and a UCLA T-shirt.

I get it, Celeste thinks. *You're in college.*

Beneath their loose, knee-length skirt, Steph crosses their legs in proper crisscross-applesauce formation. Gina has an iPad in hand. Despite her early-morning flight and drive, Gina still looks like she came off a *Vogue* photo shoot, pale pink romper, flawless skin and all.

"All right," Celeste says. "Let's put on a show."

"It can't be choreographed. We don't have time for that," Steph says.

"Late-stage One Direction," says Eva. "They sold out stadiums wandering around their stages eating, like, nachos and bananas. It'll be fine."

Celeste laughs.

"Are we going to stick with our set list from last tour, or . . . ?" Eva asks.

"Why don't we start from scratch?" Celeste says. "We don't have to think about promoting a specific album anymore."

Gina nods. "We should still definitely do some of the hits, but I agree. Let's make this special."

Celeste watches Eva's face carefully. So many of their songs—too many of their songs, maybe—were about *them*. It used to be a game with them, seeing who could include the most specific references in the lyrics. They wrote dozens of songs for each album, so plenty of those never made the cut. But some of them did.

Celeste has become used to singing about Eva, post-Eva. Eva hasn't had to sing about Celeste. Eva deliberately chose *not* to, even though she could have.

"And we should cover a song of Celeste's, and a song of Eva's," Steph adds.

"What?" Eva startles, looking up from her phone; even from the other couch, Celeste can see the open iTunes app and the album art for their debut. *Supernova* had two top-ten singles, and Celeste is still fond of the earnestness of the rest.

"We shouldn't ignore what you two have been doing. You've been making great music," Steph insists.

Gina looks straight at Celeste. "For Celeste, I think we should do 'Before.'"

"That wasn't a single," Eva says.

Celeste looks between them, surprised by how fast Eva answered. Eva never gave Celeste permission to use her as a muse post-breakup. Celeste just assumed Eva wouldn't listen.

"We can circle back to that," Celeste says.

Deciding on the main set list doesn't take as long as Celeste would have guessed, probably because she and Eva agree with all of Gina's and Steph's suggestions, and Gina and Steph are smart enough to avoid the songs that are most blatantly about them. "Girl Says Yes," "A Little More," and "You Know I Know"—it's like they never existed at all.

"I have to ask," Gina says. "We're all going to have *all* these songs re-memorized by Thursday?"

"You know music memory is different. I can still sing most of our fifth-grade choir songs," says Eva.

After some verses have been exchanged, lyrics modified for Steph as needed, and the set list ordered and re-ordered, Eva stretches and stands up. "So far, we've been all talk, no singing. We need to try this."

The rest of them follow Steph toward a baby grand piano that's tucked into one corner.

"Eva?" Celeste says.

It's not that she expects Eva to still know the piano accompaniment for any of Moonlight Overthrow's songs. For today, a single note to make sure they start on key would be enough. And, okay, any of them could do that, but Celeste wants Eva to do it.

Begin as you mean to go on is something Eva's dad said a lot, back when they were first in contract negotiations, and then every time they started work on a new project or with a new team member. Celeste hasn't seen Eva's dad since their very last show, but as soon as she got to New York, she wrote the phrase on a Post-it and stuck it to her bedroom mirror. Every morning, every day before she left for the studio: *begin as you mean to go on.*

Eva sits, runs her hands over the keys, and plays a quick succession of notes that Celeste recognizes as her "getting to know a new piano" test. Celeste aches with the half-forgotten familiarity of it, with how at ease Eva seems.

Eva turns to Steph, beaming. "It's a beautiful piano."

"Thanks," says Steph.

"'This Afternoon'?" Eva suggests.

"This Afternoon" was the first single off their second album, the number one song that nabbed them a Grammy nomination for Record of the Year and made them an international hit. Celeste and Gina co-wrote it with one of their usual professional songwriting partners. They were tired of pop music love affairs that only happened in the dark—midnight, two a.m., the middle of the night.

They were fifteen and fourteen, and even though their shows kept them up late, flirting still seemed something more likely to happen at three in the afternoon than three in the morning.

I want a love in broad daylight. I want to love in the middle of the day, Celeste said during the writing session. Eva kissed her a month later, on a sunlit rooftop patio in a city far from home. But that was years ago now.

Eva starts to play the intro. With a nod from Eva, Steph comes in right on time for the first verse.

All at once it's the chorus, Celeste's turn for the melody. The lyrics are in her veins, running through her just as much as blood. She knows she's pushing the tempo in her excitement, but Steph is matching her, grinning, Gina, Eva, and the piano right with them.

The summer sun is still pouring in through the large windows. It might not exactly be afternoon anymore, but it's close enough. It feels like it.

Celeste is in love.

JULY 2021
EVA

"I know it's not a real Shabbat dinner," Ms. Miles says apologetically to Celeste, once they've settled around the big dining room table.

Mari's already eaten, so she's playing in the living room, babbling to herself, while the rest of them have dinner. Occasionally, she toddles up to one of them, showing off her plush Elmo.

Eva looks sideways at Celeste. She remembers Shabbat dinners with Celeste's family from their pre-MO lives: the lighting of the candles, the blessing of the children, the fresh challah.

Good Shabbos, she thinks, but holds her tongue.

"This looks delicious," Celeste says. "My tour rider only guarantees one a month. I'm very lucky to be spending this one with you."

The practiced graciousness lands between Eva's ribs, and she ducks her head, hoping someone else will fill in the silence. Eva didn't anticipate sitting next to Celeste at dinner, but before she could strategize a natural alternative, Steph and Gina were already seated, and she didn't have a choice.

"Did you have a good rehearsal this afternoon?" Ms. Miles asks.

"It wasn't really a formal rehearsal," Eva says.

Maybe it should have been: the show is already sold out. It's a tiny venue, less than a thousand seats. The small seating capacity doesn't stop the worries about performing badly from lying heavy on her chest.

Grandma Marit nods. "We don't want to make you sick of talking about this benefit concert before it even happens. Steph hasn't told me what you've all been doing, since they've been home."

She means since the breakup. Eva takes a big bite of fish.

"I did tell you, Grandma," Steph says. "That's when we decided they should stay here, remember?"

"Why don't you all tell us yourselves, anyway," Ms. Miles cuts in as Mari crawls onto her lap.

Gina goes first. There is a brief round of congratulations for the *Arbitrary Deadlines* Oscar nod (on the part of Steph's family) and thanks (on the part of Gina), before Grandma Marit returns her focus to Celeste.

"And what about you, dear?" she asks.

"I'm still singing. I'm in the middle of my second tour, actually."

"I love *Silhouette*," Meghan says, blushing.

"Thanks," says Celeste. "Me too."

"You must be so proud," Grandma Marit says, and Eva realizes with a start that she's looking at *Eva*, not at Celeste.

A cold, creeping feeling starts to settle in her stomach. Grandma Marit *has* to know they broke up . . .

"Yes?" she says. "Yes, of course."

Which is the truth. Even though Celeste isn't hers to be proud of anymore.

"And Eva's been going to college," Celeste says, as if it's in any way comparable to films and Netflix and albums and tours.

(Which she didn't even want, anyway, not without them.)

Steph clears their throat. "Meghan is actually starting this fall at UMD."

Eva relaxes into her chair as Gina peppers Meghan with polite questions.

Thank you, Steph, Eva thinks.

"It'll be hard," Meghan admits. She glances at the living room, where Mari is once again lying on her stomach, patting her blocks with a careful, chubby hand. "But worth it, for sure."

After dinner and dishes, the family slowly disperses—Meghan for Mari's bedtime routine, Matt for video games—but Ms. Miles and Grandma Marit usher the rest of them into the living room.

"I've missed you girls," Ms. Miles says at one point, after the sun has set. "I was with you all so closely for years, and I turn my back for a year and you finished growing up."

"I'm only nineteen," Celeste says. "I hope I've got some growing up left to do."

Celeste is next to Eva on the couch. Being so close to Celeste again is like going to a morning class on less than four hours of sleep and no coffee. Sometimes she's hyperaware of it, and then her awareness drops away, time skips, nothing could be more natural—until her head jerks, and she's reminded that this is foreign, not familiar. She's supposed to notice this; she can't afford to get used to it again. To be lulled to sleep.

When they finally say their good nights and head upstairs, Eva trails after the others. God, she's tired.

At the top of the stairs, Celeste turns back to her. "I think we should talk," she says, her voice low.

Eva looks at her: her blue-streaked hair, her polished fingernails gleaming against the banister, the curve of that small smile just for her, no witnesses.

"Okay," she says. "Let's talk."

EVA

Celeste hops right onto the guest bed, like it's any of the hotel beds they shared over the years, like Eva is going to crawl right on top of her. Which Eva is *not* going to do. Eva is going to suffer through whatever this conversation is, then take her stuff and flee down the hall.

Gina slides into the room behind her. "Sorry, just going to grab my suitcase so I can shower in Steph's room while you . . . talk."

Eva shrugs, and Gina doesn't linger. Eva remains by the door, shut behind Gina out of habit, and, maybe, to prevent the rest of the household from hearing them argue. If an argument is coming. She's not sure.

"I don't want this to be uncomfortable," Celeste says. "It's—we haven't seen each other in a while. This isn't exactly where I thought we'd pick up again."

The old bitterness rises in Eva, threatening to flush out the lingering high of singing with the group, but she tries to force it away. It can settle in her head, her stomach, her heart, but she won't let it touch her voice.

Remember, you don't care about any of this, she tells herself. *This isn't a big deal. You're so far over this, it's funny. Laugh.* She makes herself cross the room. She sits on the bed, facing Celeste, who's leaning back against the pillows.

"Oh? That night at Olivia's doesn't count?" Eva says, keeping her tone light.

"God, I'm so sorry about that. Still. Again," Celeste says. "I had no idea . . . but I'm glad. I'm not sure you would have agreed to the benefit concert if we hadn't broken the ice between us first." A pause. "Okay, I know you wouldn't have, and I'm really, really happy we're doing it."

"Me too."

"I'm serious," Celeste says, meeting her gaze. "I missed you."

Eva wishes she would look anywhere else—the duvet, out the window at the night, the seascape on the wall. She's not sure if Celeste can still read the *same here, yes, always* in her eyes, and she's afraid to find out.

Eva glances down at her crossed legs. She stretches her arms out, placing her palms flat on the duvet. "So you mean it, that you thought about us . . . picking up again?"

As friends, she reminds herself.

"I missed you," Celeste repeats. "I just didn't know how to . . ."

"You had my number. You always had my number," says Eva.

"I wanted to give us all some space."

"I think moving to New York did that pretty effectively."

"Mental space. You know what I mean. Some time to figure out what we all wanted to do and be, after . . ."

"I thought you already had that all figured out, which is why there was an 'after' to begin with," says Eva.

It's unfair, and she knows it: Celeste wasn't the only one who wanted Moonlight Overthrow to end. But if Celeste had chafed a little bit less, if she and Eva had parted a little more amicably— maybe they could have all been friends, all this time. Maybe.

"I knew I wanted to have the chance to figure something out," Celeste corrects, but gently.

"Did you?"

Eva catches Celeste's gaze. She's still so beautiful, and god, why can't she let it go? Why can't she just let herself bask in the warmth of having Celeste back, even temporarily, for one goddamn night? Who cares about what happened—they're both here now.

Let yourself have this, she tells herself, for the hundredth time. In a week, she'll be back to L.A., back to classes and spontaneous trips to the beach. She gets one last week to drink her fill of Celeste, and to do it right this time, knowing it's the last. *Make it golden. Make it all light.*

"I think I did," Celeste says.

Eva nods. It's all she can manage. She hasn't spoken to Celeste alone since their breakup, and talking about it—it's a lot. It's too much.

"I'm going to shower, and then I guess we should grab Gina and go to bed. Long day tomorrow," says Eva.

"I'll be here."

You will, Eva thinks. *Isn't that something.*

STEPH

Now that the single's out, the timeline has accelerated. That's how Steph feels, anyway. It might not be true. None of this feels solid enough to be true.

Celeste, Eva, and Gina are swept up in it, this thing Steph thought they'd all been doing for fun suddenly being taken seriously by people with a lot of money, and a lot of lawyers. Gina tracks their stats religiously—downloads, streaming, radio play, social media engagement levels, you name it. Steph didn't even have an Instagram account until two months ago. Eva and Celeste have long sessions with professional songwriters, people whose names Steph recognizes.

But even though Steph doesn't trust this, and even though they're homesick, they don't want to go home. Not when there's this music, if only for a moment. Not when there's a chance to add more zeros to their first-ever bank account. They sent their family to Disney World with part of their first check. When Steph's mom got home, she found confirmation of a meal delivery subscription.

You shouldn't have. We're fine, she said.

It's true enough: they were never hungry; the electricity was never shut off. But even with Social Security survivor benefits, there were a lot of things Steph had learned not to ask for.

You're better now, Steph replied, and wished they felt safe giving more. Living in Los Angeles is expensive. But there will be checks from some brand sponsorships soon enough, and a new TV show wants to license the single for their credit sequence. Next on their list is buying their mom a new car.

"Steph?" a producer says. "Let's try those two lines again. Just keep doing them until I signal that we've got it."

By "it," the producer means ten seconds that are good enough to be fixed later. The lines are from one of the professionally pre-written songs, with Gina brought in at the end to tweak the bridge, so the label could say at least one band member contributed to every song on the album. The label hasn't totally decided whether they want MO to have real creative input or just the appearance of it, although Steph's already been told they'll only be allowed to drum for a few songs on tour. The label prefers bringing on backing musicians to backup dancers.

Yesterday, today, forever / we don't know what never means.

Steph sings it, but it's a lie. This band thing, whatever they're doing or pretending to do is—it's not a forever. It's today, some-how, but Steph's not counting on next year, much less infinity. They'll put out an album, apparently. The contract said it would be so. Maybe a hundred queer kids will find it and listen to it. And Steph will go back to the rest of their life. Back to Duluth, back to school. They're pretty sure that's the only possible ending.

Eva isn't used to being told no, which, somehow, has landed them here. Steph's not stupid. Eventually, someone in this indus-try is going to tell them no. Someone is not even going to let them ask.

Steph's going to be ready for that.

APRIL 2021
GINA

"Harold keeps messing up the take, so your call time's been pushed back," Georgia says, after a perfunctory knock on Gina's trailer door. She leans in the doorway, brown arms crossed in a way that shows off how much time she's spent hauling equipment across film backlots.

"I'm shocked. Genuinely," Gina says. "Is this a social call, or will they miss you if you stay a minute?"

"They always miss me. I'm a vital part of this production team." Georgia slides onto the narrow bench seat next to Gina. "So I had to really work to find you. It takes time to track down such an in-demand starlet."

"To tell me about the completely unexpected Harold update," Gina teases. She runs a hand through Georgia's dark hair, short on the sides and longer on top. "I'll vouch for you, babe."

Georgia gives her a hard look. "No, you won't. I'm on a break and offered to tell you on my way to crafty."

"I have food in here," Gina says.

"I was counting on that," says Georgia. She pulls the fruit bowl closer to her and plucks out an apple. When she bites, a drop of juice lands on her black T-shirt.

It's not that Gina didn't enjoy being on set for the two films, but acting involves a *lot* of waiting around, mostly alone in her trailer. When she was in the band, meeting other musicians was always fun, but she hasn't had to make friends since she was about ten years old. It doesn't help that so far, she hasn't had any costars within ten years of her age.

Trust Netflix to have bright-eyed production assistants.

Enter: Georgia Yang.

Georgia swallows another bite of her apple. "I did want to check on you, though. I could tell you were getting kind of irritated with Paul yesterday."

"You mean, when he was 'joking' with me about whose career I was going to sabotage to get that HBO part I've *already turned down*?" Gina huffs. Still. Pissing off the director is not a good idea. "Do you think anyone else noticed?"

"No, don't worry about it. Plus, half the cast and two-thirds of the crew are always irritated with him." Georgia tips into Gina, resting her head on Gina's shoulder. "Another week, and you don't have to work with him again. Although I am kind of hoping we'll end up on the same production later."

Gina sighs. It would be easier to decide what she wants if she *knew* she was in the opening scenes of an epic love story à la Eva and Celeste, minus the breakup she did not see coming.

Georgia taps her thigh. "You don't want that? It's okay if that's true. Business can get messy when you have friends around."

Especially friends with a habit of kissing after filming wraps for the day, Gina thinks. But it is nice not to have to worry about defining anything when they're both running on far too little sleep.

"You're the best part about this production," Gina says. Maybe that's too honest, but they've been filming since February, and Gina's tired.

"Don't say that. You're killing it as Arabelle."

"Thanks."

"You don't like the role?" Georgia sits up, twisting to face Gina properly.

"She's not the problem."

"So there *is* a problem."

"I think she's fascinating. She's nothing like me."

Georgia raises one eyebrow. "That's the point, isn't it? To immerse yourself in someone else? Actresses don't tend to become known by playing people exactly like themselves."

Actors, on the other hand, rests unspoken between them.

"No, absolutely. Arabelle is an actress's dream."

"So if it's not Arabelle . . ."

It's only having film.

It's not having her band.

During her meeting with Kayla that last spring, she thought that was what she wanted. Music and MO were her chrysalis, but she was born to be a butterfly. To take flight, she had to leave them behind. It's hard to admit that she might have been building her life on the wrong metaphor.

Gina made it to the *Oscars*, age eighteen. The Oscars are where she's supposed to be. The pride hasn't lingered, though, only the doubt. She can't put that kind of indecision into her leather portfolio. She has the whole world spread out before her, and she doesn't know which part to taste. Where to sample, where to linger.

"I miss music," Gina says, slowly, because it's not just that. "But I also miss—I miss who I was, kind of, in the band. Who I let myself be? Who I was allowed to be? I don't miss having to pretend to be some wholesome combination of Eva and Celeste, because I'm not that. But when you're in a band, part of the whole . . . spirit of it . . . is being beloved, not just admired. And even though my *role* within the band wasn't to be the funny one or the sweet one . . ." She swallows. "Even when I was like, rolling my eyes, everybody knew I loved my bandmates while I was doing it. Affection all the way down."

"You got to be soft," says Georgia.

The word seems to pierce straight through her underbelly. "Yeah. And I—I don't get to be that anymore. Nobody assumes that anymore. Nobody thinks there's anything I want except the next role, the next cover. I've been telling myself that it's true, but it's not. So when I was at the Oscars this year, the whole red carpet—I mean, all the little interviews—it was like all the questions were for this sideways version of me I didn't even realize I'd been creating." Her *Vogue* cover had praised her carefully cultivated, cucumber-cool confidence, but Gina knows better than to trust that image will hold. "If it gets one step beyond this, soon it's going to be a lot of awful coverage about how vicious or condescending I am. How dare this Black girl think she's amazing."

"Which you are."

Gina can't suppress her grin. "Which I am. And it's on the media if they decide to be racist, obviously." She pauses and looks across at the gray blinds, closed tight over the trailer windows. "You know, there was this narrative, after my first movie role was announced. About how I'm the ambitious, confident breakout star of the group. Which is true. But the hard thing is that then people started expecting *only* that from me, so I leaned on it even more. And I was standing on the red carpet in this gorgeous Vera Wang dress, on my way to be honored with all these other amazing actresses, on live TV . . . having this revelation that I think I've forgotten that this exaggerated version is an *exaggerated version*."

"Five years from now, I'm going to make a joke about the dangers of method acting," Georgia says. Her voice is like being wrapped in a flower, all velvet. "I guess you felt you had to separate yourself from the band, at first?"

"Exactly. I've spent two years convincing myself that alone, and . . . *uncontested* is the way I wanted to do my career. I'm never going to apologize for being ambitious, but I don't like this version of me. I mean, separately from whatever the hell the media decides to do. I don't like being that *inside myself*. And film—or at least how I'm doing film right now—isn't helping me get back to being a person I like being."

It's not that Gina wants to go back to the pace of her MO schedule: interviews in the afternoon, playing a show in the evening, getting more than a couple hours of sleep only if it was somebody else's night to record in a makeshift hotel studio. But her bandmates also never looked at her and saw a contract, dollar signs, a magazine cover. They wanted to hang out with her even when all they were doing was math homework. Gina didn't realize how much that surety was protecting her until she tossed it aside.

"I don't really know what to say, except that I think you're great. I like who you are. I like how hard you work. How you make me laugh when I'm least expecting it. And you're not somebody who's pushing other people down on your way up." Georgia pulls Gina into her and kisses her temple.

"I hope not," says Gina, closing her eyes.

"So now what?" Georgia asks.

"I don't know."

If Eva could hear her now, she would *hate* her. She thinks about the list she always gives: Whitney Houston. Rihanna. Janelle Monáe. The problem with basing her career on all those other icons' careers is that she isn't any of them. She doesn't want to have exactly what they have, exactly how they did it.

She wants, and wants, and wants. She has *wanted* her whole life. She points herself toward a goal, and she succeeds. But her movie star goal . . . isn't sitting right anymore. Not the *what*, and definitely not the *how*.

She's tired of being the girl who ditched her band for greener pastures, even just in her own mind. Eva did a damn good job of managing the post-breakup PR on her own. A last, maybe unintended gift from Eva: Gina can focus on changing herself, instead of trying to erase bitter MO breakup headlines. But all those reporters covering the same story with the same angle, all those trajectories where ditching your band is the inevitable, albeit mutually agreed-upon, narrative? No more.

Gina still wants it all.

JULY 2021
GINA

"Want to sit on the balcony for a bit?" Steph asks as Gina drops her suitcase by the bathroom door. They're rummaging through their dresser, pulling out pajamas.

"That sounds nice," says Gina. Her shower can wait. Even though she caught an early flight, with the time change, she's still wide awake.

They unlock a sliding patio door that leads onto a small balcony, furnished with two deck chairs and a tiny round table. Steph stretches out, resting their feet on the railing.

"You look good," Gina offers.

At the end, Steph was stick-thin on a frame that wasn't meant to be. Basic touring stress, Gina assumed at the time.

Steph laughs. "Thanks. You too."

"You know what I mean," Gina says.

Tour always exhausted Steph at a level deeper than the rest of them, and that last tour, Steph lost even more weight than usual. They've filled out since, and Gina is profoundly grateful for a physical sign that leaving has been good for Steph.

"Yeah, I do," Steph says. They flex their toes. "I had to get a whole new wardrobe. I'd never had boobs before. I had no idea what to do when suddenly my shirts were stretching in all these ways they aren't supposed to. *And* I had to buy the clothes myself."

"What was more shocking, the boobs or not having your entire wardrobe picked out for you?" Gina teases.

"Definitely the boobs." Steph rests their head against the back of the chair. "It's actually . . ."

"Actually?"

"I wasn't really sure how I felt about them, that first spring. My boobs, I mean," Steph says. "I don't like being read as a woman, but . . . I have a body, and it's non-binary, because I'm non-binary. End of story. I *like* my boobs."

Gina gives them a joking once-over. "They are pretty nice."

Steph rolls their eyes. "Right? And, like, I know not all non-binary people feel that way about their bodies. But that's mostly how I feel about mine, at least right now. It might change next year. I don't know yet."

"You're pretty badass, Steph."

They sit in silence for a moment, Gina relishing the companionable quiet she's missed so much.

Steph clears their throat. "Skylar—you remember them? Star pitcher of the middle school softball team?"

"No?"

"Lots of freckles . . . Wait, you have to remember them accidentally punching someone for real in the fall play, when you were in seventh."

"*Oh*, yes, sorry—Skylar, got it," says Gina.

"Anyway, they started T last year, and they're pretty open about what that's been like. They're actually at Lake Superior College now. We started hanging out again when I got back, and they introduced me to people."

"I admit, I've been a little worried you haven't left this house since November 2019." Gina's relieved to be wrong.

"It's been better, this last year." They hesitate now, glancing between Gina and the balcony railing. "Look, I joke about my shirts being boob-incompatible, but I lived out of Matt's clothes a lot that first winter. Until he told me that we had to go shopping. He was my cover in the 'men's' section."

"I'm really glad he was there for you," says Gina, her voice soft.

Gina remembers Steph pushing their stylists toward the butch end of things in their last year, for "candid" shots and meet-and-greets, but no one had allowed that for interviews or tour costumes. The band could be sapphic, but only in skirts.

"Me too. I didn't touch a dress for months. It was a kind of detox, until I could figure out how *I* wanted to present. And I have so many sports bras now, Kayla would die if she knew."

"I'm glad," says Gina again. She winces. "I mean . . . I'm glad that you have what you need."

She feels so stupid for not seeing any of this during their last tour. How could she have left Steph to struggle through it on their own? She doesn't blame them for not reaching out after the final show, since she knew Steph wanted privacy and to focus on their family, and Gina's post-MO life was conducive to anything but. Gina could have texted, though. A birthday card, *something*.

"Me too," says Steph. "Sports bras, my family, what more could I ask for?"

Gina's never going to get a better opening than this. She dives in. "I know we haven't been talking about what's going to happen after this concert, but I'm going to put this out there: I miss you. You were the best older"—she catches herself—"sibling. I couldn't have done Moonlight Overthrow without you, and I couldn't have done what I've done since if you hadn't helped me through MO first. I was lucky to have you then, and Meghan—and Matt, and Mari—are lucky to have you now."

"Don't be ridiculous. You could have done all that without me," Steph says.

"I thought I could. I couldn't have."

Gina resented the band for a lot of that last year, but now she understands better how valuable it was to start her career with three allies, instead of on her own.

"I never thought I'd have to say this to you, but don't sell yourself short, Gi," says Steph. They clear their throat. "What do you think Celeste and Eva are up to?"

"Think, or hope?" Gina says.

"You've got a stake in this now?"

"Did I not have a stake in it then? Didn't we both?" Gina stretches forward, her hands resting lightly on her ankles, her cheek pressed to her knees.

"Sure. But whose side are you on now?"

"Ideally . . . *their* side," Gina says. "But in the sense that I told Celeste she had to stop singing *about* Eva to twenty thousand people and actually talk *to* her—Celeste's, I suppose."

She's still going to help Celeste win Eva back. It's not like she can't tell Eva still harbors at least *some* distinctly non-platonic feelings for Celeste. But Gina always, always plays with her own endgame in mind. Gina wants them *both* back. Potential romantic reunion aside, it's going to be harder to get what she wants if Eva and Celeste can't even have a real conversation.

"Did you really? I would have paid to see that," Steph says.

Gina sits up. "It was after her Staples Center concert. You could have."

"You said it yourself: I'm a good older sibling." Steph's tone is striving for levity, but it falls flat, even to Gina's unaccustomed ears.

"We can be friends again. I think—it's your family, of course, but I think you can have friends, too. Even if you're never going to move back to L.A.," Gina says.

Steph doesn't respond.

Gina lets her ears fill with the night for a moment: birds and rustling leaves, and, somewhere down the block, the distant strains of what sounds like kids playing flashlight tag. It's more humid than it is in L.A., but not unbearably sticky.

Gina twists in her chair, tucking her knees to her chin as she looks at Steph. "Are you moving back to L.A.?"

Steph gestures back at the house. "I can't."

"But . . . what if you could?"

"I can't. They need me," Steph says.

"Okay . . . but maybe they're not always going to need you as much as they need you now. Or as much as they needed you last summer, even. What are you going to do then?" Gina asks.

Gina comes back sometimes. She has family scattered across the Midwest—a handful in Milwaukee, a handful in Chicago, some in Minneapolis, like her parents—and they've seen her since Moonlight Overthrow made it. She's paying college tuition for four of her cousins. She thinks she gets Steph's obligations more than either of the others. Eva's the only child of only children; Celeste has two much older sisters, who were already starting to settle into their own lives when Moonlight Overthrow burst into the world.

But Gina refuses to stay. She refused to stay then, and she refuses now, again and again. As it turns out, it's not a choice you make only once. You have to be a little selfish in this world if you want to make it big. You have to not care. You have to find a way to do right by people even without looking back. You have to live with however that scale balances out—or doesn't.

Steph made a different choice than she did . . . but maybe they want to change their mind.

"What would I even do, though?" Steph says.

"What do you mean?"

"It's been over a year and a half. If I left for L.A. *tomorrow*, it'd take me a year to release an album. Celeste was smart, doing it right away. I don't—I don't even have a Twitter anymore. I *hate* Twitter," they say.

"So you get a kick-ass publicity team, and they control your new Twitter, and you craft a comeback narrative. You took time off, no overexposure for random side projects . . . you reappear with a bang. As a mature musician," Gina says.

"Damn. I should just hire you," Steph jokes. "Too bad you're busy becoming . . ."

Whitney Houston. Rihanna. Janelle Monáe.

"Gina Wright."

"The first of her name," Steph says. They shake their head. "I don't know. I miss singing. I miss—the fans, everything. Well, except those long tours. But I never wanted to go solo."

Like Eva, Gina thinks, although that's not exactly right. Eva has, in her own way, as a songwriter. She might have gone properly solo if her relationship with Celeste hadn't ended at the same time, in the same way, as Moonlight Overthrow. Gina had been so sure Eva could be convinced, but she hadn't been counting on Celeste cutting all ties.

"What if . . . ," Gina starts.

"What if what?"

"What if I said I was thinking about coming back to music, too?" Gina says.

"But . . ."

Steph doesn't need to finish their sentence; Gina knows.

But what about becoming an actress? But didn't you leave the band because you were through with doing music? But then, why . . .

"I've been thinking about it, that's all," Gina says. "It felt stifling, by the end, because we were still supposed to be this unified group, and there wasn't enough space for us as individuals. And there wasn't time for me to act. Making that kind of time wasn't a priority for anybody but me, and if I waited through three more albums, through another three years? Directors wanted me *then*. But I've filmed three projects, and I miss music. I think I've bought myself some time now."

Gina hasn't said that to anyone but Georgia yet. How could she turn her back on acting when she gave up *everything* to pursue it? Gina's supposed to be the one who knows what she wants and always succeeds. There's no room for self-doubt or changing her mind in that reputation.

"I get that," Steph says. "You could still go solo. You've got an even broader fan base now. I bet a lot of people would love it if you did music again."

"Including you?"

"Duh." They sit up, swinging their legs to the side, between their chair and Gina's. "Seriously. If you want to do music again, *do it*. Your solo album can be the first non-Disney album Mari knows all the way through, once she finishes learning how to talk. It'll be great."

Gina uncurls herself, placing her feet flat on the balcony floor, her toes just barely brushing Steph's. "Babe. Can you hear yourself? If you want to do music again, *do it*."

Steph glances away. "I can't do it solo."

A heady, heavy feeling drops into Gina's stomach, some swirling mix of possibility and responsibility. If she—and Celeste, and Eva—are the ones standing between Steph and what they want, between Steph and *music* . . .

If all she had to do was say, *Let's do it together*, and fix this for Steph . . .

It's sparking and sparkling, the feeling rushing up her spine. If all she has to say is yes—if they would be in if Gina were—

She could make this work. It's the beginning of a solution, if nothing else. Where there's a will, there's a way, and no one has ever accused Gina Wright of lacking will.

EVA

When she steps back into the bedroom after her shower, the lights are off, except for a small lamp on the bedside table. Celeste is already lying down on the left side of the bed, eyes closed, although she's still on top of the duvet. The blue in her hair shines under the soft yellow light.

"Bathroom's open," Eva whispers.

Celeste's eyelids flutter open. "Thanks." She slides off the bed.

Eva zips her suitcase, hauls it upright, and hastens down the hall to Steph's bedroom. She knocks softly, hoping not to disturb any of Steph's family. Gina doesn't answer, so she knocks again.

"Gina?" she hisses. "I'm coming in."

When she opens the door, the room is dark. Gina is splayed out in the middle of the full-size bed, her head angled away from the door.

"Gina?" Eva tries again.

The light from the hall is enough for Eva to see the duvet shifting with Gina's even breaths, but her silk head wrap covers her ears, making it impossible to tell whether she's wearing her customary earplugs.

Either way, she's fast asleep.

Well, shit.

If Gina's asleep, Steph's probably gone to bed as well.

Eva returns to the guest bedroom, frowning at the bed. There's nothing for it. She slips between the sheets.

Celeste can figure out how to solve the problem for once, she thinks.

Eva lies still on her back, head tilted away from the lamp. The sheets are cool against her skin, and fresh-smelling, just washed. Eva has stayed in nice hotels over the years—*very* nice hotels, that last tour—with off-the-charts thread counts and fancy water and personalized notes waiting in the rooms. But this is homey. It knows her in a way that no hotel could, no matter how many instructions her team sent on ahead. There, she's always a guest, handled with kid gloves; here, she's . . . not exactly family, but pretty close. It's good to be back.

When Celeste opens the bathroom door, Eva freezes beneath the covers, her heart racing, even as she tries to keep her breathing steady.

"They went to bed without telling us?" Celeste says.

"Yeah," says Eva. "I wasn't going to wake anybody up. We'll fix it tomorrow."

It would be so easy to tell Celeste, *What's one more night, what's one more week of nights*, but Eva can't do that to herself.

Celeste gets into bed without another word. Out of the corner of her eye, Eva watches as she straightens the pillows behind her, then settles more comfortably into the mattress.

"Okay if I turn the light off?" Celeste asks.

"Yeah."

The mattress shifts as Celeste moves to turn off the lamp; there's a soft click, and then darkness. Eva's breathing seems thunderous in her own ears. Her entire body seems too loud, too big, even though there's at least a foot of space between them.

"Have enough blankets?" Celeste says.

"Yeah. You?"

"Yeah. Feel free to steal them back, if I hog them."

"Same. Uh, you too."

She hasn't bothered to shut her eyes again. Instead, she stares straight ahead into the darkness, toward the half-open bathroom door.

"Hey, Eva?"

"Yeah?"

"Thanks for doing this. You really, really didn't have to."

"I'm happy to." Eva turns her head toward Celeste, who's curled on her side, facing Eva. "You're the one who . . . well, you might not be thanking me after tomorrow, if it turns out I can't sing anymore."

Eva has mostly been able to ignore the issue of getting onstage again. Performing. Again. But the fact is, she hasn't, not in years. She was okay this afternoon, definitely not the best she's ever been. She's trying not to remember that her best wasn't enough to keep Celeste.

"Don't be ridiculous," Celeste says. "You can still sing. Your voice is gorgeous, okay? Don't ever doubt that."

Eva shifts fully onto her side, toward Celeste. She's not used to arranging herself like that. They used to have whole conversations with Celeste's nose brushing against the back of her neck, Celeste's hand on her hip or waist or stomach, slipping along her skin as they talked in the dark.

"Thanks," Eva says.

"I'm serious. Do you know how many people I've talked to who are, like, beyond jealous that I got to sing with you? That I got to *write* with you? A lot."

Of course I don't know that, Eva thinks. *You don't talk to me.*

"I don't remember her name now, but an A&R rep from the label called me last year, to ask if I'd write something for *Silhouette*," Eva says.

"Oh god," Celeste says. "I'm so sorry. I had no idea—I didn't—I wouldn't—"

"I know," Eva says.

There's a pause, and Eva wonders if they're going to leave it at that, if those will be the last words spoken before they will themselves to sleep.

But then Celeste says, "What did you tell her?"

"She left a message. I didn't even call her back. I mean, I didn't have to. She called again to say . . . sorry, never mind, it wasn't your idea. No harm, no foul."

"Oh."

"Yeah. So . . . I guess now you know. It's a great album," Eva offers, then winces. She didn't mean for that to slip out.

"You listened to it?" Celeste sounds . . . hopeful, and a little shy, and something else besides. Almost embarrassed, maybe, but Eva can't assume she knows how to read Celeste's tone anymore.

"I hope that was okay? I didn't know you didn't want me to. And, like, radio singles, kind of hard to avoid entirely . . ."

"No, I wanted you—I mean, I didn't not want you to . . . it's fine. You liked it?"

"I have a feeling another Grammy is headed your way," Eva says.

It's way less revealing than, *I listened to it on repeat for two whole weeks after it came out, I cried and I laughed and I reblogged so many promo posts on Tumblr, you have no idea.*

And she clung hard to every quote Celeste gave about being a storyteller, crafting fiction, weaving songs out of other people's stories. It hurt to think about Celeste writing songs for some other girl.

"We'll see," says Celeste. "You might, too, the way you keep racking up number one writing credits."

"We'll see," Eva echoes.

It's hard not to remember the last time she was at the Grammys. The way they didn't win Best Pop Duo/Group Performance. It meant she didn't have to give a gracious speech, all by herself. It also felt like proof the others hadn't had a reason to stay.

"It's going to be great," Celeste says. "The show. Because we're great and we love Duluth and we love our fans."

Every "we" and "our" hits Eva like a full-body blow. She's grateful for the dark, how Celeste can't see her expression.

"Yeah?" Celeste prompts.

"Yeah," Eva says quickly. "Fans, Duluth, great."

"*We're* great," Celeste says insistently. "Together. We are. You heard us downstairs."

"I was there," Eva agrees.

If we were so great . . .

But it's a thought that's crossed her mind so many times, it's worn out.

CELESTE

Eva's words play on repeat in Celeste's mind: *I was there, I was there.* What does that even mean? With the lights off, there's nothing to cushion them: no smile, no gesture.

Celeste sighs. "Do you even want to be here? At all?"

Every conversation with Eva feels like tug-of-war. Push, pull. Forward, back. And, okay, it's not like Celeste thought this would be easy. She hoped it would be easy. But she hadn't expected it to be easy one second and hard the next.

"Of course I do," Eva says.

"I know I do. I know Steph and Gina do. I'm not sure about you." It's not something she would have dared to ask earlier, but the whole conversation feels unreal. In the dark, Eva curled up beside her on the bed. Unreal and all too familiar, at the same time.

"I want to be here," Eva says, her voice very soft. "It's just . . . I was the only one who wanted to be here, back then. So it's hard to be back, after I found all these other places I liked being, too."

A hot rush of shame runs through Celeste and settles, sour, in her stomach. And, okay, a little jealousy, too.

She tries to tell herself the pride evens everything out—she's happy Eva has been happy without them . . . without her. Really. She couldn't expect Eva to be *waiting*. But a small part of her still wishes she were necessary for Eva's happiness. Even though that was part of the whole damn reason she left in the first place.

But see, she thinks, *maybe this means you can listen to Gina. Maybe you'll both be okay this time.*

"I'm sorry," Celeste says.

"Don't—"

"I am. I'm so glad you're here, and I'll do—whatever, anything, to make this easy for you. To make this *good* for you, okay?" Celeste swallows. "I know we're here because of a shitty situation, but . . . I'm having fun with it. And I really want it to be something you can enjoy, too."

And then she waits for Eva to say something. Is this how Eva felt that night, waiting for them to explain that nobody was staying? God, Celeste had messed that up. It's not that she regrets her decision, but she should have talked to Eva about it earlier. Way earlier. Way more nicely.

"I'm working on it," Eva says. "I want to be having fun with you all. It's just . . . letting myself have it. I don't know."

Letting herself have things never used to be a problem Eva had, not back when she thought she had everything and was going to get to keep everything, Celeste thinks.

"Anything I can do to help you with that, I promise, I'll do it, it's yours," Celeste says.

"Don't say that."

"I mean it."

The mattress shifts as Eva rolls onto her back.

Come back, Celeste thinks. She's missed Eva, okay? She's missed her voice and her laugh and her body, beside and beneath her own. She's missed waking up in the middle of the night with Eva still tucked against her, or at least within arm's reach, her hair tickling Celeste's nose. Her soft breathing, that gentle rise and fall, the heat of her.

"We should probably go to sleep," Eva says.

"Yeah. I set an alarm for the morning, while you were in the shower."

Celeste almost reaches out to her. She thinks about it. She thinks about finding Eva's hand beneath the covers, linking their fingers. Or brushing a hand along her shoulder. Something, some small touch. Intimate, but not necessarily romantic.

Instead, Celeste says, "Good night."

Eva murmurs her own good night, then rolls away, her back to Celeste.

Which is actually how it should be, only Celeste is left staring at the dark shape of Eva's body, unnaturally far away on the bed. Even when they were annoyed with each other, they didn't sleep this far apart. Even when they were irritated, they touched. It was a way of saying, *I'm still here with you. We're still in this together.*

It's harder to miss Eva up close than far away. The distance is more apparent, more immediate, than when she's onstage. Than when she's pretending she's not singing about Eva, even though, okay, yes, she really, really is.

It's instinctive to pull Eva close to her, but she can't. She's gotten used to sleeping alone, but it's different tonight, because she's not alone. Eva's right here. Eva is *in bed with her*, because . . . Celeste is an idiot, and Gina probably timed her own falling asleep to ensure that she couldn't switch with Eva.

I miss you, she thinks at Eva's back.

She closes her eyes.

MAY 2021
GINA

"I'm glad we're taking this chance to catch up now that filming has wrapped," says Kayla. "You're sure you don't want to go out for lunch? I can have my assistant call ahead, get us a booth."

"You know me," says Gina. She offers a sweet smile, nothing overdone. "I like to treat business as business."

"That's the Gina Wright we know and love," says Kayla. She holds open a door that leads into a small conference room.

As Gina settles into a chair and pulls out her black portfolio, Kayla says, "Tea? Coffee? My assistant should have—"

"She offered," Gina says. "I'm good, thank you."

"Well, then. Let's get to it, shall we? We're both busy women." Kayla pauses, leaving a space for Gina to agree. When Gina says nothing, Kayla continues, "Although you could be much busier than you are."

Now we're talking, Gina thinks.

"You've passed on every script that's been sent to you in the last three months," says Kayla.

"I have," says Gina.

"There's such a thing as being *too* selective, especially this early in your career. You have to choose something. You need to start going to auditions again." It's obvious that Kayla is trying to layer her scolding with indulgence, but neither rings true to Gina's ears.

"Nothing felt right," says Gina.

"In this business, you don't get to wait for the perfect project that ticks all your boxes. You have to convince casting directors that you tick all *their* boxes. You have to do the work." Kayla softens her expression. "I know you know how to do the work."

Gina has spent the entirety of her teenage years ensuring that the Kaylas of the world know she can do the work. She always knows she's at least getting that right.

"They weren't right for me," says Gina.

"You look tired. I know you've just come off filming, but we've got to catch these opportunities while they're coming. You can take a vacation once you've had some callbacks."

The easy response is on the tip of her tongue: *I don't take vacations until I've signed some contracts.*

Gina is no longer interested in the easy response. She's been in this rat race since she was thirteen. Almost five years nonstop, her life planned to the hour a year or two in advance. What if she wakes up one day and can't point to the decisions that led her there?

"I hope I don't look unprofessional," says Gina. "I haven't been to this office without makeup on . . . ever. But I've got to let my skin breathe, after all that heavy makeup during filming."

She very nearly wore a suit to this meeting, before switching to a sleek, knee-length skirt and a silky blouse. A pap walk is arranged for her exit from the building, and she knows the limited-edition three-inch heels are likely to be sold out within the week.

"You always look exactly as you mean to," says Kayla, her words a little slower than before. "But maybe we can talk about some of these roles. Not even *Bayahibe Rose*? You've done a big studio film that gave you an Oscar nod, your indie's coming out this winter . . ."

"It's the sequel potential that concerns me," says Gina.

"Concerns you! My point was that now might be the perfect time for a franchise. The first book won that big prize, the second topped the *NYT* list . . . It's not superheroes—you'll still be up for awards, if you do it right—and you'd get to film on location in Jamaica."

"The Dominican Republic."

"The Dominican Republic, sure," says Kayla. "I'm glad to hear you've done some research. And isn't it perfect for you?"

The thing is, *Bayahibe Rose* is perfect for her. Perfect for Gina if she wants to keep being perfect. For the first time in her life, that sounds . . . terrible.

"It's a long shoot, with potentially more to follow, if it does well," says Gina. "I can't commit to that right now."

"Are you pregnant?"

Only years of media training keep Gina's jaw from dropping. "No."

"Then I don't see what the problem is. You haven't had a problem committing before," says Kayla.

Gina cocks her head. "Actually, I think that's exactly how we got here. If we think back to the first time I declined to sign on for another three years of the same thing."

Kayla throws up her hands, letting them land heavily back on the conference table. "Yes, that's exactly how we got here. You wanted this. You sat down that hall"—Kayla points toward the door—"and told me this was how it was going to be. They're offering you first dibs on the *perfect* role. You know these kinds of parts don't come around every day, every *decade*."

Bayahibe Rose is right there, hers for the taking.

Gina has always taken.

"I can't be trapped into that kind of schedule," she says.

"Give me a reason. Help me out here. Two years ago, you sat across from me and said you wanted to be an actress. You can't be an actress if you don't act. Not even if you're Gina Wright." The lines around Kayla's mouth are taut.

Gina *knows* this.

"Show me what's in that binder of yours. You're the girl with all the answers." Kayla tries for a laugh. "You come in here, you know exactly what you want out of every meeting. Just tell me whatever it is."

"I don't know." It's only half a lie.

What she *wants*? She wants more than a week to take a step back and figure out what the hell she's been doing. Where she really wants to go from here. She loves acting. She loves music. But they don't feel like choices anymore, and she wants them to, desperately.

"Don't give me that. We've known each other too long," says Kayla.

"When I think about the people whose careers I want to emulate, it's not all acting or all music. It's both."

"Everyone has a main thing. Is yours going to be acting or music? Because if it's still music, it would have been good for me to know that two years ago," says Kayla.

I don't know, Gina wants to scream.

What do you do when you just *don't know*? She has tricked herself into certainty for so long. She has risen to every expectation, and now she's been running too fast to keep up with her own damn self.

"Are we talking about a solo album, now that you've shown the world who you are without the others holding you back?"

"They were never holding me back." Gina doesn't snap. Her tone is low and sure.

"That's not what you told me."

"That's what *you* told *me*," says Gina.

"It's 2021. Don't be afraid of your own ambition."

"I'm not."

"You're going to sacrifice this amazing, perfect series . . . for what?" Kayla raises her eyebrows.

"I want to devote my energy to something else—*all* of it," she says.

To being a person, not only a prodigy, she finishes, just for herself.

She hopes part of that means finding her way back into friendships that mean more than Insta likes. Gina's never going to trust Kayla with Celeste, Eva, and Steph again.

"*Bayahibe Rose* isn't going to wait for you. They need to lock down a lead. Save your soul-searching for preproduction."

"They'll lock down somebody else. If they don't know any other dark-skinned girls to call, I can make a list," says Gina.

"Look, Gina. Can I be blunt with you?" This time, Kayla doesn't wait for an answer. "This industry isn't going to wait for you to decide to get off your high horse. If you walk out this door, no new projects on the horizon—"

"Netflix might order another season."

Kayla waves this away. "If you don't take anything, they're going to stop asking. Then they're going to stop letting you audition. You just said it yourself, there are other girls. This industry moves on."

"I know Hollywood won't be waiting," says Gina. "I know a film career won't just be *waiting* for me. But I also believe in my ability to make it happen later. I've got time."

"You won't be eighteen forever. You don't have time, not in film."

"I'm Gina Wright. I make my own time."

"That thing you do, right there? It's cute, until you are *so wrong*. I admire you, I do. You're poised, you're articulate—"

I'm done, Gina thinks, with total clarity.

"—you're always great in interviews. Such confidence! But the world isn't wrapped around your little finger. And if it is right now, just a little, it's not going to stay that way, and it's especially not going to stay that way if you walk away."

Are you done? Gina wonders. She waits for the space of two breaths. She doesn't want to be interrupted by a continuation of Kayla's lecture.

"Either you trust me or you don't," she says, with a light shrug.

"I have had the utmost trust in you, until this very moment. Who even are you right now? Because it's not the Gina Wright I know."

That's . . . fine by Gina.

"There's something else I want," says Gina.

"More than *Bayahibe Rose*."

Gina's heart squeezes. Why is she being so stupid?

She thinks back to the night of the Oscars. Exactly where she was supposed to be, and still watching it all like her own life was someone else's film.

"More than *Bayahibe Rose*," Gina confirms.

"And this something else you want is . . . ?"

But Gina just shakes her head.

Kayla sighs. "I don't know what to say."

"I'll call you, if anything changes."

"Maybe a vacation would be good for you," Kayla says. The air of fake defeat doesn't nearly hide her true irritation. "You're right, you've still got two projects forthcoming. You won't get *Bayahibe Rose*, but we'll see what's out there later this summer. Spend some time with your family. Remind yourself why you're doing this."

"That's great advice. I think I'll do exactly that," says Gina.

She shakes Kayla's hand and sees herself out.

In a single-stall bathroom on the ground floor, she pulls out a few essentials: lipstick, mascara, eyeliner. Just a little something for the camera.

As she steps onto the sidewalk, she adjusts the strap of her Kate Spade handbag, smiles at the photographer, and calls her PA.

"Hey, Sofia? I don't want to do anything to interfere with the album promo, but can you figure out when Celeste's going to be here in June?"

Gina doesn't have time to read scripts right now. She has friendships to rekindle. She's under no illusions that she'll have a real chance to reunite the band, but every plan has to start somewhere, and it might as well start with her.

EVA

When Eva wakes up, there's a horrible moment of elation when she thinks that she's fallen into some parallel universe where nothing went wrong, because Celeste is right there, in bed with her. She blinks again, though, and remembers where they are—Steph's guest room, Duluth—and how they got here—breakup, storm, benefit concert. There's only this reality, where she's curled on her side, facing Celeste, who's still asleep. A few strands of brown hair have fallen across Celeste's face, and it takes everything in her not to brush them aside.

Wake up and sing with me, Eva wants to whisper, even as she thinks, *Stay asleep so you can't break my heart again.*

Eva rolls over and watches the sun advance across the carpet until the alarm on Celeste's phone goes off. The mattress shifts as Celeste fumbles for her phone, turning it off and then sitting up. Eva takes a deep breath before copying her, twisting in the covers and pulling them up with her.

"Morning," Celeste says, in that soft, just-woken-up voice. "Sleep okay?"

"Yeah," says Eva. "You?"

Celeste nods. "Ready for today?"

"I guess." She tilts her head. "You know what? Let's go have some fun."

Celeste answers with a grin.

A knock on the guest room door startles Eva, and she drags her eyes away from Celeste's bright eyes and mussed hair.

"Come in," Celeste calls.

To Eva's surprise, Meghan ducks inside, wrapped in a fuzzy bathrobe.

"Can I use the shower in here?" Meghan says. "I know you're rushing off to rehearsal, but Mari kind of had a fit about her oatmeal this morning. I just need to get it out of my hair, and Steph's in my bathroom right now."

"Of course, go for it," says Eva.

As Meghan steps farther inside, Eva notices the pale, gloopy remains of the unappreciated breakfast, clumping strands of Meghan's hair together.

"I'll be fast," Meghan says.

"Whatever you need," says Celeste.

Eva slips out of bed and pulls out some casual rehearsal clothes from her suitcase. Celeste is quiet, and Eva thinks back to their argument the night before. *Letting herself have this.* What would that look like?

She hears the shower turn on.

Eva abandons her suitcase, flopping onto her stomach across the end of the bed. Her legs dangle, and she makes grabby-hands toward the pillows until Celeste tosses one her way. She's got a few minutes while they wait for Meghan to be done in the bathroom. She wants to show her brain—her heart—a way to cling on to the lightness of the morning. She wants to find some peace or joy in this mess of a situation, and she won't get that if she doesn't begin that way.

"So tell me about it," Eva says, before she can talk herself out of it.

"About?" Celeste's tone is half-wary, half-surprised at being addressed at all.

"Your life now. Funny tour stories. Whatever."

"You sure?"

"Don't leave me hanging. What'd I miss?"

Celeste laughs. "Well, for one, there's way less babysitting on tour now, compared to ours."

"Fewer water balloon fights, I'd imagine," Eva says.

"Hey, that was not even our fault. What did they think was going to happen?"

"Probably not four absolutely drenched kids who were supposed to be—"

"You're telling me that SoCal college kids are above water balloon fights?"

Eva throws her pillow at Celeste, who clutches it to her chest. "Mine now."

"Heyyy!"

"All of them!" Celeste tips sideways across the pillows stacked against the headboard, wrapping her arms and legs around as many as possible.

Eva crawls toward the head of the bed, then throws herself forward, trying to get at one of the pillows beneath Celeste. Celeste shrieks and twists, trying to hold on to all the pillows even as Eva tugs—until one final pull ends with both of them tumbling off the mattress onto the floor.

"Ow," says Eva, and bursts out laughing.

Celeste is half on top of her, her fall partially cushioned by pillows, partially by Eva.

"Okay," Celeste says between giggles. "I guess we can share."

"Oh, you guess. So magnanimous."

"You and your four-syllable words." Celeste is smiling at Eva, lazy and open, like they never have to get off the floor, like they have all the time in the world to hide here and grin at each other.

Idiot, she thinks suddenly. There's trying to be friendly and enjoy the moment, and then there's nose-diving into old habits.

"Anyway," Eva tries, not wanting to completely spoil the mood but also needing to find her way out. "You were hogging the pillows."

"Should've thought of that before you started this," says Celeste, teasing.

Eva shrugs.

Celeste rests her head on her arms. "So Steph's grandma might think we're in a classic teen comedy, morning-after-sleepover pillow fight included, and Gina and Steph probably think we're killing each other."

"And the truth is somewhere in the middle," says Eva.

"Yeah," says Celeste, finally rolling off Eva. "Somewhere in the middle."

Eva lets herself look at Celeste for another moment—hair in her eyes, pajama T-shirt askew—before she pushes herself to her feet.

The bathroom door opens. Meghan emerges, hair wrapped in a towel.

"All yours!" she says.

"You can go first," Celeste tells Eva.

Eva doesn't hesitate to close the door between them.

EVA

It's not like her life goal was to end up crying in the back staircase of an academic building after her morning lecture. She doesn't cry on campus, ever. Not when girls (and some guys) kept coming up to her during fall quarter, saying how much they loved MO, the brave ones even inviting her to parties. Not when one of the LGBTQ clubs asked her to speak about homophobia in the entertainment industry, and she couldn't once reference the comfort and worthwhile complexity of dating her (former) bandmate.

But like every other part of the last fourteen months, Eva's here regardless. Unlike every other part of the last fourteen months, now that she's crying, it's not because she's sad.

The door to the stairwell opens with a snap, and before Eva can turn away—pretend to be fumbling in her bag, anything—she's face-to-face with one of her environmental science classmates, a white girl with blond hair that's always twisted up in a messy bun.

The girl halts, assessing Eva's tear-streaked face before glancing at the stairs beyond her, the door shutting with a thud.

Before Eva can do more than lift her chin, the girl says, "Ocean acidification. It's a real tragedy. They should've passed out tissues at the exits."

Eva's startled into half a laugh.

The girl tilts her head. Loose strands of hair brush against her brightly patterned T-shirt. "You good? Any professors I need to prank, frat boys I need to beat up . . . ?"

Eva's pretty sure she's never spoken to this girl before (L-something. Lisa? Louisa?). She's also somehow certain that the offer is genuine, not an effort to tease out a story she can leverage for social media followers.

"No," Eva says. "I just, um . . ." She waves her phone. "One of my English profs emailed us comments on our first paper."

"I thought you said there *weren't* professors you needed—"

"I got an A," says Eva.

Her first A in college. And more than the letter grade, her professor's feedback is . . . like getting a really good album review from a tough-to-please music critic. A delicious high.

One she's been trying not to feel since she started college in September.

And it's not that she's worked out how to make normal friends or how not to miss the band, but somehow . . . her English professor doesn't see her as a flighty pop princess, someone dabbling in college for a weird publicity stunt. She's taken seriously here. The A is proof that she belongs.

Standing in this concrete stairwell, Eva's done resenting college for not coming to her the way that she dreamed it would. It's not just a rebound. It's here, and she's here, and that weight of could-have-should-have has rolled off her shoulders and tumbled down the stairs. That feeling welling up inside her?

Relief.

Long-delayed joy.

"Well," says the girl. "Congratulations."

"Thanks," says Eva. She blots her wet cheeks with the back of her hand and waits for the girl to leave.

"We have lab together, don't we?"

"I think so. Thursday afternoons," says Eva, still searching for the girl's name. Laine? Lynn?

L-something continues to scrutinize her. "We're picking lab partners for the rest of the quarter this week. Do you have one yet?"

"No."

"Well . . . do you want to be mine?"

"Seriously?"

"Gosh, it would be a real imposition to be partners with someone who always does the reading."

"I didn't take AP . . . any science," says Eva.

"And?"

"I want you to know what you're signing up for?"

"I work a lot of hours and don't have time to handhold someone who doesn't pay attention in lecture. Just so you know what you're signing up for." She props her hands on her hips.

Eva grins. "Okay. So, partners?"

"Deal." L-something holds out a hand. "I'm Lydia, by the way."

"Eva."

"Really, now? I had no idea," says Lydia. "Anyway. I've gotta run, but if there's an NDA or whatever, email me, I'm on the course list."

There's not an NDA, Eva wants to say, but, well, she's a two-time Grammy winner and a lawyer's daughter. "Thanks."

Lydia adjusts the straps of her backpack on her shoulders. "It was nice to meet you, completely unknown Eva, about whom I have never read nonsense on terrible websites."

"Sounds about right," says Eva, smiling. "See you Thursday?"

"I'd better. I'm not getting stuck with a straggler until spring break," says Lydia, hopping past Eva and heading up the stairs at last.

"Bye!" Eva calls.

Instead of descending the stairs toward the exit, though, she falls back against the poster-covered wall, stealing another moment to compose herself. Not because she's crying anymore, but because she thinks she might be about to make her first college friend—her first friend at the place she fled to after she lost . . . everything she thought she would always have.

Like the relief that preceded Lydia's entrance, it's a pretty good feeling.

Finally.

JULY 2021

EVA

Downstairs, they find Gina, Steph, and Grandma Marit sitting around the kitchen table, nursing tea or coffee.

"Did you sleep well, girls?" Grandma Marit asks. Her tone is courteous, but Eva blushes, then blushes even harder as she catches Gina's gaze.

Gina merely raises her eyebrows, but Eva bursts into giggles. Instinctively, she turns to hide her face in Celeste's shoulder, just as Celeste pulls her in, wrapping an arm around her.

"Very well, thank you," Celeste says.

Eva ducks out of Celeste's embrace, sobered by its casualness and intimacy. Clearly they both need some practice at recalibrating from flirty to basic friendliness.

"We're meeting everyone at a studio downtown in an hour," Steph says.

Eva nods. The rhythm of rehearsal is familiar, although this one is absurdly accelerated. A full show in a week—she would have laughed in the face of anybody who suggested that in their heyday, back when their voices were all strong and polished and practiced—but taking out the choreography should let them pull this off, more or less without making complete fools of themselves.

Fingers crossed, she thinks, as Steph leads them to the egg bake sitting on the counter.

After breakfast, Steph offers to drive them all in their car.

"Shotgun," Gina calls, hand already on the door to the front passenger seat of Steph's Prius.

As Steph drives, Eva concentrates on looking out the window and not at Celeste. Most yards have been cleared of the downed twigs and smaller branches Eva saw on the news, but there are still larger branches—and, here and there, whole trees—yet to be cut up and hauled away. There's a dumpster in front of one house with a blue tarp over one section of the roof, and another with some sort of durable plastic over a few of the windows.

This is why we're here, Eva reminds herself.

Despite her long absence, despite her too-big L.A. house, something about Duluth will always be *home*. And her home is hurting right now.

Steph navigates around a cordoned-off sinkhole, and there's a twisting ache in Eva's gut that runs at least as deep. She wants to fill it in with her bare hands, go house by house to fix it all.

"We're running late, or I'd take you past the worst of it," Steph says, breaking the silence in the car. "We can go on the way home tonight."

"Thanks. That'd be good," Gina says.

A fierce wave of protectiveness crashes through Eva, the kind she's only used to feeling about the other three, and not since the breakup. A storm is not a homophobic journalist, is not an executive with wandering eyes, is not even a grueling tour schedule that no amount of coffee can fix. But that doesn't shake the sense that *nothing* should be able to do this to Duluth.

But it has, she reminds herself. *So now you have to sing.*

They reach the building where they'll be rehearsing a few minutes later. Gina grabs her bass from the trunk; someone from Celeste's team will have her guitars waiting for her here.

The rehearsal room is a large dance studio, with the stage lines marked out in bright red spike tape. There's a drum set for Steph off to one side. The other half of the room is crowded with people. Eva recognizes Alicia, one of their vocal coaches from their second and third headliner tours. She looks around for Celeste's tour manager before remembering that she's helping to coordinate from afar while prepping for the next leg of Celeste's tour. Finally, Eva spots Pip, who breaks away from the assembled group of organizers to greet them.

"It's so good to see you," Pip tells each of them, but she reserves a hug for Celeste.

Eva keeps forgetting that Celeste has been working with Pip all this time.

Pip flashes a brisk smile. "Let's get started. I've somehow ended up in charge"—they all wince, because entirely coordinating benefit concerts is definitely not in a publicist's job description—"so we're going to start with introductions, quick updates from leads, and then jump right into actual rehearsal. Apparently, you all need to sing or something."

"I didn't realize. Are you sure?" Gina quips.

Pip turns back to the rest of the team, clapping her hands and calling for attention. "We've got a lot of work to do in the next week to pull this off, so I want to thank you all for everything you've been doing so far . . . and remind you we need to keep up this pace until the end. But our talent is here, so I'm very happy to once again introduce you to Moonlight Overthrow."

EVA

"Why did I offer to drive us?" Steph asks as they pull out of the parking lot.

The summer sun hasn't fully set yet, and the storm-damaged buildings downtown cast long shadows on the pockmarked streets. Eva tips her head back against the headrest, a water bottle held loosely between her hands.

"Because you're very generous and not at all diva-like, so you didn't think we should ask for someone to pick us up," Celeste says.

Eva tries to push away the memory of their late rehearsal lunch: Celeste pulling Pip away for a private conversation, Eva firmly watching Steph twirl drumsticks in their hand instead of trying to figure out whether Celeste was complaining about them all or just discussing the infinite number of more important things she's putting on hold this week.

"I vote we all be divas tomorrow," Steph says. "Just on this one thing."

"What's Matt up to?" Gina asks. She lets her head loll to one side, then rolls it to the other. "He could take us, maybe, if you don't want to ask anyone else. Because I don't think we should take a Lyft to rehearsal."

Nobody's PA came out, and Celeste didn't even bring any security. It really was like middle school again.

"I'll ask him when we get back," Steph says, turning onto a new street.

It's not the way back to their house. Eva sits up straighter in her seat.

"You wanted to see," Steph says.

A lump rises in Eva's throat as she looks out the window. The roads have been cleared, for the most part, although there are still patches of glass outside a few buildings. Two multistory apartment buildings, part of the skyline for as long as Eva can remember, are now burned-out shells, thanks to the fires. Eva knows from news reports that these people aren't the only ones who lost their homes; even if they had been, the community still would have needed this concert.

Steph keeps driving, taking them past two big business buildings that sustained heavy damage, then along the harbor, where storm-tossed, hail-damaged boats wait for repairs. They double back on the frontage road, passing the movie theater where Eva went with Gina and another girl in their grade to see *Star Wars: The Force Awakens*, her first movie without a parent supervising. Next is the convention center. The parking lot is full, although Eva isn't sure of the exact breakdown between people coming to help and people coming in need.

There's Playfront Park, a favorite for elementary school birthday parties and post–Girl Scouts playdates, and then—a still-flooded field, scattered with downed limbs and other debris.

"Stop," says Eva. "Steph, can you—pull in here."

Steph turns into another parking lot. As soon as they're stopped, Eva tumbles out of the car, the others following. On the far side of the field is a small stage, with four concrete-and-red-metal pillars holding up the high roof.

"Our first headliner show," Celeste says.

In her bottom desk drawer, Eva keeps a scrapbook her mom made of clips from MO's first year. Their Bayfront Festival Park show garnered them an above-the-fold headline in the *Duluth News Tribune*.

"I was so nervous," Steph says. "I kept almost dropping my drumsticks."

"I rambled so much between songs that show. I thought we'd figured it all out when we were opening, but as soon as we got home, once it was *our* concert . . ." Gina laughs a little.

"It's different, your hometown show," says Eva.

So much of that show is now just an adrenaline-blurry haze in her memories, but she remembers looking to her right throughout the evening and being able to see the Aerial Lift Bridge, a kind of North Star. The breeze coming off the harbor basin behind them cooled her sweaty palms and whispered its own melody in her ears.

You have no idea what's coming, Eva thinks, as if some ghost of her younger self is still standing on that stage, microphone in hand and every dream within reach.

"It's . . . weird to realize that was only four years ago. You know?" Celeste says. "It looks so small now, but back then . . ."

"Still a great venue," says Steph.

"C'mon, then," says Gina, and Eva thinks she means to herd them back into the car, but no: Gina's heading down the curving service road, the only dry way remaining to reach the stage.

Eva follows.

This backstage lot is normally for equipment vans—or semis, depending on the size of the act—but today it's empty. They clamber onstage, Gina still leading the way. It's different, somehow, seeing everything from this angle, slightly removed, slightly above. The gaps in the skyline seem starker, and Eva clings to that wrongness. She never wants to forget what *right* looked like. She doesn't want to forget what's supposed to be there. The last time Eva saw this view, the field had been cheerfully covered by familiar faces:

classmates, neighbors, old music teachers. If you tried to lay a picnic blanket in the field now, you'd lose it in the mud.

"I wish we could play here," Gina says. She's half turned away from the field, facing the lift bridge instead.

"Our Shop-Vac is good, but not this good," Steph tries to joke, but their heart's obviously not in it.

Eva turns too, taking in the calm waters of the harbor basin. It feels weird to put her back to where the audience should be. But there's no one there to charm. She wonders what it was like here the night of the storm, when Eva was lounging in the Pacific's salt spray. Did the waves reach the stage? Surely not—the water hadn't risen nearly that high—but she's drawn to the idea somehow, of the stage slipping straight into the lake.

What really happened is bad enough, she thinks.

She spins back toward the field and the view into town.

You should be full, she thinks at the empty audience. *You should be here*, she thinks at the burned-out spaces.

She wants to sing them back into being, let every note be a brick. It doesn't work like that, she knows. Singing's not magic, not in that way. Eva hopes what it can do will be magic enough.

Back in the car, Steph continues their winding loop through Duluth. They maneuver around potholes deeper than Mari is tall, pass holes where mailboxes should be and shallow ponds where a week ago there were driveways, yards, community gardens.

I lived here, Eva thinks. *This was home.*

She can feel the tears gathering behind her eyes.

She doesn't deserve to cry. She's like those reporters who swoop in, swoop out. When was the last time she spent more than a few days in Duluth? When was the last time she was in Duluth, period? She left, and now she's only back for the show.

"Hey," Celeste says in a low voice.

She reaches across the back seat to place her hand over Eva's. Eva bites her lip, squeezes her eyes shut, tilts her head against the window. She doesn't deserve this, either. This comfort. This Celeste.

Steph turns on the radio for the last few minutes of the drive. Eva braces herself—it's going to be one of theirs, or one of Celeste's, or one Eva wrote for someone else—but the song that comes on isn't any of theirs. She hasn't heard it at all before, can only guess at the title and artist. She doesn't so much try to commit the chorus to memory so she can look it up later as let herself sink into it, let the hook catch her and keep her.

JULY 2021
EVA

"There's stuff for tacos out if you want some, when you're ready," Ms. Miles says as they enter through the garage door and line up their shoes in the mudroom.

It's like being thirteen again, before any of this happened, when they were still four of thousands of kids out there with castles in the clouds shaped like Hollywood stars.

It's maybe, Eva thinks, what nineteen is supposed to look like: coming home from college over the summer, hanging out at your high school friends' houses. Your high school friends' parents' houses, anyway. Dinner you cook yourself, or at least cooked by someone you're not paying in anything other than gratitude. But Eva likes her nineteen all the same, despite everything, because of everything, and she suspects Celeste does too.

"Thanks, Mom," says Steph. They lead the way into the kitchen.

A cursory glance at the two pots still warm on the stove reveals them to be half-full of beef and chicken, respectively. A dozen dishes on the center island contain every taco fixing and appropriate side dish a Midwesterner could want: salsa (not too hot), shredded cheese, sour cream, coleslaw . . . A lot of dairy that Celeste won't eat with meat, but at least she's always liked tomatoes.

"You didn't have to do this for us," Celeste says.

"It looks great," Eva says.

"It *smells* great," says Gina.

Ms. Miles waves this aside. "I'm used to cooking for a crowd. I'm going upstairs to talk with Meghan about some college things, but holler if you need me."

Matt is sitting at the kitchen table, idly eating a few last salsa chips and doing something on his phone. He looks over as they start to fill their plates. Eva scoops chicken onto her tortilla, then hands the serving spoon off to Celeste. They're so close together, Celeste's hip presses against her own.

"Well?" Matt asks. "Am I living with pop stars or what?"

"Looks like," Steph says. "Sorry."

Matt shrugs and stands to clear his dishes.

Eva hands the sour cream spoon to Steph without offering it to Celeste. When she catches Celeste's smile, she startles, wondering if Celeste's habits have changed, but Celeste shakes her head. Eva knew that Celeste hadn't kept strict kosher, the kind that required separate dish sets and sinks, not at home in middle school and not in the band. She'd still had to make an info sheet for their small squadron of PAs on tour, with notes like, *If we send you out on a secret fast-food run, 1. Do not tell our nutritionist. 2. Do not get me a cheeseburger.*

"You could do us a favor, though," Steph says.

"Who, me?" Matt closes the dishwasher and straightens up.

"Yeah, you," Steph says. "Want to drive us to and from rehearsal?"

"Uh, why?" He leans his elbows on the center island. "You can drive."

"Because rehearsal is exhausting, and if one of us falls asleep at the wheel and crashes the car, the concert will be off," Steph says.

"You think you're going to fall asleep driving in the ten minutes it takes to get from downtown?" Matt sounds mostly skeptical, but also a little impressed.

"I'll pay you," Steph says.

Matt perks up, which Eva thinks is funny, because there's no way he's short on cash: Steph (or their mom, or both) is definitely paying for his video game consoles and expensive shoes and whatever all else Eva hasn't seen. "Actually pay? Not just in 'I drove Moonlight Overthrow to their reunion rehearsals' stories? Because Cold Stone does not accept those as currency."

"Actually pay," says Steph.

"Okay. Let me know times and stuff later," Matt says as their grandma walks into the kitchen.

"You must tell me all about rehearsal," she says.

"It was great. Everyone killed it," says Celeste.

A slight exaggeration, but Eva will give her a pass. Grandma Marit doesn't need to know that rehearsals aren't exactly a walk in the park. This one definitely wasn't: everyone's rusty, on harmonies or breath control or the words themselves. It was frustrating, given how good they used to be together, but it didn't seem a lost cause, either.

"It was—incredible to be back, just doing the work, measure by measure," says Gina.

"I'm sure you all worked very hard," Grandma Marit says.

"We should check in on social media, then get to bed," Gina says.

"You're right." Celeste stands, taking her plate in one hand and Eva's in the other. "I need to call Pip quick, but I'll catch up with you guys in a minute."

What is with Celeste and these private conversations with Pip?

Just her solo life that isn't actually on hold while she's here, Eva answers herself.

Fifteen minutes later, they're all gathered in the big guest room. Gina's perched on the desk chair; Steph is sprawled across the foot of the bed. Eva and Celeste are leaning against the pillows.

"Pip posted on Instagram twice, once from the MO account and once from the concert account," Gina says, scrolling rapidly on her tablet.

"So we each like at least one of them, and then post something ourselves," Celeste says. "I've got that selfie we took over lunch—everybody okay if that goes on Insta?"

A murmur of assent.

Celeste leans into Eva to show her a tweet by someone offering short fic rewards if people message them screenshots of donations ten dollars or up. Eva's stomach lurches. It could be because Celeste's arm is pressing against hers, warm and familiar, and the scene could be from any night on tour, the four of them gathered into one room, Celeste and Eva cuddling at the center. It could be because she recognizes the username, although not from Twitter. Enough of the big fic writers are also big general fans that she's been following this particular one for years on Tumblr, even before the breakup. And even though she tries to blacklist fic entirely, summaries sometimes trickle through.

Do you know she wrote a Persuasion *AU of you and Gina?* Eva thinks about saying to Celeste. Unbidden, another thought arises: *We're supposed to be the* Persuasion *AU.*

Take that back, she orders herself. She and Celeste can't be anything. *Won't* be anything, because no matter how sweet Celeste acts at rehearsal or in the kitchen, Celeste doesn't want her anymore. And Eva will never let her heart be broken all over again.

Eventually, Gina sets down her tablet and looks at Eva. "You want Steph's room tonight?"

"Yes, thanks," she says. "I'll just grab my stuff from the bathroom."

While Gina is in Steph's room gathering her own things, Celeste says, "So? Fun? Agony? Missing your smart college friends yet?"

Eva texted Lydia a little today and yesterday, but it's hard to know how to sound, now that she's not just a college student with a wild backstory and a cool freelance job. This week, she's the big story, or a quarter of it, anyway. But Lydia's taken it in stride. Eva will spill everything once she's back home . . . once she's figured out what she has to say. For now, though, there's Duluth and rehearsal. And Celeste, still waiting for an answer.

"Really, really fun," Eva says.

"Good," says Celeste. "That's really—I'm—good."

"Yeah," says Eva, pulling her suitcase upright. "So, good night?"

"Sweet dreams."

After she's settled in Steph's room, Eva logs into her secret Tumblr. She and the others may have taken care of all the other fans earlier, but there's still a friend she's been neglecting for two days. As she suspected, there are about two dozen messages from Kay waiting for her. She takes a deep breath, preparing herself to slip into celestial-vision's mind. What would a fan think?

What does Eva think?

celestial-vision: So first: I am SO SORRY I missed all these messages. Real Life showed up with a bang this week and I haven't been able to really log on in a couple of days

celestial-vision: But believe me I have been following along (I got a freaking CNN alert about the concert!)

celestial-vision: Thanks for all this <3 <3 <3 I feel like I got to be part of the live reaction

That's . . . fine, right? It's all true.

celestial-vision: DISCLAIMERS ASIDE

Eva glances around the room, ceiling to dresser to the en suite bathroom's open door. If she were a fan . . . and she *is* a fan . . .

celestial-vision: oh my god. oh my GOD. I feel so much I almost don't know how to feel, except . . . oh my god. PINCH ME? This is happening? I won't believe it until it happens

celestial-vision: I was definitely one of those people who cried a ton when they found out. Maybe we're not in the darkest timeline after all

celestial-vision: You're probably out or sleeping or something but, you know, slkdfjlksfjs talk about the best things being out of the blue

celestial-vision: Not sure when I'll be on this week, but 'til the moon crashes into the sea

Eva wonders what Gina and Celeste are talking about in the guest room. Their post-MO careers? New celebrity friends they have in common?

Eva tries to settle her racing thoughts.

Rehearsal tomorrow.

Sweet dreams.

CELESTE

Eva released her second single yesterday, so it's probably fitting that today, Celeste is supposed to be writing material for her next album. Okay, it's not technically *Eva's* second single. To everyone else, it belongs to the singer who performed it, but Eva *wrote* it. Record of the Year versus Song of the Year.

Celeste doesn't really care about the artist. She doesn't have anything against her—other than rampant jealousy over getting to sing an Eva-penned song—but in her mind, the song is Eva's alone. She toys with tweeting out congratulations, or making an Insta story of her jamming out to it in the kitchen, but Pip would probably take her social media control away. God, she gets it, okay? She was an asshole, and now she has to stay in her own lane.

Celeste readjusts her guitar and tries out a few chord combinations.

Nope.

She tries again.

The sound dies flat against the walls of her New York living room.

Eva had posted a short video of her writing the song—that first moment where the chorus came together—and she was so damn pretty in it. The light from an unfamiliar window bringing out the subtle red undertones in her dark hair. A T-shirt with a sunflower in the center.

A sun, not a moon, so Celeste understands the message for what it is: fuck you, and fuck Moonlight Overthrow, too. Except maybe it's not. Maybe it's just a T-shirt Eva likes. Maybe she doesn't even like it, but it's the first shirt she pulled out of her closet that morning suitable for a day at home, and not an awards show. Celeste should probably stop going to so many, so Eva can have a turn.

Pip has vetoed this idea already.

God, she *misses* her.

Celeste thinks about sending a message, not to the group chat, just to Eva. Something like, *Hey, sitting here trying to write a song by myself, doesn't it suck??? How do you do it???*

She'll have co-writers on this album, too, but she likes to walk in with rough drafts. She's never been comfortable with the idea of an album where she only contributed lyrics, never melody. None of the tracks her primary producer has sent her are really clicking anyway. And she loves being a musician. She loves *Landlocked*. She wants to love whatever this next album ends up being.

She wants Eva.

She calls her oldest sister. They don't do a lot of spontaneous calls, but Jenna also knows Celeste's schedule is both crammed and constantly changing.

"Hey, Celeste," says Jenna. "What's up?"

"You and Daniel married pretty young," Celeste blurts.

"Um." Celeste knows her sister's eyebrows must be practically at her hairline. Even for Celeste, that was a pretty strong non sequitur. "I mean, yeah, compared to the average. That's not really new information."

"But it's good, right? Or—"

Crap, she thinks. *What if it's* not. Either way, she needs to know.

"We're good. More than good," Jenna says. Celeste can hear her smile. "Did you just call to question my marriage or is there something else going on?"

"I just . . ." Celeste pulls her knees into her chest. "Mom and Dad married pretty young."

"Daniel and I aren't our parents."

"But how do you *know*?"

Jenna sighs. "Because Daniel is—what we have, there's a steadiness there. I don't have to keep looking back to check that he's with me. I'm sure of it, all the time. Even when we disagree, I know we're both trying to figure out how to get to a shared place. You know when I studied abroad in college?"

"Yeah," says Celeste. Jenna had done a semester in Warsaw and a semester in Budapest.

"I was really worried about being gone for the whole year. I asked him if he wanted to break up."

"I didn't know that."

"Well, I did. He said no. I was never going to get a better chance to study there. I didn't want to give that up for us, and *he* didn't want me to give that up for us. Our rule was that we had to talk— not just messages—once a week, but neither of us could give up doing something for that call. We had our own lives."

That, Celeste thinks. *Exactly that.*

"But I didn't forget about him, either. My feelings didn't fade. And that helped me to realize it wasn't just a strong crush. This wasn't just a college thing. This could last, if we let it."

All of Celeste's words are caught in her throat.

It's been a year since she broke up with Eva. There's not a day when she doesn't think about her, and not just in a nostalgic, old-friends way. She tries to be angry with Eva for *not getting it*, but she's starting to wonder if her anger is just a way to keep convincing herself she was right.

"And when I got back," Jenna continues, "it's not like I never got butterfly feelings, it's not like we didn't try to be sweet to each other. But we weren't trying to *win* each other. We were already won, you know?"

I know.

"It's a different thing. It's—*comfortable*. Our senior year, he would go to CVS when I got my period. I helped him with a bunch of the paperwork when his mom's identity got stolen. You don't do that with someone you just want to look pretty for at the dance. You have to let them into your mess. And that's part of how you know."

Eva was a planner. Good in a crisis. Celeste never let her in for the biggest mess. She wanted to come up with the plan on her own for once, you know? She didn't want to use Eva like a crutch her whole life. But she never gave Eva the chance to allow her that space—to step back without letting go.

Jenna clears her throat. "Mom and Dad were never steady, not when we were kids. Maybe before, but nothing I can remember."

"Mom was always trying to win him again. She wanted to get to the shared place," says Celeste.

It was terrible to witness. Heartbreaking and somehow humiliating. And lonely, with her sisters already off at college by the time the divorce proceedings finally began.

"Yeah. But seriously, why are you thinking about all that?"

"I can't do that," Celeste manages. She tries to swallow down her tears.

"Can't do . . . ?"

"Mom. I can't—I could never—"

There's a pause. "I don't want to make assumptions . . . But is this about Eva?"

"Always." Celeste tries to laugh. She tries to be bitter.

"I'm really sorry you're still hurting."

"Will it stop?"

"I don't think I can answer that for you," Jenna says.

"You're supposed to know everything. That's your job, right?"

"I hope not!" Her voice has all the lightness and teasing Celeste can't quite reach.

After they hang up—after Celeste actually asked about Lila like a normal aunt—she stretches out on the couch, one arm dangling over the edge.

She and Eva, they'd had steadiness. They hadn't had *separate*.

What about now? she makes herself ask.

She reaches for her guitar.

CELESTE

When Celeste's alarm goes off on Sunday morning, Gina is already awake and in the bathroom. Celeste lies in bed as she waits her turn. Yesterday was probably the last morning she'll ever wake up with Eva again. And it's still one more than she thought she'd get. She wants to be grateful for the extra morning, but mostly she just *wants*.

It's hard to remember now just how scared she was at the end. Figuring out how to keep going without Eva—that was scary. Making two albums by herself—also scary. But Celeste has managed both. These feelings surging inside her, even when she's not onstage? They're not scary anymore. Maybe Eva will break her heart. Somehow, that's not nearly as frightening as the idea of going back to tour without letting Eva know her heart is prepared to break.

Steph and Eva are already in the kitchen when Celeste and Gina arrive downstairs, plus Matt and Grandma Marit, who, from her perch at the breakfast bar, mostly seems to be telling Matt when to pay attention to the scrambled eggs on the stove and when it's safe for him to ignore the pan in favor of his phone.

Matt lifts the spatula at them in greeting.

Eva is sitting at the table, her eyes shut against the bright morning sunshine.

"Hey, sleepy," Celeste says.

"Mm," says Eva.

"Songs to sing. There'll be a piano for you to play today . . ."

"Well," says Eva, eyes fluttering open. "If there's a *piano* involved."

Despite the early hour, Celeste's own phone is buzzing in her pocket, hopefully with updates from Pip on their secret mission. Celeste has been trying to get them into a bigger venue. The venue choice was first made in the immediate post-storm panic, when they were scrambling to find somewhere, anywhere, to perform. Between the news that the show sold out and the additional days since the storm for other venues to evaluate damage and begin repairs, Celeste hopes an alternative can be found. Normally, she wouldn't even think to try—you'd never be able to book somewhere this last-minute—but everyone in Duluth wants to be part of the relief effort. She hasn't told the others about the search yet; she's hoping to give them a grand reveal, with none of the stress, worry, or logistical wrangling along the way.

"Anything I can do to help with breakfast?" Eva asks Steph, her voice soft.

Celeste instantly recognizes that pitch: it's a singer who can't afford to strain her voice before a show. The compressed rehearsal timeline is not exactly best practice. While Eva and Gina busy themselves with setting out silverware and pouring orange juice, Celeste discreetly quizzes Steph on the tea options. When Eva turns away from fiddling with the forks on the table a few minutes later, Celeste is right in front of her. She presses the warm mug into Eva's hands.

"Tea," Celeste says.

Eva lifts the mug in a silent toast before taking a first sip. Her eyes widen in recognition, no doubt at the sweetness, and she takes another, longer sip. The tea is herbal, and Celeste stirred in honey to soothe Eva's throat. It's nothing difficult, nothing particularly specific to Eva, but Celeste wants her to know that she's paying attention. That she cares.

"Thanks," Eva says. She presses a hand to Celeste's shoulder as she passes her.

The touch seems to go right through her T-shirt, burning her skin.

Celeste wants to burn always.

Everywhere.

When Celeste looks up, Grandma Marit is watching her. The older woman gives her a small nod, the moment broken only by Steph handing out plates.

After breakfast, they troop into the garage and negotiate seating in Steph's Prius. Gina ends up behind Matt, Eva behind Steph, Celeste in the middle. Steph plugs in their phone as Matt backs out of the driveway, starting them off with a Kehlani track they used to blast on the tour bus. Eva's wearing shorts today, athletic chic, and Celeste's eyes catch on the expanse of exposed, muscled thigh. She wishes they had time to add in choreography. Eva could seduce with her voice alone, of course, but her power trebled if you let her move.

Eva turns her head away from the window. Her eyes meet Celeste's. "It's like old times," she says.

"Hmm?" Celeste is caught on her small smile. The flecks of hazel near the center of her blue eyes. The fact that she still has freckles, even though most makeup artists cover them for photo shoots.

"The four of us, squashed into one car, on our way to sing . . ." Eva leans into her, pressing the whole length of her arm against Celeste. Their knees bump.

"Not for that long," Matt says from the front. "You got snatched up pretty quick."

"Long enough," Gina says.

"And those first tour buses? Tight quarters," Steph adds.

"Yeah, yeah," Matt says. "Whine to your Grammy."

"Grammys," Gina corrects.

Eva muffles a laugh into Celeste's shoulder. It's almost a kiss.

EVA

They start with "Standstill," one of the songs they'll be singing a cappella during the show. Steph taps out the rhythm on their thigh; Celeste hums the starting pitch; Eva and Gina leap into the first verse. There is a lot of eye contact involved in a cappella singing, especially when you aren't used to singing with your partners. Eva watches for the crisp cut-offs, for the added riffs, as much as she listens for them.

Celeste's rib cage is a marvel to watch, precise and practiced in its expansion, but she doesn't hold back as much as she should when she's supposed to be backing Gina. Steph flubs the words on their verse. Gina misses her harmony on the next chorus. Eva comes in too late on the bridge.

Every time she's knocked off course, the song slips a little further out of her grasp. By the time Celeste cuts off their last note with a sharp but subtle movement of her hand, Eva is shaking. Her stomach plummets, a cold, guilty feeling curling around her heart and clogging her throat.

"So. We've got some work to do," Celeste says. Her voice is light, no hint of frustration, no undertone of superiority.

Eva's stupidly grateful. It's no use being mad at herself, much less at the others. They didn't know this was going to happen. They couldn't have prepared. They came as they were, all of them, and this is how they are. A little off balance. A little off beat.

"We know how to do this," Gina says. "Just like yesterday, just like two years ago."

Except as the morning drags on, it's clear that they don't. Panic starts to drown out everything Eva's supposed to be paying attention to: the words, the notes, her breathing.

"We could just cut the song," Steph says at last. "Cut our losses, move on to the next."

But who's to say they won't have this problem with the next? Maybe yesterday was the false-hope fairy tale, and they really can't do this anymore.

"Let's get out of here," says Celeste.

Eva's jaw drops. "What?"

"Like Steph said, we're getting stuck. So let's move. We need to regroup, and, honestly, I think it just needs to be the four of us. Right now, it feels like a performance we're bombing, not a rehearsal. We need to go somewhere else." Celeste glances at each of them in turn.

When did she get so *smart*?

"I'm in. But where? Steph's house?" Eva says.

Celeste shakes her head. "Not if we can help it, anyway. Steph? Can you think of someplace we could go?"

Twenty minutes later, Celeste parks Pip's rental car in a visitor's spot in their old middle school parking lot, and Ms. Pha, the principal, rushes out to greet them. Her black hair has a few more gray strands than Eva remembers, but, she realizes with a start, it hasn't actually been all that long since she was a student here.

"Welcome, all of you!" Ms. Pha exclaims with a wide smile. "It's so lovely to see you all again."

"Thanks for letting us come," says Celeste.

"We're delighted to help however we can," she says, ushering them inside. Eva's quiet as they follow Ms. Pha. They pass the library and then the science wing. Eva's main memory of middle school science is crushing on a girl in her class, Nora, who had thick brown hair and had once given a presentation on manganese. Ms. Pha stops outside the choir room's double doors.

"And here we are! Please don't hesitate to ask if you need anything."

They thank her, and then Eva pushes open the door.

The choir room seems exactly as they left it. Everywhere Eva looks, a new memory arises, turning through her mind like a kaleidoscope. Just inside the door are two huge bookshelves, crammed with sheet music. The four of them painstakingly looked through almost every song before they settled on one to sing at Eva, Gina, and Celeste's eighth-grade graduation. There are still posters of solfège on the wall, the *do-re-mi* their teacher had them learn before they were allowed to practice a song with the real lyrics. Two old computers sit on desks against the back wall. Before Steph left for high school, they would sometimes spend entire lunch periods at one of them, carefully constructing their songs in GarageBand.

Everyone is hushed, as if they've just entered a holy space.

The last time Eva was in this room, she had no idea their Spotify album was about to blow up, no clue they were going to spend the summer reading contracts instead of Great American Novels. She's startled by the force of her protectiveness toward the girl who knew this room so well—and then almost starts giggling when she realizes her middle school self would feel the same way about her now. No Celeste, no performing. Who would want to grow up knowing that was ahead?

Eva sits down at the upright in the center of the room. Celeste bounces toward the three tiers of red plastic chairs. With Eva's eyes mostly focused on the keys, Celeste is a blur at the edges of her vision, partially obscured by the piano. It could be 2016 again,

Celeste's notes soaring toward the fluorescent lights, Eva about to fall in love.

Eva's heart aches and aches, the loneliest kind of beat, no melody to soothe the gaps.

"Better check that it's in tune," Steph says. They take a seat in the front row, on the side where the tenors sit.

Eva settles her fingers on the worn keys. She plays through the key of E, then G, before her fingers slip into a song. She doesn't choose "Standstill," or even another one of the songs they need to learn. Instead, she stumbles through "America the Beautiful," the first song she learned how to sing in this room. It feels right: the beginning is, after all, a very good place to start.

A few bars in, Celeste starts to sing the melody. Gina jumps in with the alto harmony. Steph sits up straighter, inhaling like they're about to join, when Eva's fingers jerk into a wrong, jarring chord. She stops playing abruptly, then bursts into laughter.

"Oh god," Eva says. "Definitely not that."

"That was pretty good, for a song no one's touched since 2014," says Gina.

Celeste hops down the risers, reaching for Steph and spinning them out of the chair. Eva slides off the piano bench to join them.

"And on that note," Celeste says, "let's do this."

Line by line, note by note, two bars over and over, then a different three, then all five together. Even with the laughter in Eva's throat instead of panic, it takes some time to coax an acceptable a cappella version of "Standstill" into being. But when it *works* . . .

"This one's going to be it," Celeste says. She's been saying something similar the last two or three times: *We're close, we've almost got it, this might be it.*

"This one's it," Gina confirms, and it's like *let there be light*, because Eva knows, from the first inhale she takes, before she releases a single note, they are beyond bright.

When it ends, and the last note has faded above them, there's a moment of silence. The four of them look at each other, marveling, in awe.

We did that, Eva thinks. She knows the others are thinking the same thing. *We can do this. We can* still *do this.*

Gina starts to clap. Before Eva can copy her, Celeste's arms are around her waist, squeezing, and then Gina's there, and Steph, and they're a tangle of arms and hair and euphoric laughter. It's the kind of hug that says, *we were amazing* and *I love you all no matter what* and *thank you*. The kind of hug they should have had at the end of their last concert. Maybe they couldn't do it then, and maybe it wasn't the kind of hug meant for fans' beseeching eyes. But they had it now, where it really mattered.

I needed this, Eva thinks. She didn't just want them playing nice on Twitter, hitting notes for a crowd. There is no crowd here, no cameras. Just their friendship and their joy.

"Okay," says Gina. "Onward?"

They all step back, still grinning widely, in the way you can't while you're singing. When Eva dares to look at Celeste, she's blushing.

"'Sweeter' is next, unless we're changing the order again," Steph says.

"Piano time," Celeste says, looking at Eva.

Eva ducks behind the piano, tuning out the others' chatter. Her first few warm-up chords are utterly exuberant, too jaunty and loud by half for the song she's about to play. She lets herself have a few more of those, then deliberately slows her breathing. She can't play "Sweeter" the way it's meant to be played if she's a live wire, all spark and heat running through her fingers and into the music.

Celeste sits on the floor next to her, leaning against the piano bench. Eva resists the urge to keep playing with only her left hand, leaving her right to run through Celeste's hair. She wishes she didn't want to. She and Celeste are long over; shouldn't her feelings have dissipated by now? It's hard to dismiss her feelings as meaningless echoes of old interactions when Celeste is leading them out of musical crises . . . while wearing a pink V-neck T-shirt emphasizing that her personal trainer must have decided to embrace her curves.

When Eva's through with her warm-up, Gina and Steph drift over. Celeste stands and walks around the back of the bench to join Steph and Gina. As she does so, she brushes a hand along Eva's back. It's so much like before, it's almost physically painful, a clenching around Eva's heart and in her stomach.

I want this, I want this, she thinks.

Let yourself have it echoes back.

But Celeste could be doing it because that's how they all are, or were: comfortable together. Celeste might not even *realize* she's doing it.

It's not real. Or it is, but not in the way she wants. Not that she wants to want this. There's so much grief wrapped up in this concert already, she can't add losing Celeste a second time.

Eva starts to play. With the three of them arrayed on the other side of the piano, it's exactly like they really are back in middle school, messing around in the choir room before class. It's playing in front of a hundred people, then a thousand, then thirty thousand. It's being right here, right now. With them, again.

If Pip called and said the concert was off, Eva would say, *Let's keep going.* They could commandeer this room, sing a hundred songs badly, order pizza without worrying about dairy affecting their voices. Have a marathon of all their favorite music movies from elementary school, the ones they loved on their own and later learned the others had watched too.

For Duluth's sake, Eva wants the benefit concert to go well. But she's starting to think Duluth might be okay with a few forgotten lyrics or missed harmonies. The point is that they came back, all of them. The point is that they first met because of songs, and they're back because of songs, but Eva thinks that they might keep showing up for each other. Stage or no stage, song or no song.

The bridge is Celeste's. She retraces her steps, coming to stand right behind Eva. The hair on the back of Eva's neck stands up. She can't actually feel Celeste's breath against her neck, but there's still the ghost of it, the memory of it, the possibility of it.

Celeste's voice is a siren song, and Eva willingly drowns.

Eva doesn't turn her head but pretends to stay focused on looking out toward where the crowd will be, even though the room around her is a blur. She knows if Celeste took a half step forward, maybe less, her body would curve against Eva's back.

When the song ends, Celeste takes that half step. Her arms wrap around Eva's shoulders, her chin resting on Eva's head.

"How was that?" Celeste says, and Eva feels the words as much as she hears them.

"You tell me."

"Never heard it sweeter."

FEBRUARY 2019
CELESTE

"How come you never let us do this on your piano at home?"
Celeste asks.

She's lying stretched out on a Steinway grand piano, Eva smirking up at her from the bench. Steph and Gina are being positioned standing up, in the piano's curves.

Most of the time, their photo shoots are very girl-next-door. Today, the artistic vision is ethereal, a grown-up kind of elegance. Not too grown-up, of course: their team sets strict limits on the allowable amount of skin and male gaze fuckery. They get away with it because they're all still under eighteen, and someone's parent is present more often than not. They're all a little on edge already for June, when Steph will jolt into legal adulthood and the media will stop even *pretending* not to sexualize their eldest member.

Celeste pushes the low-level thrum of anxiety over paparazzi tactics and shitty press away, focusing on the smooth polish of the piano beneath her. She's definitely not complaining about the genre switch of today's photo shoot. Eva is drop-dead gorgeous in the lilac evening gown, her shoulder-length hair smoothed into an updo. Celeste's desperate to pull out every bobby pin, for an excuse to slide her hand against Eva's silk-clad curves.

"I play that piano," Eva says, looking at Celeste through new eyelash extensions.

"We could play on that piano, if you know what I mean." Celeste waggles her eyebrows.

Okay, the suspense is delicious.

Eva adjusts her position on the bench, a subtle change of the arch of her back. She tilts her chin up. Celeste follows the line of her jaw down the line of her throat down to her breasts, tastefully covered but more than hinted at nonetheless.

Eva knows what's she's doing.

"*You*," Celeste accuses.

"Later." Eva sends her a Cheshire smile.

The photographer claps once. "Steph, release the tension in your face for me, relax your shoulders . . . You're beautiful, you're happy, that's it. Gina, stay just like that. Everyone, focus, please."

"If you two are done eye-fucking . . . ," Steph says, poking Celeste's foot.

"Are we ever?" says Celeste, although she's careful not to turn her head away from the focus point the photographer indicated.

"Quiet on set," Gina murmurs.

At the photographer's direction, Eva shifts her shoulders and changes the position of her legs. Before she turns toward the cameras again, she mouths, *Never*.

SEPTEMBER 2019
STEPH

"Steph, stay on a moment, would you?" Kayla's voice is neutral, but it's hard to pick up on her facial micro-expressions in a video call.

Steph repositions the laptop so they're centered in the frame. "Sure."

"You okay?" Eva whispers, already on the other side of the hotel suite's coffee table.

"I'll catch up with you in a minute," Steph assures her.

Celeste, Eva, and Gina depart.

Kayla doesn't speak until she hears the thud of the heavy door shutting. "So." She says the word like a complete sentence.

Steph waits. Kayla has been uncharacteristically restrained about the additional albums, barely hounding them at all. Maybe one of the girls told her they weren't thinking about the last part of their contract until the end of tour. Someone must have, back in the spring when they all had their individual meetings with Kayla. Steph can't gather the energy for retroactive gratitude.

"So," Kayla starts again. "Steph. How are you doing?"

"I'm fine."

Steph wonders if any of them answer those kinds of questions honestly.

"You're looking a little worn down. I worry about you."

A year ago, Steph might have believed her. Kayla *thinks* she means it, which is more than can be said for some others in the business. But mostly Kayla wants Steph to assure her that they just need a cup of coffee and they'll be ready to make her lots more money. Kayla could be counted on to send very nice coffee.

"Tour, you know." Steph doesn't try for a smile.

What can Kayla do, honestly? They're leaving this band, this whole life, by Thanksgiving. Steph's not counting on a good reference. Their family's house is bought and paid for. Steph has plenty of money in savings, to pay for Meghan and Matt to stay in their private high school, continue on to private college, whatever they want. Steph may have messed up everything else, but at least there's money now. Their mom hasn't had to worry about whether she can afford full-price groceries for three years. Matt hasn't had to hide pinched toes in too-small shoes. Meghan's after-school activities aren't all free.

Steph did that. Music did that, but Steph would have found a way. Music just led them there faster.

You should have paid me less, Steph thinks. They don't need to stay anymore. The band was temporary, as Steph always knew it would be. But family is forever.

"The fans have noticed. You're less engaged during shows. I'm happy to send you some footage so you can see for yourself. Sometimes it helps to have that outside perspective."

"I'm sorry they've noticed," says Steph. "I don't need the footage."

"I see. It's unfortunate that you've let it get to the point where we need to have a conversation about it. Whatever it is, it's better to be honest. Do you need a doctor? A psychiatrist? Rehab?"

"It's not drugs or alcohol. And I'm not . . ." Steph shifts on the pale green couch. "I don't need a doctor."

"I trust you, Steph. But whatever it is, I can find a way to help. I'm happy when you're happy," Kayla says.

Except Kayla is happiest when they can be as wholesome as their band can hope to be: fresh-faced Midwestern girls, *gay* but not *queer*. No fuck-you. She wouldn't like Steph messing up that neat narrative.

"Just tired," Steph offers.

So tired. They stopped reading their press this summer. They don't read posters during shows anymore, leaving that to the girls. It's stopped being easy to chat with fans during M&G who just want Steph to know how happy they are to have found a girl band that sings about loving girls.

There was a "girl power" song from their second album that made it onto the set list for this tour. Steph stopped being able to sing the harmonies, then their melodies. In July, Celeste suggested they switch it out for a different song from *Supernova*, "just to mix things up." Steph's been heading to their drums earlier and staying there longer every show, even when the arrangement doesn't call for them to play. Maybe it's not fair to the fans, or the girls, but it's the only way Steph knows how to get through this.

"I understand. Touring is hard, and you girls are very young." Steph flinches. "You'll have a little time off this month, for Rosh Hashanah and Yom Kippur. Use it wisely. Get some rest. Be ready to come back and give it your all."

"Got it," says Steph. They look past Kayla to the abstract painting on the wall. Lots of pastel colors. Nothing tying it down to earth.

"Wonderful," says Kayla. "I'm glad we had this chat. And of course, if you think of anything I can do to help, just let me know."

Kayla ends the call before Steph can think of a polite response. She might have gotten the last word tonight, but what does that matter? In two months, Steph's getting out.

JULY 2021

lesbianbayyy:

I've never been cagey about where I'm from, everybody here knows I'm Minnesotan af, you can pry the Étoile du Nord out of my HOCKEY FAN HANDS, Minneapolis is the best and Chicago can suck it. And you know that I got concert tickets because let's be real that's basically the best thing that's ever happened to me, no way could I keep that to myself. What you *don't* know is that my aunt lives in Duluth, and I drove up this morning to spend the week with her.

Guess who all went out for Cold Stone tonight?

Me. My aunt.

OT4.

(Plus people I assume are all related to Steph. I'm kind of a latecomer to the fandom, so I just realized I've never actually seen a picture of their siblings & co before? But like the family resemblance is super strong.)

They were SO NICE about taking pictures. It was pretty close to closing time, so there weren't a whole lot of us there, and it was just so friendly and relaxed. Celeste paid for their whole group, and Gina left a huge cash tip.

I couldn't actually hear what they ordered (sorry everybody for my failure here), but I can tell you that they were all sharing, totally comfortable with each other. Celeste actually fed Eva a bite of hers FROM CELESTE'S OWN SPOON, I have no fucking idea what kind of ice cream I was eating, that moment wiped out all other sensory input for like, a solid thirty minutes on either end.

Ummm I'm pretty much dead from adrenaline right now so I'm skipping a bunch of stuff but like you can see what they're wearing from the pics and everything . . . I asked them how rehearsal was going, Gina said great.

!!!

!!!!!!!

I'm going to go scream into my pillow for a while.

#WTF IS MY LIFE #that time when I met OT4 #in fucking cold stone

ginestebest:

They're out there living their best life??? Getting Cold Stone after a day of rehearsal??? They just look so chill in the pics. It's honestly kind of startling, given that it really seemed like they hadn't hung out since Nov 2019 . . . But there's so much we don't see. I know I harp on that all the freaking time and sometimes you guys are like "let us have our fun okay" but it's so clear here. And I'm so happy for them. And for us. Obviously.

#duluth #ot4 #I can't believe that tag has NEW CONTENT in it

JULY 2021

CELESTE

The way Eva looked at Celeste when she tried Celeste's ice cream—through her lashes, blushing—lingers longer in Celeste's mind than the taste of any sweetness on her tongue.

They're gathered in the guest room again, checking the fan photos that have been posted online. Celeste is so tempted to like the one of that moment, Celeste's spoon held between them. Tempted, definitely, but it wouldn't be nice to Eva. You don't stir shit up online without the other person's consent, not if you like them.

Steph drops their phone onto the bedspread, just as Celeste's starts vibrating. It's a video call from Pip.

Please, please be good news, Celeste thinks.

"I gotta take this," she says. She slips off the bed, phone in hand. "Hey, Pip. I'm with the band, but if you give me a sec—"

"No, that's perfect," says Pip. "That last option was a gamble, but it paid off."

"For real? *Yes*," exclaims Celeste, forgetting to modulate her voice. She hopes Mari is a deep sleeper.

"What's going on?" Eva asks.

"You tell them," says Pip.

When Celeste pictured this moment earlier, she imagined she would be full-on thrilled, but now that it's actually settled, she's nervous.

"C?" Gina prompts.

Celeste sits back down on the edge of the bed. "What would you say if I told you I got us a bigger venue?"

"What?" says Eva. Her tone is surprise through and through, the pure shock burning away any clues to subtler emotions.

"How much bigger?" says Gina.

"They're still digging up numbers for how many people they can put on the field, but . . . at least six thousand," Pip says.

This is happening, a good thing is *happening*, because she asked if it was possible.

"Oh my god," says Gina. "When? How?"

"Yesterday. Well, Pip and I started asking around yesterday."

Eva's quiet, but her eyes narrow.

"Hang on," says Steph. "Field?"

"Wade Stadium," says Celeste. "They'd already switched their games to 'away' until next Monday, because of the storm."

It's not the stadium size Celeste normally thinks of when she dreams of an all-stadium tour, but for a small metro area in the Midwest, she'll take whatever baseball venue is available.

She glances at Eva. Her face is still, her jaw set. Celeste just can't figure out *why*.

"When we were making plans earlier, we didn't want to go with an outdoor space, because most of them had a lot of damage, and in case the weather report changed," says Pip. "But the stadium didn't get hit too badly, and we're close enough now to trust it's not going to rain again until after Thursday."

"They'll have enough people to finish the storm cleanup and get set up? This fast?" Eva frowns.

The knot in Celeste's stomach unclenches a little. Eva's worried about staffing, that's all.

"That's what they just confirmed now. It's owned by the city, which helps with coordination," says Pip.

"That's awesome," says Gina.

Celeste blushes.

"They're going to announce and release the new tickets tomorrow morning, maybe early afternoon," says Pip.

"More locals are going to be able to come. That's good," says Steph.

Gina nods, bouncing a little in the desk chair. "And more people from the Twin Cities. We can have more sections now that are open to anyone. That should help, economically."

Celeste wants to pull Eva up from the bed and spin her around. Only . . . Eva's biting her lip, hesitant instead of happy like everyone else.

"I'd better get back to this," Pip says. "But Celeste—good thinking. It was smart not to settle for the smaller venue."

"Thanks so much for your help." Steph waves at the phone camera.

"We'll see you tomorrow," adds Celeste. She hangs up and looks back at the others. "I didn't want to get your hopes up if it couldn't happen, and I thought it might be a nice surprise." Celeste's words could be meant for everyone, but she's only looking at Eva.

"It's exactly what I wanted," says Eva, finally, although her smile doesn't reach her eyes.

"Good," says Celeste. If she can just stay positive, maybe she can plow through whatever doubts Eva has. "I wanted to do that for . . . us. And Duluth. If I could."

"This means a lot to me," says Steph. "Thank you."

"Any time," she says, regretting the words as soon as she's said them. They're not really true, are they? She's the reason they had to put together the concert so quickly, and why they can't just do a second show this weekend.

"But maybe not this big of a surprise again," says Eva. Her eyes widen a little, as if she didn't realize she was really going to say anything until she did.

"Well, no," Celeste starts, because probably this is the only time they'll agree to put on a slapdash charity concert for their storm-swept hometown.

"You didn't give us the chance to say no." Eva's tone loses its hesitancy. "You didn't ask us before you just went ahead and did this. Like, hello, we're *all* playing the show? You didn't let us have an opinion on whether an indoor show might still be better. Steph's local—they might have known something about why using the Wade wouldn't be a good idea. Gina or I might have had some other objection."

Celeste's stomach twists as she tries to think about it from Eva's perspective. How much does bigger and brighter matter if you didn't get a say in it?

Way to ruin your winning streak, she thinks. *Shit.*

"Do you?" Celeste makes herself ask. "Not want to perform outdoors?"

"No, it's fine." Eva pushes off the bed, opting instead to stand against the wall, her arms crossed. "But you didn't give us the chance to have any input."

"I was trying—"

"Please let me finish. I know what you were *trying* to do. I know you were trying to do this amazing surprise, and hopefully it'll work out perfectly—I really am glad we'll be able to help more now. I'm just saying that for things this big, you can't leave me out of it. Even when you're trying to be nice. I am *right here*. I have been with you all day, and all day yesterday." Eva stops abruptly, her cheeks pink. She squares her shoulders before continuing. "I mean, we've been with you. You had every chance, so now you have no excuse. You're used to being able to coordinate whatever you want with Pip and the rest of your team, but you can't act like a solo artist when all four of us are doing something together."

Celeste swallows. She thought—she thought she was rebuilding some goodwill with Eva. Inching toward being in the black. But Eva's hard tone is red all the way down. Celeste struck the one nerve she wasn't supposed to hit again. Right in front of Steph and Gina. As if this could be any more humiliating.

"You're right," she says. "I'm sorry."

"'Sorry' doesn't matter if you don't change."

"What do you want me to do? It's done, and it'll be better for Duluth. I *am* sorry, but there's no 'fix' now."

"Isn't that convenient," says Eva.

"Your intentions were good, and the outcome looks great," says Steph, before Celeste can reply. They sound like they mean it.

"But the process?" Celeste says. She's looking at Eva.

It's Gina who answers. "Room for improvement."

Celeste nods.

"Thanks for getting the venue," says Eva, but her voice is stiff.

Celeste tries to settle her twisting stomach.

Chill out, okay? she tells herself. *If she didn't care, she wouldn't say anything in the first place.*

But Eva doesn't move to retake her place next to Celeste on the bed.

EVA

"So. Now that that's taken care of, I think we were about to go to bed?" Eva prompts.

She doesn't wait for good nights, just lets the lingering adrenaline carry her out of the guest room and down the hall.

You're right, Celeste said. Eva wouldn't have to keep being *right* if Celeste would just stop being *wrong*.

She thinks back to the shaky candid she saw online, Celeste's spoon an inch from Eva's lips. That was so stupid of her, to let Celeste get that flirty, to flirt back. It's all fun and games until someone's heart gets broken. Celeste is a bad idea. Celeste has *been tried*. It didn't end well for Eva. And if Celeste feels she can still make decisions without her, she needs to stomp out whatever sparks she's let fly.

There's a knock on Steph's door, and Gina slips inside.

"I'm sorry I didn't switch with you on Friday," she says without preamble.

Eva sighs and slumps onto the edge of the bed. Gina sits beside her, her toes just barely brushing the carpet. "Water under the bridge."

"I still think it warrants an apology. I told you we would switch, and then I didn't make it happen."

Eva nods. "Thank you."

"To be honest . . . I did want you and Celeste to have to talk things out. I thought it might be helpful for the two of you, for all of us. I shouldn't have done it behind your back like that."

Of *course* Gina would never do something as innocent as accidentally falling asleep early on a day when she'd traveled halfway across the country. Of course it was part of a scheme.

"You're not supposed to plot against your friends."

Gina winces. "I know, I'm sorry. Like I said, I thought . . . it was for the best?"

"For whose best? Mine? Or yours?"

Gina's quiet for a few moments, then says, "I miss you, both of you, all of you. I miss being in a friend group."

The Gina who crosses Eva's Tumblr dash is never this vulnerable. Still—talk about Hollywood problems.

"I'm sure there are plenty of squads that would love to have you."

"That's not what I meant. I miss—and I know other people figure it out. Find real friends, people who aren't just looking for an introduction to someone else. But I already had that. And I feel like I'm not gonna get it back if you and Celeste can't even have a polite conversation."

"That's not my problem," says Eva. "And, like, for the record? You want real friends again? Try treating me like one. I'm not Kayla, or a journalist. Don't manipulate me."

"I'm sorry, I am," says Gina. "And now you know, so. That's done with."

"Sure."

"I wouldn't have told you if I wasn't going to stop," Gina says.

Despite herself, Eva laughs. "Okay . . . but for real, no more."

"For real," echoes Gina. She sighs. "I'm not renewing with Kayla, actually."

"Why?" Eva brings her knees up to her chest.

Gina's the only one who stayed with Kayla after the breakup, and if *that* didn't prompt a change in management, what would?

"She treats me like I'm still thirteen. I want to have more control over my career."

"Oscar-nominated films and Netflix aren't doing it for you?"

"I'm not sure."

Eva lets her feet drop back to the floor. "What the hell?"

"I don't know. Acting is . . . there's a lot I like about it. I love the research and trying to do justice to a character and all of that. But I don't know if it can be the only thing for me."

"So write a script. Start a fashion line."

Gut reaction aside, it makes sense for Gina to talk to Eva about this. Eva's the only one who has tried to do more than one thing.

"I was thinking music." Gina's voice is hesitant.

It's as if ice has instantly covered all of Eva's insides. Without meaning to, she shivers. It's not like she wasn't expecting it necessarily, but at this point she didn't anticipate being told to her face. She thought she'd wake up one day to headlines about Gina's solo record deal and, a year later, begrudge all the fans who could attend a show.

"Great. Okay." Her words sound hollow, even to her own ears.

"Maybe . . . we could work together?"

Eva choses her words with care. "I'd like to see if we can be friends again. I've had a lot of fun singing with you this weekend. But you can't ask me that. It's not fair, and you know it."

"I had to ask." There's a small, sad smile on Gina's face.

"Let's just go to bed," says Eva.

"Kicking me out. I see how it is." Gina makes a show of kissing the top of Eva's forehead. "Mwa."

"Good night, Gi." She rolls her eyes, but she's smiling a little, too.

FEBRUARY 2020
STEPH

Matt glares at them from his seat at the kitchen table, slumped and arms crossed. "Mom already told me she's not fighting the suspension. You don't get to yell at me, too."

"I'm not going to *yell* at you." Steph pushes a mug of hot chocolate toward him.

"He was calling her a slut. To my face. What was I supposed to do? You wouldn't just let that go." Matt ignores the steaming cup.

Steph strategically waited for this conversation until Meghan was upstairs with their mom and grandma, who promised her a back massage and foot rub. They've managed to keep the news away from the tabloids, but there's no controlling all the kids at her high school. It's been a constant fear since Meghan started showing. She has enough stress even without the possibility of *Us Weekly* speculating on the pregnancy of the younger sister of a now conspicuously absent queer pop star.

"You almost broke his nose. There's a difference," says Steph.

"He wouldn't stop saying it. You don't know what that's—" Matt cuts himself off.

"I've heard people say all kinds of things about Celeste, Eva, and Gina to my face," says Steph. For the last few years, they've had five siblings, not two.

"That's different." Matt sets his jaw. "Those are just random idiots, and you always had security and stuff. I go to *school* with people who call Meghan names."

"You won't, if you get suspended one more time. And this *would* have been the last straw, except they're willing to recognize he was trying to provoke you." Steph sighs. "Look. You and Meghan can both switch again next year if you want to. Maybe that would be better. But you *can't* get into any more fights. Meghan doesn't want you pulling some white-knight routine anyway, and punching a douchebag fifteen-year-old because he called her a slut does not qualify for the no-violence exception."

"Nazis," Matt supplies.

"Yeah. But John's not a Nazi. He's just a teenage asshole."

"It wasn't like it was the first time he said it. He always made it into a big thing, whenever he saw me, for a *week*."

Steph is already aware of this. They'd gotten permission from the school to sit in on the meeting with the principal, and Matt was vocal in his protestations.

"He sucks," Steph agrees. "But what would suck more is if his family had decided to go to the police, and you got an *actual* assault record, instead of just a suspension on your transcript. You're not a little kid anymore."

"And I can't get in trouble with the police. What if the *press* found out, what if your stupid little brother messed with your perfect *reputation*?"

Steph was on tour when Matt was becoming a teenager, and they're continually startled every time they expect childish petulance and get a sarcastic attack instead. It doesn't suit Matt. Steph can't help but wonder if, without Moonlight Overthrow, Matt might have launched into adolescence without losing his sweetness.

"That was never, ever about protecting me," says Steph. "I didn't want anybody bothering *you*. The Grammys were last week, and none of us were there besides Eva, so, yeah, people are asking questions, poking around. I don't want them to find out about this fight, because that's going to have consequences for you. You don't want a future roommate, or partner, or employer to search your name and find a TMZ article about this. Trust me."

Matt remains silent.

"Give it another few months, and nobody will care anymore. I quit, it's over. I'm not going back. I'm sorry it completely messed up our family. I'm here now, and I'm trying to fix it as much as I can, but these things take time."

Sometimes, when everyone else is asleep, Steph tries to imagine what that time will look like. The nursery's already set up for the baby, who will soon inherit Steph's dad's role of Miles family spring birthday. Starting in the fall, Steph and their grandma will take care of the baby during school hours, while Meghan does her senior year. Steph will drive Matt to hockey practice and accompany Grandma Marit to the cemetery. They'll keep learning Pro Tools, but they'll never professionally produce. To really become a producer, Steph needs some singers, and the only three they want to work with probably don't want anything to do with them right now.

"You got to leave." Matt's voice cracks, and they both ignore it. "For every kid who thought it made me so cool to have this famous older sibling, there was somebody—and the teachers tried to stop it when they heard it, but every year, all the time, there was some kid who was calling you and the girls names. Saying stuff to me and Meghan about you. Grandma told me they were just jealous, but that doesn't actually help, you know?"

Steph's heart clenches. It's not like they didn't know. But Matt's still clearly so hurt about it.

"You think I didn't get called those names when I was in middle school? To *my* face, when they were talking about *me*? When Moonlight Overthrow wasn't anything yet, and I was just an ordinary queer kid with no money, no security team, hoping Mom wouldn't find out because she was trying to raise three kids by herself and I knew she'd make a fuss about it with the school—" Steph takes a deep breath. They adjust the cuffs of their green plaid overshirt.

Matt's sneer slides away as his face falls. "She was gone a lot."

"Yeah. Because I was fifteen and spending months on end away from home. I didn't have soccer games for her to go to, I had shows. Other than MSG, I never once asked her to come. You can be mad at me for not saying no every other time she came to a show or music video shoot or whatever, but I didn't ask her to. If you need to talk about that, talk about it with Mom, not me." Steph doesn't bother to try to keep their voice from shaking. The circumstances are their fault, maybe, but on this one point they're sure.

"Sorry," says Matt. He flicks a finger against the mug. "I did think it was cool. Your music and stuff."

"Thanks," says Steph. "These fights are not."

Matt nods.

"We good?" Steph asks.

"If you warm up my hot chocolate. Please," says Matt.

Steph stands. They would never deny him that.

CELESTE

Pip greets her with a tight hug on Monday morning. Her fuchsia blouse is wrinkled, but that's the only indication of the ridiculous workload Celeste has asked of her.

"You don't look like someone who just increased the seating capacity by several thousand," says Pip.

Celeste shrugs. She glances at Eva, who turned away as soon as Pip approached.

Pip follows her gaze. "Chin up. The rest will follow."

It's hard to feel excited about the show when Eva keeps a careful, calculated distance between them at all times.

"Everything good?" Celeste says, during a quick break. Eva is tucked against a wall, texting someone.

"Yup." Eva waves her phone in her hand. "College friend."

"Friend like Gina's 'friend'?" Celeste winces at the edge in her own voice.

"Friend like friend. Don't you need to check in with Pip?"

Celeste doesn't, actually, but she takes the hint and chats with someone from the sound crew instead until it's time to start again.

One by one, the songs left between them and "Before" disappear.

"You ready to teach us your harmonies?" Gina asks. "It's next on the set list, if we're sticking with that order."

Celeste has kind of been hoping that they would forget about the plan to sing one of her songs and one of Eva's, or that they would decide to cut them, for the sake of time.

It's not that she isn't proud of "Before." But "Before" . . . it's for Eva. Or maybe it's for Celeste, two years ago, when she was deciding she had to break up with Eva. The pre-chorus is definitely what she almost wishes she said, at the end, or right after.

Be back before I miss you.

Be back before I say goodbye.

"I guess," says Celeste.

When Celeste meets Gina's eyes, the message is clear: *Get your ass into gear. Get your girl, or get out.* She should be grateful Gina and Jenna don't cross paths anymore. Her oldest sister had a way of backing Gina's every play and getting what she wanted in the process.

"Ready for this?" Celeste hears Gina say, but when she looks up from tuning her guitar, Gina is standing next to Eva.

"Hmm?" Eva asks.

Gina hums the first bar of the chorus.

"Yeah," Eva says, but she pivots toward Celeste. "You're sure you don't just want to sing it yourself?"

Celeste flinches. "If you don't want to, I can, but—"

"We want to," Gina says.

"Eva?" Celeste prompts.

"Yeah," says Eva, to Celeste's surprise. "As long as you're okay with us taking over your song. Temporarily, I mean."

"Absolutely," Celeste says.

"This is getting a little too Midwest, even for me," Steph says.

"Very funny," says Eva.

"Eva," Celeste says, quieter this time. She doesn't look at Gina or Steph. "We don't have to."

"It's a great song."

Which means Eva hates it.

"Let's get started," Gina says.

Dutifully, Celeste counts them in.

It's excruciating. Not the singing itself, not like yesterday's early fiasco. But listening to *Eva* sing it.

I'm back, I'm back, I'm back, Celeste thinks. Or she would be, if Eva asked.

Eva, of course, is brilliant. She *gets* it. She adds in harmonies Celeste hadn't thought to arrange; she does a new interpretation of the bridge. But she doesn't look at Celeste unless absolutely necessary.

Celeste is a musician. She knows you can only mess around with a song like that once you've inhabited it. Once you really, really know it.

"She hates it," Celeste tells Gina, on a break a while later, while Eva's in the bathroom.

"Yes," says Gina.

Celeste's heart clenches. She knew it already, but that doesn't mean she wanted Gina to confirm it.

"She hates it because she thinks you wrote it for *some other girl*," Gina says.

"What?"

"Babe." Gina casts her gaze upward, as if seeking divine assistance for Celeste's incompetence. "The song is amazing. Eva will love the hell out of it after she realizes it's not about someone else. And after she forgives you."

"There's no other girl," Celeste says.

God, of course there isn't. It's not like she didn't try, but . . .

Inside, maybe she always knew, as much as she tried to ignore it. She always had this stupid little seedling of a plan. Less of a plan, more of a wish, the kind you don't even articulate to that first-star-you-see-tonight, because it's your own damn fault you don't still have her. That Eva would come after her. That Eva would go solo, and, three years from now, write them a duet. That five years from now, they'd reconnect at a Grammys after-party. She wanted Eva later; she just didn't see how she could get from Eva *now* to Eva *then*.

First loves don't work out. But if Eva just happened to also be her second . . .

Celeste might see how to get there.

EVA

Eva runs into Celeste on the way out of the studio bathroom.

"Hey," Celeste says. "I wanted to talk to you about the song."

"There's nothing to talk about," Eva says.

This whole thing was so embarrassing. How much she loved showing the others the live arrangement of the bridge she created and hadn't sung for anyone but her piano. How obviously she liked the way Celeste's eyes stayed on her as Celeste sang about missing someone.

"It's brilliant."

It would help if Celeste could stop sounding so earnest. Suddenly Celeste's litany of compliments isn't dreamy anymore. It's not a soft escape, a gentle transition that will ease her way back to L.A. once this is over.

"Stop it," she says. "Steph's family isn't here. We don't need to play nice."

Celeste looks abashed, but she still says, "Well, I want to be nice. And I mean what I say."

Eva resists rolling her eyes, then thinks, *Screw it,* and rolls them anyway. "You're going to leave again. You get that, right?"

"What?"

"On Friday morning, you're going to get on a plane and go back to the life you really want. And you're going to stay there."

"Eva—"

"No. We're not doing—whatever this is that we've been doing, even when we don't have to. I'm not—" Eva cuts herself off. She still can't bring herself to say *I'm not the girl you broke up with*. In some fundamental way, she still is. She still loves Celeste, after all. But there's more to her than Celeste. There always was, even when she couldn't see it.

"You're not . . . ?" Celeste frowns. "Are you—are you dating someone? That college friend, the one you've been texting?"

"If I were dating someone, we definitely would not have shared a bed on Friday."

"Right. Okay," says Celeste.

"You left."

"I know, I'm—"

I wouldn't finish that sentence if I were you, darling, Eva thinks. *I wouldn't have fucking started it.*

"And you know what? I am also going to get back to my life. I'm getting a degree at the best public university in the country. Come November, I'm going to be a Grammy nominee. *On my own.*"

"I'm happy for you. I wanted that for you."

"Did you, though? Did you really? Or did you just want me to be waiting for you, ready to start holding your hand once you decided you had time for me again?" She keeps her tone hard, harsher then she really feels, so she can't walk this back. She doesn't want to leave herself the option of running after whatever Celeste is offering.

"No, I didn't—that wasn't . . . We were too wrapped up in each other. You get this now, I know you do. We couldn't function on our own, and we *needed* to, we needed to be able to be our own people." Celeste's voice is pleading, a grotesque echo of Eva's as she tried and tried to give Celeste everything she wanted the night of the breakup. As she tried to persuade Celeste to stay.

"You have—and had—the right to decide what *you* need, for

yourself." She makes her voice even now. Not gentle, but calm enough that she could claim to be the mature one later on. This fight has been building for a year and a half, the words reshaping themselves in Eva's chest every month, every time she found she didn't need Celeste to finish a chorus or make her laugh after an awkward encounter with a classmate. There is a terrible victory in getting to say them now. "You don't get to dictate that to me. You didn't get to decide *for me* what I needed. You were my girlfriend, not my parent."

"But now you've done it," Celeste says, insistent. "You've gone and done so much, so much that you wouldn't have—"

"You don't get to take credit for that," Eva snaps. "You don't get to claim *any* of that. I wrote my application essays. I go to office hours. I sit at my piano and do the damn work. That is *all mine*. All this stuff in my life that you couldn't even imagine—I built it. I wrote it all. You do not get a producing credit. You are not in the fucking liner notes."

Eva is not going to fall into this again.

Being lesbian is not a choice. Loving Celeste is not a choice. But pursuing Celeste is a choice, and Eva tries very hard not to make the same mistakes twice. She hopes she loves herself enough not to set up her heart for another fall.

"I was scared," says Celeste, her voice small and raw.

"Of?"

"I loved you *so much*, Eva."

Eva shakes her head, covering her face with her hands until she's taken a few deep breaths. She cannot, she cannot with this, she cannot with Celeste.

Celeste clears her throat. "We were so young."

"We're still young."

"Even younger," says Celeste. "And I loved you so much, and I didn't know what to do with that. I didn't want us to crash and burn later on because I didn't know how to handle feeling so damn much. And you were—you were *everything*, my songwriting partner, my best friend, everything. I couldn't handle one person being all that, having so much of me. What if you left, and I never learned how to sing on my own?"

"But it was okay with you to make me figure that out?"

"I was trying to protect myself. Maybe in the most hurtful way possible, but . . . looking out for yourself isn't a crime."

"So you thought you'd go for the preemptive scorched-earth policy. Instead of giving us a chance." She wants to be vicious, but the words come out tired. Sad.

"I was my parents' chance. That's why I'm here. And they couldn't do it. My mom was seventeen when she fell in love with him, and they couldn't do it. They were desperately in love, each other's everything, and look at them now. I thought I knew that was going to happen to us, and I couldn't bear to wait it out."

It's hard to hold her own pain and accept Celeste's at the same time.

"Um . . . guys?"

Eva spins around. Gina's by the door to the rehearsal studio, grimacing.

"Sorry to interrupt, but we should probably keep going. If . . . you're ready."

Eva walks away from Celeste without another look. "I'm ready."

It won't be the first time she's sung while upset with Celeste, but if Celeste can just keep her mouth shut for a few more days, it can at least be the last.

JULY 2021
CELESTE

Dinner is . . . uncomfortable. Eva is aggressively cheery with everyone else, laughing loudly at Matt's stories about soccer practice, gushing over the non-binary-flag socks Grandma Marit just finished knitting. She won't look at Celeste.

After a few attempts, Celeste stops trying to join the conversation. She spends most of the meal staring at the whiteboard that's on the wall near the mudroom entrance. The top half is divided up month-style, the bottom half like a week. Every member of the family has their own color, so you can tell at a glance when Grandma Marit has doctors' appointments and when Mari and Meghan have day care orientation. Thursday is circled in bright purple. Someone has written *CONCERT* sideways, so it takes up most of the day—and between getting ready, pre-show interviews, and sound check, they'll be busy long before their openers finish at eight.

Three days.

Celeste gets to perform with them in *three days*. She knows that Eva isn't exactly as excited as she is.

Celeste hopes she has a chance to show Eva that the life she really wants isn't the one where she always sings alone, sleeps alone, brings her sisters as her dates to awards shows, and lies to her songwriting partners about why this lyric or that really needs to stay in. But if she can't show Eva all that, she at least wants Eva to have fun performing again. Celeste owes her that much.

When Celeste turns around after loading the dishwasher, she's surprised to find Eva is the only one still in the room, examining a parade of family vacation photos on the wall on the other side of the kitchen.

"Hey," says Celeste, crossing toward her.

Eva starts, her eyes darting around the otherwise empty space as she faces Celeste.

"I was going to shower, but . . . you want to hang out for a while? We can talk? We didn't really get to finish, um, our conversation earlier," says Celeste. Her heart is beating faster than it did while she waited for the last Grammy nominations to be announced. Asking to finish a fight with someone she's known since middle school shouldn't be this scary, right? Except this is Eva, so maybe her heart's frantic pace is exactly right.

Eva crosses her arms. "I said everything I wanted to say."

"Oh. Okay then. I just thought I'd offer. In case—you're still okay with this, right?"

"With what?"

Like singing with Celeste doesn't even register as something to feel anything about.

"Performing with us, I guess," she says.

"Yeah, sure." Eva tosses her head. "After today . . ."

"After today?"

"It just reminded me of a lot of old days."

Old days on tour? Old days after the breakup? Neither of those featured fights. They only really ever had the one.

Shit.

"You need to finish that sentence for me," Celeste says. She bites down on the *love* that threatens to slip through. "After today, you realize you can't wait to get back to college? After today, you remembered you hate us all . . . ?"

"There wasn't really an end to that sentence. Just figuring out my own head," says Eva. Her tone is cold, a clear do-not-enter sign.

Maybe she just hates me, *not Gina and Steph*, Celeste can't help but think. How do you say, *I'm sorry for everything and I'm thrilled we're doing this don't ever leave* without coming across as pathetic and desperate and so, so fucking hypocritical?

"Go on," Eva says. "I've got—something I need to do."

Celeste heads upstairs on her own.

The fight itches like a fresh scab. She can't face rehearsal tomorrow knowing Eva is still mad at her. Really, actively mad, not just the baseline bitterness Celeste guesses she's been carrying this whole time.

Celeste knows Jenna's at a work conference this week, flying straight from Philly to Duluth on Thursday, or else she'd call. Celeste needs to make this right.

They rotated bedrooms again after rehearsal, so Celeste has Steph's room tonight. When she knocks on the half-open door of the guest room after her shower, hoping to clear the air with Eva, there's no response. Celeste taps it open.

Eva's gone.

No no no no no, she thinks. *You can't do this, you can't leave—*

But Eva's things are still here, Celeste notices. Her suitcase is in the corner, her chargers coiled on the floor next to an outlet. It's just Eva who's missing.

Celeste darts into Steph's room, throws on a sweater, and plunges back into the hallway. There's a light on in Meghan's room, and a quiet murmur that means someone's talking. Celeste knocks, then enters at Gina's "Come in."

Gina's the only one in the room. She's sitting cross-legged on the bed, on a video call with someone.

"Oh, sorry," Celeste says. "I didn't mean to interrupt."

"No problem, babe," Gina says. "I thought I'd come in here in case Eva wanted some privacy in our room. Steph's in with their mom, talking about some church thing. Do you want to chat, or were you just . . . ?"

"Looking for Eva."

"If she's not in the guest room, I don't know where she is. I told Eva I'd stay out of it, but I think it's fair game to say that you should apologize for whatever happened today."

Celeste shakes her head. "She won't even let me do that."

"Don't wait too long," Gina advises.

I'm already a year and a half late, Celeste thinks.

She walks through the ground level, passing from the thick carpet in the main living room to the cool hardwood of the kitchen. Eva's not in any of the rooms—not in the dining room or the tucked-away, smaller living rooms, or even the mudroom. There's no light emerging from beneath Grandma Marit's door, and the muted noise from Matt's room suggests *Avengers: Endgame*, not Eva. It's weird, walking around somebody else's empty house at night, like being an archeologist. All the artifacts of the family's existence are still scattered around: a big bin of Mari's toys, a few skeins of yarn that belong to either Steph's grandma or their mom, a comic book Matt is reading. But only Celeste is awake and walking through their world.

She backtracks to the stairs leading into the basement. When she opens the door, she hears it: the somewhat staccato sounds of someone trying to play a piano very softly while working through an unfamiliar piece. Celeste hesitates at the top of the stairs. She should probably leave Eva alone. She can try apologizing again in the morning. If Eva wanted her downstairs with her, she would have asked.

But Celeste has come this far . . .

She should check to make sure Eva's all right, anyway, even if she leaves straight after. That's what friends do. She might not have been the best girlfriend, but she hopes she can at least be a dependable friend now. She heads downstairs. Her ankles crack. Eva replays a measure, with a few note changes.

Eva's back is toward her. Her laptop is open on the piano bench beside her, a notebook lying across half the keyboard.

She's writing, Celeste realizes.

She's halfway across the room when Eva turns to write something down, sees her, and drops her pen. It rolls off the notebook and onto the carpeted floor.

"Celeste," she says. Her eyes are wide.

It makes Celeste think of that night at Olivia's, the dramatic shadows on Eva's face making it impossible to read her eyes.

They used to write together.

Celeste has written with world-class songwriters for her two solo records. And they lived up to their reputations, and it was good work, good experience. But Eva made her spoiled. It requires effort to learn how to work with someone new, creatively. It requires vulnerability to let someone know what feelings you want to express in a song.

"Sorry," Celeste says. "You weren't upstairs, and I wanted to check . . ."

"I just wanted to finish writing this," says Eva.

"Oh. That's great," Celeste offers.

Eva looks at her expectantly, her eyebrows raised. Celeste can't seem to make her body move. All her apologies catch in her throat.

"It's been in my head since the Fourth, and I finally figured out the last verse tonight—I think, anyway—so I thought I'd come down, and . . ."

And now you're not leaving, Celeste finishes.

"Right. Cool."

"I was trying to be quiet." There's an edge to her voice, one that

Celeste has no trouble reading: Eva was doing fine on her own, and Celeste just had to track her down and interrupt.

"You were. I mean, I couldn't hear you until I opened the basement door. They probably put in some soundproofing," Celeste says.

Eva nods. She bends over to pick up her pen; her hair falls over her face, and she brushes it away with the back of her hand.

"Is this for somebody I know?" Celeste blurts. "I mean, um, you don't have to tell me, just curious."

"It's not for anybody else yet," Eva says. "There's a couple people it could work for, I think, when it's ready, but . . ."

But not me, Celeste knows.

"Cool," she says again. She tries for a smile. "I look forward to seeing it on the charts next summer."

"Thanks." It's just one syllable, but it's prickly enough that it might as well be a whole angry breakup song.

Celeste is still standing awkwardly a few paces away, not so close as to loom, but too far away to feel natural. Her toes are cold, despite the soft carpeting. In another universe, she didn't push during rehearsal, and Eva wants her to be here.

Celeste wants to crowd into Eva on the piano bench, kiss the sensitive spot behind her ear. She'd settle for lying on the floor, right here, listening to Eva rework hooks and choruses until she fell asleep. Until Eva woke her with a kiss and said, "I'm not sleeping on the floor. Let's go to bed."

Kiss me, Celeste thinks. *Sing with me.*

Let me sing with you.

Stay.

"I guess . . . ," Celeste says. "I'll just go back upstairs, then. Don't stay up too late working on this?"

"Good night," says Eva. Dismissive.

"Good night."

Celeste leaves the room slowly. Hesitates on the stairs. She wants Eva to call her back. To say she works better with Celeste here, or since she's still awake, she might as well stay, or *anything*, but the piano starts up again.

At the top of the stairs, Celeste shuts the door behind her.

EVA

Eva has a problem.

Well—in terms of her Five Year Plan, she doesn't.

Moonlight Overthrow is five weeks into their first tour as a support act. Their album debuted at number fifteen, which is about sixty places higher than Eva's most realistic wildest dreams, and only ten places below her wildest-wildest-wildest dreams. But their initial contract is for two albums, which means they'll have another chance. And a chance after that, if the label thinks they're still worth it. And *three* more chances after that, if they do really well. Her dad spent ages explaining the contract to them, but it boils down to this: the label has *options*, times when they can decide if MO can continue with them or not. If they can, they must. Eva intends to make sure they're so successful, the label will demand all six and then beg for more.

Celeste, meanwhile, had used the number fifteen to make golden album jokes about Eva's age.

"Never again, though," Gina said.

Gina will be fifteen when their next album comes out. Gina means: only up from here.

None of that is the problem.

"Eee-vaaa," Celeste whispers across the tiny aisle in the middle of their tour bus. She says *Eva* like the *WALL-E* character, the sleek and shiny robot that dazzles the lonely trash compactor.

Eva feels more like the trash compactor. She's embarrassed every time her skin-care routine is changed, which is every time a zit dares to appear, which is more frequently than anyone cares to acknowledge.

"It's just stress," one of their makeup artists assured her a few nights ago.

It's just my skin, Eva thinks. Only now that's not acceptable the way it was last year.

"What?" Eva whispers back.

"You're so far away."

Normally, they get on the bus together and immediately crawl into one or the other's bunk. Tonight, they had one-on-one debriefs with their vocal coach; Celeste had gone before Eva.

"And you didn't sit next to me during signing," Celeste says.

Eva slips out of her bed and into Celeste's. Given the narrowness of the aisle in this part of the bus, it's basically a single movement. Celeste is sitting with her back against the bus wall, slumped low so she doesn't hit her head against the bunk above her, and she lifts up her blanket to tuck Eva in next to her.

"Someone moved my name card," Eva says.

"Well, move it back next time. Or pretend to be Steph. Can you do Steph yet?"

Celeste means Steph's signature. It's something they messed around with in a hotel room one night, all of them taking turns to learn the others' autographs. They've never used their admittedly terrible forgery skills on anything that will get into real fans' hands, but there may be a sexist radio host or two (or three, whatever) proudly displaying a glossy photo covered in wobbly signatures.

"The *S* is impossible," Eva says. "I'm the easiest."

"Hey, now." Celeste pinches her arm lightly. "Friends don't let friends call themselves 'easy.'"

Eva flushes, grateful for the dark. *I am for you*, she thinks.

Everybody's easy for Celeste. Eva might as well be one of those queer girls hyperventilating from the casual hugs Celeste passes out at meet and greets. *I feel you*, she thinks at them. Except Celeste doesn't joke with them quite like she jokes with Eva. She doesn't pout at them when they don't sit next to her. She'd never, ever invite one to share her bed on the tour bus.

"Tomorrow," Celeste whispers. "Promise."

"Promise."

Eva tips her head onto Celeste's shoulder. Beneath the blanket covering their legs, Celeste begins to trace something on Eva's bare thigh. After a minute, Eva realizes Celeste is practicing their autographs: the tight *S*, loopy *G*, round *E*. That big *C*, the confident sprawl of the longest name of them all. In the dark of the night, the stillness of the bus, every sense is concentrated on whatever bit of skin Celeste is naming. There's the cool brush of the blanket against her legs, Celeste warm beside her, their shoulders pressed together, Eva's heartbeat fast and loud, pounding out a beat that sounds like *hope*.

The next night, their name cards are out of order again: Gina, Celeste, Steph, Eva.

"No, no, no," Celeste says, not even stopping as she breezes by, picks up the cards, and switches them in a single efficient movement, like she's been practicing the choreography in her head all day. "Eva sits next to me."

Steph raises a water bottle in salute and sits down on the end, as usual. An assistant smiles brightly at the fans close enough to hear, the ones who probably left their set early to be at the front of the line. The half-hour break between their set and the headliner was long enough for them to get through everyone that first week, but not since. *Good problems*, Eva's parents call this.

Celeste slides into her seat, then pushes out Eva's with a sandaled foot. Her toenails are a glossy, bold blue, seven hours old.

Eva sits and uncaps her Sharpie. Steph looks down their row, waiting for Gina's nod before signaling the assistant, who waves the first group of fans forward.

Steph signs the poster the first girl sets on the table, then slides it neatly toward Eva. Eva barely glances down as she signs; eye contact is more important.

"Did you all have a good time?" she asks.

Steph's already covered "How are you all tonight?"

They've settled into a rhythm for these things.

"You were amazing," the girl says. She's wearing a concert T-shirt, clearly thrown over the tank top she wore to the show. "So good, oh my god."

"Wasn't she?" Celeste chimes in, leaning over into Eva's space.

The girl startles, eyes going wide as she pulls at her friend's hand, an insistent order to *watch this, they're just like how we thought they'd be.*

"Your solo in 'Standstill' killed me," the girl says, half to Eva, half to Celeste, like she's looking for Celeste's approval of her praise for Eva.

"Every night onstage I just want to, like, end the show after she sings it," Celeste says. "Like, go home, everybody, nothing tops that. Every night!"

"I'm glad you don't?" the girl says, hesitant.

Eva laughs. "Don't listen to her," she tells the fan. Mindful of the assistant, mindful of the line, she passes the poster over to Celeste.

"Listen to me," Celeste says. "I should be on the other side of this table. Why don't I get Eva autographs?"

"You get—" Eva cuts herself off. If she says *to write* all *of our autographs across my thigh* or even just *nightly bus cuddles*, that's exactly what the fan will post online. Enough fans will take that in a direction Eva's not ready for that she keeps her mouth shut.

"I think we should fix this," Celeste says, winking at the fan but turning toward Eva. "Will you sign something for me?"

"You're holding up the line," Gina calls, but without heat.

"Sorry!" the fan squeaks.

"Not you, babe. This one." Gina pulls the signed poster from Celeste.

Celeste pushes her own Sharpie into Eva's hand. "Well?"

"Sure? What am I signing, though?"

"I have some ideas . . ." Celeste raises her eyebrows.

Eva very, very pointedly does not look away from Celeste's eyes.

Celeste grins and taps her bicep. "Here?"

Eva signs.

STEPH

The best Steph can say about rehearsal on Tuesday is that it's better than yesterday.

Better than yesterday does not actually mean all that much. It's honestly more miserable than the last seven shows they did as MO. Even though Steph wasn't confident about anything else during that time, they knew their cues, their beats, their lyrics. They knew they were going home.

Now, Steph is home, trying to find a way to maybe leave again. It's not going to happen while Eva keeps giving Gina this sticky-sweet smile and refusing to look at Celeste. It's clear that each note reminds Eva of every objection and every betrayal. More than ever, Steph can appreciate just how much work Eva put into those last shows. Fans didn't only come because they thought MO could sing: they came because they liked to see how much they all liked each other. With a rotten center, what is Duluth going to think of them?

They still have two more songs to learn that afternoon when Steph's phone begins to ring. They leave their drumsticks on the seat and dart over to their bag.

"I'm so sorry, guys, I swear I put this on do not disturb," they say over their shoulder.

Steph starts to automatically decline the call, but stops when they realize it's Matt. They huff. Steph has been available 24/7 since the end of MO, and now they're taking one week for a charity show, he has to interrupt?

"What?" Steph answers. "I'm in the middle of rehearsal."

"Grandma's in the hospital."

Steph drops to their knees. "What?"

"She just collapsed. She was breathing but she just—she collapsed, so I called 911, and they wouldn't let me come in the ambulance, and Mom's phone is off because she's at work—" Matt's voice is high and panicky.

Oh god.

Steph doesn't want to even think about if—to name, just in their own mind—

Pull it together, Steph instructs themself. *Pull. It. Together.*

"You did good, calling 911. Where are you now?" They stand, pulling their bag over their shoulder as they rummage around the pockets for their keys.

Actions, movements, yes, that's how to do this, the only way out is through, they need to *go.*

"In the car, on the way. Meghan was at the park with Mari. She doesn't know yet."

"Is it safe for you to be driving? You can pull over, I'll come get you."

Shit. Matt drove them to rehearsal. Steph doesn't have a car. Why did Steph let him do that? Why didn't they just *know* it would end badly?

The girls are approaching, wary but concerned.

"Steph? Is everything okay?" Gina asks.

No. No, no, no.

But "no" isn't enough. "No" is fucking useless. "No" alone won't get them what they need.

"How can we help?" says Eva.

"I need a car. I need to go to the hospital. Right now," says

Steph, holding the phone away from their mouth. Their words are jerky as they try to control the trembling in their voice. They can't bring themself to say why, not just yet.

"Done. I'll get the keys from Pip," says Celeste, turning away.

Eva's and Gina's faces are parallel studies in horror, but they don't ask follow-up questions; they just move with Steph as they head for the door, their attention back on Matt.

"I'm okay, I'm almost there," he says. "What should I do?"

Call Mom back, Steph thinks. *I don't want to do this again.*

Immediately, guilt surges in their stomach, acidic. Steph is the oldest. There is no choice. They have to be strong for Matt.

"Go to the waiting room. Wait for me there. Um, introduce yourself to the front desk staff." Steph swallows. "But Grandma probably wasn't able to consent to sharing information with extended family, so they won't tell you anything anyway. I'll get ahold of Mom."

Celeste reappears in their field of vision, dangling keys from one hand. Steph reaches for them, but Celeste shakes her head.

"I'm driving."

Steph doesn't argue. Eva and Gina follow them out of the studio and into the parking lot.

"It was so scary, Steph." The words come out choked. Matt needs to get off the road.

"I know. You've done great. You got the paramedics there, you called me. I'm going to hang up so you can concentrate on driving, okay?" Steph folds themself into the front seat of the car Celeste unlocks. Their free hand is trembling so much, it takes three tries to fasten their seat belt. It's a good thing Celeste offered to drive.

Gina and Eva are in the back seat, whispering quietly. Eva hands Celeste her phone. Steph catches a glimpse of Google Maps.

"Okay," says Matt. "You're coming?"

"I'm on my way. Be safe, wait for me."

"Okay," he repeats.

Steph hangs up. They tip their head back into the headrest. Can nothing go right, ever? They wanted *one* week, and the goddamn universe couldn't even give them that. At least Steph knows better than to wish for something like that again.

"St. Luke's, yeah?" Celeste says, glancing at them as she turns right.

"Yeah." Steph sucks in their cheeks, then lets out a breath. "Grandma. Collapsed while just the two of them were home. Matt had to call 911."

"Oh my god," says Eva.

"Steph, I'm so sorry." Gina reaches around the front seat to squeeze Steph's shoulder.

"He's on his way there now. He doesn't know anything except . . ." Their breath catches. "She was breathing. He said. She was still breathing. So."

"She's a fighter," says Eva.

"I wish people wouldn't say shit like that," Steph says. It's not even Eva's fault, it's just a dumb social platitude, but now that they've started, they can't seem to stop. "Like, I get there's probably some research out there about a positive attitude and whatever being important, but it doesn't always matter. You just die. You die *anyway*. Or even if you were 'fighting'—you get tired, and you can't blame people for that."

This is why Steph has to stay, no matter what pretty things Gina has to say about music and Mari growing up. What if they were holding the charity concert in Minneapolis instead? They were really going to make their family wait alone for *hours* while Steph got on the highway? No.

"Of course. I'm sorry," says Eva.

"Don't even with that," Steph snaps. "You don't get it. You are *never* going to get it. My grandma is in the hospital and I wasn't even there, and I'm tired of having to explain it to someone whose mom doesn't ever need you, whose lawyer daddy can just do whatever it takes so your life is exactly what you want—"

"Hey, stop," says Celeste. "You're upset, but you can't talk to her like that. This isn't Eva's fault."

"And of course you're defending her. When you get right down to it, it's always really going to be about the two of you, isn't it? You don't care who you throw under the bus along the way." Steph blinks back tears. They can't cry yet. They don't know anything. They definitely can't cry because it's the same shit all over again.

"That's unfair. And not true, and I know you know that," says Gina. "Let's just all take a couple of deep breaths."

"Breathing does not solve the fucking problem," says Steph.

"Neither does yelling at us!" says Gina. "I know you feel useless because until we get to the hospital, there's nothing you can do, but please hold off on lashing out until we're there."

Steph feels themself deflate against the hot fake leather of the seat.

"I need to let Mom and Meghan know," they say. Their voice sounds hollow even to their own ears.

"Do you want us to call? At least Meghan?" Eva offers.

They know it's meant as a peace offering. They're just not interested in peace right now.

"No. That's not fair to you or her. It has to be me."

Steph's phone lights up in their hand: *Mom*, it reads, but remains silent. They hadn't forgotten to put it on DND after all. During rehearsal, Matt must have called twice in a row, so his second call was allowed to ring.

"Mom?"

"Honey, what's going on? I just stepped away and saw a bunch of missed calls from Matt. Now he's not picking up."

"Maybe the lot was full and there's a dead zone in the hospital parking ramp," Steph says.

A fraction of a pause. "Hospital?"

Steph explains the little that they know.

"Where are you now?" Steph's mom asks. They grimly recognize the question. They asked Matt the same thing only a few minutes ago.

"On my way, with the girls."

"Good, all right. I'll call Meghan and have her meet me at home. I don't want her driving. She'll be too upset. Is that okay? Do you want me to come straight there?"

Detouring home to pick up Meghan and Mari will mean an extra ten minutes.

"Up to you," says Steph. "I'll be all right, so it's just—what you want to do."

Celeste makes another turn. They recognize the route now. Only a few minutes to go.

"Steph? I love you so much."

"Love you, too, Mom."

They hang up, gripping their phone tightly in their hands. They can't bear to go through this again. Not another stroke or—or. They just can't.

"I'm going to drop you off at the entrance, okay?" Celeste says.

"I'll come with you," says Eva. "In case you need someone to take messages, or just . . . for whatever."

"Fine, okay."

They're quiet for the time it takes Celeste to pull in front of the emergency room entrance.

"We'll be in as soon as I've parked," she says.

Eva follows Steph into the hospital and up the wide entrance staircase without a word.

Matt is already sitting down in the waiting area, but he springs up when he sees Steph. His face is tear-streaked.

"Are you okay? Do you know anything?"

Matt shakes his head. Steph pulls him into a tight hug.

"I'm sorry you had to be here by yourself," Steph says.

"You came right away," says Matt.

See? Steph thinks, as if Gina can read minds from wherever Celeste's parking. *Any delay would wreck him.*

"Of course I did."

"I need to, um. I need to find the bathroom," Matt says, almost tripping over a chair as he maneuvers around Eva.

Matt is still gone when Gina and Celeste rush in. Celeste tries to sit in the chair he vacated, but Eva stops her. "Matt's sitting there."

Celeste sits next to Eva. Gina sits on Steph's other side, glancing from Steph to Eva.

"I know they can't say anything until Mom gets here. You guys can go back to rehearsal," Steph says.

"What the *hell*?" says Celeste. She glances around the distinctly non-empty waiting room and lowers her voice. "We're not just leaving you in a *hospital waiting room*, Steph. If you don't want us here once your mom comes, we understand. We'll wait at a coffee shop, or we'll go back to your house. But we're not rehearsing without you, especially not if you're here."

"Well, I need to be here, and you need to put on a show. I think that's what they call 'irreconcilable differences,'" says Steph.

Celeste flinches. "We're *not* leaving you."

"My family *needs* me. You think you can waltz back to Duluth, and put on this shiny concert, and all my problems will just be conveniently on pause for a week. Maybe that's how your lives work, but it's not how mine works. Just go, and let me deal with this on my own."

Just like before, they think.

"We don't want to leave you," says Eva. "We want to help. She's your grandma, but we love her, too. And if you want to yell at me about how I don't know what it's like, because *my* grandmas both died before I could do division, much less drive, *fine*. But that's not going to make me leave. It's not going to make me want to help less."

"We're friends," says Gina. "Fuck rehearsal."

And then Steph starts crying. They fold in on themself in the stupid hospital chair, digging their fingers in their hair. It's too much, and they're tired of it, but at least if they get these tears out of the way while Matt's in the bathroom, they can pretend they never cried at all.

"Hey, we're here," Eva murmurs. Steph feels a hand rubbing across their back.

"I don't want to ruin the concert," Steph says to their knees.

That's the sticking point, isn't it? It doesn't matter what Steph may want, how much they've enjoyed being back at the drum set, their sore arms giving their girls the tempo they need. Steph will never be able to guarantee they'll be around for the band. Something like this is always going to happen.

"You're not ruining the concert. We already knew we might have to cut some songs," says Gina.

"Not just that," says Steph. They sit up, tucking their knees to their chest and curling their arms around their legs. "If . . . if she's not released, then I can't rehearse tomorrow. I can't do the show on Thursday. They'll need me."

Steph looks at Eva as they speak, waiting for the betrayal to appear in her eyes, just as it did that terrible November night. But it doesn't come.

"Of course they will," Eva says, her tone soft instead of the sarcasm Steph expected. "We'll make it work, however you want it to. And maybe 'making it work' means not doing it at all. That's up to you."

"That's not fair to you. You came all this way—"

"For you," says Eva. "And for the band, and for Duluth. But not just to get on a stage and sing."

"But the show. All those people who bought tickets, especially now with the bigger venue. We made a promise, and just because I can't be there—"

"Maybe," Gina cuts in. "We don't know anything yet. You have time to decide. And it's okay to decide that your family needs you, I promise. But I don't think you should make any decisions until you know what's going on."

"But if I can't."

"Celeste could do it," says Eva.

"What?" Celeste's eyes are so wide with shock, it's almost comical.

"You know your set. You'd have to do more acoustic versions, and that would be a bit of a hassle, maybe, but you've got a whole show. Cut the songs that you really need your tech or musicians for, and I'm sure you've still got enough. Your set is already longer than some people's." Eva leans back in her chair.

At this point, Steph can't even be surprised that Eva knows Celeste's set length. Is there anything she doesn't know, other than that Celeste wouldn't dare to break her heart again?

"But . . ." Celeste looks to Steph. "This was supposed to be *our* show, for Duluth."

"Eva's right," says Steph. "If we can't do it as MO . . . you have a show. Use it."

"I didn't come here to do solo stuff, to—take over. I'm here for *us*, I promise," says Celeste, almost a plea.

"We know," says Eva. "But in this case? Your solo set might be the solution. It might be the only one we've got."

"Gina?" Celeste says as Matt returns and slumps into the empty seat between Steph and Eva.

"Listen to Eva, babe. *A* show must go on, and you're an excellent backup plan." Gina stands. "I'm going to see if they can get us a private room to wait in, okay?"

"Whoa, what?" says Matt, looking between them all.

Celeste follows Gina to the front desk. They make for a good co-ambassador team, two magazine cover stars with high-engagement Instas.

"Nothing," Steph says, then amends, "Later."

"What about the show?" Matt says.

"Later," Steph says again. "Mom's here."

Matt's head whips around. "Mom!"

He gets the first hug, which Steph doesn't begrudge him. They weren't the one who had to call for an ambulance. After a moment, though, Steph's mom pulls them into a tight group hug.

"Mama!" Mari commands, squirming in Meghan's grasp.

"In a minute, baby," she says.

Steph's mom's gaze sweeps over the assembled group: Eva hovering on the edges of their family circle, Celeste and Gina making their way over with a nurse who reminds Steph strongly of early Wolverine Hugh Jackman.

"Ms. Miles?" says the nurse, extending his hand. "There's a private room for you all to wait in. It might be more comfortable."

"Thank you," says Steph's mom. "That would be great. And then I'd like an update on my mother."

"Of course. Right this way."

They follow the nurse Steph has privately dubbed Nurse Logan down a hall, until he ushers them into a small conference room. High windows let in natural light. The late afternoon sun only serves to make the oblong table's fake wood appear even waxier. Celeste sits down in a plastic-backed chair near one of the table's tapered ends and pulls out her phone.

"I'm going to go talk to her doctor," Steph's mom says to the room at large. "I'll come back once I have an update."

Mari runs around the table once, taking great delight in crawling under Celeste's chair, before deciding that Meghan's lap is really where she wants to be. Steph passes a book from the baby bag to Meghan, then takes a seat beside Celeste, who's still frowning at her phone.

"Is it on social media?" Steph asks.

Celeste hesitates, then nods. "They don't know who's in the hospital, but a couple of people in the waiting room posted on Twitter about seeing us all. No pictures, so it's easily ignored as a rumor, at least for now. Pip's asking me what I want to do, but— what do you want?"

"Could you ask Pip to keep an eye on things? My instinct is to let it be a rumor for a while longer. If it spreads, then we'll say something once we know—what's going on."

"Sounds good," says Celeste.

They all lapse into silence, with the exception of Meghan and Mari. Everyone startles when the door opens and Steph's mom enters. She looks tired, as she almost always does, but her face is free of dire news.

"Grandma's all right," she says, closing the door behind her.

Matt exhales sharply.

"Come sit down, Mom," Steph says.

She takes a chair near Mari's spot on the floor. "She's awake, a bit upset to be in the hospital, a bit embarrassed that she fainted."

"So, what was it?" Matt asks.

"Right now, they're thinking her blood pressure dropped. They're running a few more tests to rule out anything more serious. And they're going to keep her overnight for observation, given her medical history. She'll be moved to a different floor soon." She gives them a bracing smile.

Steph's glad they're already sitting down. Their bones, the whole structure of their being, can be forced upright in a crisis. But now that it's passed, mostly, they feel like crumbling to dust. They slump further into the chair, collapsed under the weight of relief.

"Blood pressure, that's . . ." Matt nods, seemingly more to himself than anybody else.

"You were really brave, sweetheart. You did the right thing, calling right away. I wish I had been there instead, but I'm proud of how you handled it." Matt nods again. "I'm going to stay here, but you all might want to go home. I know you want to see her, but she's not up for more visitors tonight. I'll call if there's any news."

"I'm staying until the rest of the tests come back," Steph says. Matt and Meghan echo them.

"We'd like to stay, too," says Eva. "But only if we won't get in the way. If you'd rather we go, maybe pick up some dinner for the rest of you, just let us know."

"Stay," says Steph. "If you're sure."

"We're sure," says Gina.

Her answer doesn't come as a surprise, and gratitude threatens to restart the tears Steph has been holding at bay.

STEPH

The doctors rule out any connection to their grandma's stroke.

"I still want to be there, when she's released," Steph says to the girls. "I know that will mess with dress rehearsal."

"Don't worry about it. We'll rehearse when you're ready," says Eva.

Eva goes with Celeste as she drives Meghan and Mari home. Steph follows with the rest, minus their mom, about an hour later. Eva ordered delivery for dinner, and it arrives shortly after Steph.

They stare down at their plate. "I *am* sorry. For what I said in the car."

"It's fine," says Eva. "You were really scared."

"That doesn't make it okay. You've all been really helpful, and really nice. Not just today, but this whole week. You didn't deserve that," says Steph.

"We're good," Celeste says, waving their apology away. "Let's just focus on the fact that your grandma's all right."

No one talks much for the rest of the meal. Steph still feels dazed; the girls are presumably quiet out of awkwardness, or respect.

Meghan comes back to the kitchen after putting Mari to bed. A few strands of hair have escaped from her ponytail. Mari likes to touch her hair, especially at bedtime.

"Steph? Can we talk to you?" Meghan says.

Matt stands up from the table, like he's been expecting this.

"Yeah, of course," says Steph, confused.

While there have been some big Family Talks among them over the past few years, it's not something Steph's siblings have ever arranged.

"We'll go upstairs," Eva says.

"Oh, we can go." Steph makes to stand.

"Nah, we're gone." Celeste closes the dishwasher. She and Gina follow Eva out of the kitchen.

Matt sits back down with Meghan next to him, across from Steph.

"What's going on?" Steph asks. Before they can answer, though, Steph adds, "I'm really sorry I wasn't home today. I'll be at the hospital tomorrow morning, and I've already told the girls I might not be able to do the show at all. Grandma's the priority."

"Please stop talking," says Meghan.

"You're doing the show," says Matt. There's a stubborn look on his face, but not with the same sullen sheen from all those meetings with the principal when Steph first got back to Duluth; instead, there's the shadow of a smirk.

"That's nice of you, but Grandma's health is more important. Celeste can do her usual set. It's not like there won't be a show at all." Steph rolls an unused fork between their fingers. It hurt enough to make that decision, and now their siblings are forcing them to defend it?

"Can you stop being a martyr for five seconds?" Meghan snaps.

"Three days," Matt says. "Or three years."

"I'm not making myself into a *martyr*," Steph says. "Grandma is in the hospital! Matt had to call an ambulance! What about that is hard to understand?"

"And she's going to be fine," says Meghan.

"Mom already left early today. She can't take off the rest of the week."

"I'll be here," says Matt. "I don't work. I can drive. I managed calling 911 today just fine, thanks."

"And then you called me, freaking out," says Steph.

"I had a minute of panic when I couldn't reach Mom right away, okay? So yeah, I called you. That doesn't mean you need to cancel Moonlight Overthrow again." Matt crosses his arms.

"It's not fair to put that responsibility on you, when something goes wrong," Steph says.

"If," says Meghan. "And you put all that responsibility on yourself, back when you came home. You were eighteen, trying to solve everything. I'm eighteen now."

"You have a *baby*."

"Who is no longer nursing, who wakes up once a night. It's still hard, and I'm not saying I'm not glad you came home. You've changed more diapers than anybody but me. But you don't need to keep hovering." Meghan props her chin on her hands, elbows on the table.

"We've got our shit figured out now," says Matt, ignoring the Look Steph sends him for the swear word. "I'm always going to call you. But . . . sometimes all you need to do is answer and tell me to breathe and help me call somebody else. You don't always need to show up."

"Gee, thanks."

"I mean that in a good way. We're okay. Meg and I can handle things." Matt sends them a Look right back. "And now you've got your shit together, too."

"We're not saying you didn't come home for us. But you also came home for you, which is totally fine. And now you know who you are and who you aren't, so maybe you don't need to stay," says Meghan.

"You're kicking me out of my own home?"

Matt rolls his eyes. "You're a musician. You want to perform at festivals and pull all-nighters fiddling with production stuff I don't understand. You want to be interviewed by *Rolling Stone* as part of a feature on non-binary singers. You can't do that staying here."

"It doesn't matter," Steph says. They can't bring themself to say *what I want*.

"You gave up a lot to be here with us," Matt says. "We know this. We're not Mari's age. So maybe you could just believe us."

"There are probably going to be times when we wish you were around. But it will be *worth it* for us, if you're doing music again. We want to do this for you. We'll work to make it work, just like you didn't work so you could stay here all this time." Meghan raises her eyebrows.

Not for the first time, Steph thinks that becoming a mom gave Meghan a backbone of steel.

"You're not just talking about the concert on Thursday. You mean . . ."

"Moonlight Overthrow. Or you on your own, or with a new group, whatever you want. Stop being afraid of wanting too much," she says.

"Having it all is a lie," says Steph.

"You're telling that to me?" Meghan counters. *Touché.* "But you can choose to shift the balance. You can try."

"Just remember we're not the little kids we were when you left the first time." Matt sticks his tongue out.

"You're really sure about this? Both of you?"

"We've been talking about how to bring it up since May," says Meghan.

Steph glances at the kitchen wall, where the family vacation photos are hung. Their grandma's all right, as Celeste said. Matt didn't freeze up when it mattered.

"I need to do some thinking. And probably talk with the girls," Steph says. "But . . . thank you. Just—thank you."

"Don't get sappy in your old age," Matt says.

After a few more traded barbs, Steph heads upstairs. They stop outside the door to their room, which is cracked open.

"Celeste?" they call.

"Just me," says Gina. "Come in."

Gina's sitting at the desk, laptop open. Sometime during Steph's conversation in the kitchen, she changed into linen pants and a dark red top.

"Where are Celeste and Eva?" Steph asks, wandering in.

"In the guest room. Talking." Gina fails to suppress a smirk.

"Yeah? Well, good. I was kind of worried about them, after everything."

"Same here." Gina stretches her legs out. "You want to sit out on the balcony for a bit? Let's talk."

"We should," says Steph. They unlock the balcony door.

JULY 2021
GINA

The night air is cool, a light breeze ruffling the leaves on the trees that line the backyard. Overhead, a scattering of stars is already visible, more than Gina would be able to see in L.A., where all the stars are on the ground. They sit quietly for a few minutes. Steph doesn't bring up the hospital or whatever Meghan and Matt wanted just now, so Gina follows their cue.

"Your parents coming up for the show?" Steph asks eventually.

Gina pauses. "Is there a show?"

"If you'll all agree to it, considering I cut rehearsal short today and I don't want to start the dress rehearsal until Grandma's home tomorrow." Steph's lips twist, nervous.

"I'm really happy to hear it. And of course if you're still in, I'm still in," Gina says.

"'Til the moon crashes into the sea?"

"Exactly."

Steph nods. "Okay, then. I guess we're doing this."

Gina laughs. "Just a last-minute show, no big deal."

The whole process of this concert is such a change from how things were done with Moonlight Overthrow. They didn't get real input into the set list until their *Lunar* tour. As for design, styling, work schedule—forget about it. If Gina had had this much control back then, maybe she would have contented herself with a film cameo or two. It wouldn't have fixed everything, but it might have felt like enough, at least for a little longer.

"So, your parents?" Steph prompts.

"Yeah, they're driving up Thursday morning, plus a couple of my cousins." Gina takes a deep breath. "Georgia can't make it."

Georgia texted that afternoon with the final "no," followed by a dozen crying emojis.

"Georgia?"

"She was a production assistant on my Netflix show," says Gina. "We're not officially dating—I'm not talking public, I mean even between the two of us—but we're not *not* dating."

Steph props their chin on their hand. "That does not sound very Gina-like. The not-not bit."

"I like flirting with her. She likes flirting with me. We'll see where it goes," says Gina.

She wants it to go somewhere. They're both busy, though, and Gina plays the long game.

"But she's not coming?"

"She's working, couldn't get off."

Flight, hotel, backstage pass, it's all yours, if you want, she texted, days ago.

I'll try and still trying and one day I'm going to be successful enough to make film productions wait for ME so I can go to your shows from Georgia.

"Did you tell her to name-drop?"

"I said she could, obviously. It's not a secret we're friends—she's on my Instagram," Gina says. She knows there are shipping rumors. She doesn't technically know if Georgia's seen them, but that's like saying they're not technically dating.

"Gina Wright, in love at last," Steph teases.

Gina wrinkles her nose, even though Steph is right: she's never been one to traipse from crush to crush. But she wanted to talk to

Steph about more than her just-beginning love life. She thinks about how she's felt during every rehearsal—cool in a way she doesn't feel most of the time, when she's busy being Gina motherfucking Wright, first of her name, all clean lines and polished elegance. Let it be heard: Gina motherfucking Wright can also play a mean solo.

"I've been thinking . . . so Georgia's missing this show. But maybe there could be others," she says.

There. She's said it. There's no *Bayahibe Rose* to stop her. All that's left is the follow-through.

Steph has the grace not to feign surprise. "As in . . . a show or two a year kind of thing?"

"As in Moonlight Overthrow, take two," says Gina.

Despite the sometimes rocky rehearsals, the trip to the hospital, Eva and Celeste's arguments—it's been the best week she's had in a long time. She has them all back now, and she has no intention of letting them go. She may not be the official smart one anymore, but she's still smart enough not to make that mistake twice.

Steph exhales sharply.

"I want music. You want music," Gina presses.

"I want music," Steph agrees, their voice catching, like it takes everything they have to admit it.

"We can give this to each other."

Let me do this for us, Gina thinks.

"It couldn't be the same. I can't tour like we did before. I already know being out isn't going to be enough to change how much touring messes with my head."

"We'll figure it out." Gina leans forward. "Please say yes."

Steph pretends to glare, then breaks into a grin, almost laughing. "Yes, okay. I feel like . . . there should be champagne and speeches and everything. Fancy shit."

Gina stretches to hug Steph. It's so good to have a goal again.

"That'll come later. For the fans." Gina shrugs. "We don't need that. It starts here."

Duluth. Steph's house. Loving the music, loving each other.

"We need to bring in Eva first, this time," Steph says. "Not even both of them together. Eva first."

"Agreed. After the concert. We're not throwing anything new into the mix last-minute."

There won't be much time after the concert, though, not if they want to ask Celeste after they've had at least first-round negotiations with Eva. Gina has a certain, panicked feeling that if they don't talk about re-forming, or whatever this will be, in person, before they leave Duluth this week, it'll never happen. Eva will never agree, and without Eva, Celeste won't do it, not this time. It's now or never.

"What, you don't think a concert we're not prepared to do isn't a volatile enough situation?" Steph says.

"We're prepared," says Gina.

"In your dreams," says Steph.

"Tell me about my track record of making reality match those dreams," says Gina. When Steph has no response but to roll their eyes, Gina says, "That's what I thought."

EVA

They're both perched on the edge of the guest bed.

"Sorry," Celeste begins. "About yesterday. I didn't meant to say all that. I don't want to fight."

"I'm glad you did. And . . . this fight was coming."

"I know. Even so," says Celeste.

What surprises Eva is that despite their arguments this week . . . Celeste is still here. She wasn't just setting things aside for Steph's sake at the hospital. She wants to talk about it, instead of running far away as fast as possible.

"You left me on my own, with no warning. You shut me out. You didn't even try, not once, to talk with me about what you were feeling. And if you wanted to break up with me just because you didn't care about me anymore—"

"No. I still cared about you. I've told you that. It wasn't that my feelings changed. You'd have to throw a lot more at me to make me forget that."

And what about your feelings now? Eva wonders. "Am I supposed to feel bad about your capacity for self-sabotage?"

Eva's the one who had to figure out a whole new plan for her life, without her friends, without her girlfriend.

"I'm not asking you to feel sorry for me. I don't want that."

Celeste bites her lip. "You'll probably be mad at me for saying this, and that's okay, I get it, only—I still think it was the right thing to do. It was selfish and I wasn't nice about it, but I couldn't trust that I knew how to do anything on my own. I didn't trust that I could be anything without you, not a person, not an artist. Now I know I can."

"So my heart was the collateral damage for your personal growth," says Eva.

Celeste winces.

At least she's being honest. And it's not as if—well. It's not as if they were married. They were seventeen, and Celeste had the right to break up with Eva for whatever reason she wanted. Eva didn't have to like it.

"I'd like for us to be friends again. If you want. I understand if you can't do that anymore, or need more time, or . . . anything you want," says Celeste.

Eva's heart seems to twist in her chest. Here comes Celeste, offering (almost) everything Eva wants on a silver platter.

"Let's say we're friends again. What happens this winter, when you're making your new album? Are you going to decide you've forgotten how to create on your own if sometimes we hang out before you go to the studio? How do I know you're not scared anymore?" Eva doesn't let herself say this to her knees, the carpet, the walls. She looks straight at Celeste.

Celeste meets her gaze, but she hesitates before answering. "I don't know. I wish, I really wish, I had an easy answer for you. I wish there was something I could say that would let you trust me. All I can say is . . . I won't forget what it was like to be *alone* so much. I did it. I could do it again if I had to. But I don't want to. Knowing that I can—that's enough for me, I think. I'm ready to be scared now. I can handle it."

Eva can't help but also wish there was an easy answer, but maybe this is better. Honest uncertainty. Hopeful determination.

"Okay. That's—thank you for that. But there's also what you said to me on Monday. You can't take credit for what I've done since. That's not fair," says Eva.

Four songs for other artists, three completed quarters of college: those are hers.

"I'm sorry," says Celeste. "You're amazing. You were amazing then, and you're amazing now. And you did that despite me, not because of me."

Eva lets out a long, slow exhale, and the last of the fight leaves her. If Celeste can be brave enough to be vulnerable, Eva can reciprocate. Not because she owes it to Celeste, but because she's tired of not being completely honest in order to shield her own scarred heart.

"I haven't been able to write an upbeat dance track since, so part of my 'amazing' in Moonlight Overthrow was definitely because of you. When we write together . . ." Eva trails off.

It can't be put into words, the magic spark of it. Or maybe it can, in a song, and Eva couldn't stand the thought of writing that song without the process—the partner—that inspired it.

"I noticed. I didn't even realize how good we had it until after. I had no idea it just wasn't . . . always like that in the studio. Turns out you knew me way better than anybody else." Celeste's smile is small and wry. "And that, um . . . It wasn't a bad thing, you knowing me like that."

"Back at you," says Eva.

"I'm really sorry if I made you uncomfortable this week. Seeing you again was just—anyway, that's on me, and I'm sorry."

Eva places her hand, palm up, on the bedspread between them. After a moment of hesitation, Celeste puts her hand on top of Eva's.

"I wanted to see you, too, and be friendly, and everything. Except for yesterday. Which I told you." Eva looks at the seascape. "It's been a long day. Let's just go to bed."

"Yeah? We're . . . we're okay?"

"We're okay," says Eva.

As crappy as it felt when Steph was mad at her in the car, it felt good when Celeste defended her. Celeste running interference with Pip to try to give Steph's family privacy was even better. Celeste actually *apologizing* to her was certified gold.

After Celeste returns to Steph's room, Eva heads down to the basement again and messages Kay. She sits on the piano bench, rather than lying beneath it, the way she probably would if she were having this conversation at home. The curtains are still open; the backyard stretches infinite in the darkness.

Wouldn't everything be easier if she could just fall in love with Lydia? Lydia cares about college, even more than Eva does. She'll never ask Eva for a song. She's in L.A. and is going to stay there and has never broken Eva's heart. Everything would be safe and happy and normal. Not that Lydia has ever indicated she wants Eva like that, though the pieces would line up so neatly if she did. But what if Eva could work on a remix, instead of a whole new track?

celestial-vision: You know how I said I was back home dealing with some stuff?

Eva's on a seriously compressed timeline here, and, as if sensing this, Kay responds almost immediately.

kaystar: Yeah, is everything okay?

celestial-vision: Weirdly good, I think. Mostly

She checks herself: Is that how she really feels?

Yes, she decides. Mostly.

Then she takes the plunge.

celestial-vision: I'm thinking about my ex. I mean, I'm pretty much always thinking about her, but trying not to? Like every thought has a giant warning label, DO FUCKING NOT. And . . . I'm kind of wondering what would happen if I let myself take that label off. And just . . . thought about her

Holy crap. Did she really just type that? Does she really mean that?

Yes, and yes.

celestial-vision: Not necessarily actually getting back together with her (not at ALL sure that she'd even want to). But . . . the feelings are still there, on my end. Really, really there

It was hard to admit to herself these past days with Celeste, but it's easier now to confess to Kay.

kaystar: Ooh, that's a tough one

celestial-vision: Bad idea, 100% of the time?

kaystar: I don't know your ex, I don't know what all happened between you, it's hard to say

Eva almost laughs. It's so very true, and so very not true, all at the same time. Immediately, she feels mean, and ashamed of that meanness. Even though she's not asking Kay what to do so she can laugh about the fact that Kay does actually know of Celeste. She's asking Kay what to do because she's not sure she's ready to ask Gina or Steph or Lydia.

kaystar: Don't let either your head or your heart take over. If what went wrong was just a lot of outside shit . . . maybe try again

kaystar: But I really have to say this bit: somebody who was shitty to you before is going to be shitty to you again

Does not telling me until she didn't have a choice count as being shitty? Eva wonders.

Yes. She just had that very argument with Celeste. But maybe not, like, chronic shitty.

celestial-vision: Thanks <3

celestial-vision: Sorry for the exes drama, I know that's everybody's least favorite lol

kaystar: Don't even worry about it, you never have relationship drama, so I'm happy to help! Friendship level goal reached ;)

celestial-vision: Haha

celestial-vision: Anyway, tell me about how it's going with Cute Library Girl??

kaystar: OMG. She knows my name now!

celestial-vision: What! Tell me *everything*

Kay fills Eva in on the bumbling conversation that culminated in this information sharing, and then Eva signs off. She wants to run through her song a few times before heading back upstairs. Last night, she sang it as an anthem, but maybe tonight, she'll make it a little softer. A comfort song. A lullaby. She'll sleep better after she's tried it.

EVA

Morning dress rehearsal happens.

Eva thinks that's the best, most diplomatic way to summarize it. They started two hours later than they planned last week, so Steph could help their grandma get settled at home. Eva doesn't begrudge Steph a minute of that, but once rehearsal started, none of them seemed to be able to stay on key.

"I'm going to take five," Gina says, departing for the bathroom immediately after they've finished the last song. If you could call what just happened a song, anyway.

Steph sits down in the middle of the "stage." They're moving to the real outdoor stage that afternoon, but the openers' dress rehearsal is there now.

"Well," says Eva. She snags her water bottle from a table and heads into the hallway.

It's going to be okay, she tries to tell herself. Eva thinks about messaging Kay or Lydia. Instead, she texts her parents: We might suck tomorrow night. Just as an FYI.

Within ten seconds, her phone is ringing in her hand.

"Hey, Mom."

"Hey, honey. Do you want us to come up tonight instead?"

Eva swallows past the lump in her throat. "No, it's fine, don't change your flight."

"We can be there in four hours."

"It's fine, just . . . hard morning." She tips her head back against the wall. "I really wanted this to be good."

"I'm sure it's going to be amazing."

"Mom."

"Don't be so hard on yourself, or the others, all right? It's been a long time. Of course you're a little rusty. Let yourself enjoy it. That's what counts."

"This was supposed to be the easy thing." The words come out as a whisper. "College was supposed to be the hard thing. This was supposed to be the thing I know how to do."

Three years of her life, and years of dreams and plans before that. And now she comes in late, and Steph fumbles harmonies, and Gina's fingers stumble on her strings. God, they can't be washed up at *nineteen*. This was supposed to be waiting for her if she wanted it on her own.

The door to the main rehearsal room opens, and Celeste walks out.

"I've gotta go," Eva says. "I'll see you tomorrow."

Celeste hovers by the doorway, not heading for the bathroom, not heading outside for sunshine and space.

Eva hangs up and wipes at her cheeks with the back of her hand. For fuck's sake, she's a professional. She's not some kid who just lost *The X Factor*.

"Hey," says Celeste, moving to stand in front of her. It's a soft *hey*, like *hey, it's okay, I'm here*, not *hey, idiot, why are you messing this up for me?*

"Hi."

Eva sniffs, trying to get herself under control, but the sniff turns into a gross hiccup-cough-sob. Celeste pulls her into a hug. Her arms are gentle without being tentative. Eva tucks her chin onto Celeste's shoulder and wraps her arms around Celeste's waist.

I'm still not perfect. But Celeste is out here with me this time, Eva thinks.

Celeste doesn't speak, but one of her hands rubs slow circles on Eva's back. After another moment, she says, "Black hole/supernova, go."

"What?" Eva pulls back. Celeste's hands fall to her waist.

"Oh! It's, um . . . kind of this game I started playing with myself, after. Black hole is the worst possible outcome of whatever I'm nervous about. Supernova is the very best. Maybe it's stupid, but it helped me sometimes."

"I don't think that's stupid," says Eva. She's touched, actually, that Celeste would share this with her. "Black hole/supernova . . . all right. Black hole: It's terrible? Off-key, missed lyrics, piano out of tune in the middle of the show, a thousand headlines about the fall from grace, a thousand more Instagram comments about how it's a good thing I'm in college." The words come fast.

"Mmm," says Celeste. "College, you say."

Meaning: Eva has someplace to fall toward. Someplace to catch her. Unlike real matter, Eva would come out the other side.

"And supernova?"

Eva takes a deep breath, slowly letting all the brightest possibilities rush through her, one by one lighting her from the inside out. "Supernova: It's amazing. We're brilliant. We raise a ton of money for Duluth. I have the time of my life, and—" She stops. Because the opposite of the worst-case scenario . . . is that people say they miss her voice.

"Yeah," says Celeste. "And from listening to you this week, and all that time in MO—I know which one I'd bet on."

Celeste quirks a half smile at Eva. *Now you*, Eva almost says, but she hears the bathroom door at the end of the hallway open, and Gina appears in her peripheral vision. Celeste steps back.

"You okay?" Gina says. Her eyes are clear, so maybe she's not mad at anyone, either.

"What? Oh." Eva finishes wiping the half-dried tears from her cheeks.

"C'mon," says Celeste, just as Steph opens the main studio door, beckoning them all in.

Gina turns to walk back down the hall. Celeste takes Eva's hand.

A cry, a hug, a hand.

Eva's ready to try again.

JULY 2021

EVA

After Wade Stadium's event manager introduces them to the local openers, the four of them follow him around for a tour: bathrooms, ad-hoc dressing rooms, the side entrance they should use when they arrive tomorrow.

"And here we go, the stage at last," the manager says, gesturing grandly.

The four of them cluster at the entrance. There's a tiny backstage area on the platform, behind a scrim on which pictures of them and Duluth will be projected during the show. It's already cluttered with sound equipment and a dozen hard, heavy instrument cases.

Gina pushes Steph forward, then follows them onstage.

"You okay?" Celeste asks.

Eva's still lingering on the threshold. She hasn't been on a stage since that last concert. It's absurd, this lingering, she knows. There's no crowd today, adoring or otherwise. It's just a rehearsal. A dress rehearsal, but a rehearsal all the same. She's done this a thousand times before.

Eva steps forward. Without glancing back, she can hear Celeste's footsteps, following.

She walks the stage alone. The empty outfield stretches in front of her, wide and flat. After a week without rain, the ground is firm and dry, ready for thousands of hopefully dancing feet. Tomorrow, she won't be able to see the ground. Tomorrow, there will be fans again.

Tomorrow, she's going to sing again.

She can't wait.

Eva plucks a mic off its stand, then sits on the edge of the stage, letting her legs dangle. She plays the right-hand notes for "Sweeter" against her thigh, her fingers moving through the harmonic tension, the resolution. A crew member standing on the ground waves to catch her attention, then flashes his fingers, *one, two, three*.

"Hello, Duluth?" she says into the mic. Her amplified voice echoes back.

"Hello, Eva!" Gina calls from behind her.

"Blow us a kiss!" Pip is standing in the grass, an assistant next to her with a big camera.

Eva does as instructed, then says, "Watch for it."

She turns so she's half facing the rest of the band, without ruining the camera angle. She blows a kiss at them, too. Steph is bent over their drum set; Gina is replacing a broken string. But Celeste looks up in time to catch the kiss.

"You're a gem, Eva," Pip says.

"A star," Celeste shouts back.

"Hush, you," Eva says, walking toward her.

Or walking toward the piano, where she needs to finish warming up, but actually-and-also Celeste.

"Tell me I'm wrong," Celeste says. She follows Eva to the piano.

Instead of answering, Eva plays the opening chords of "Sweeter."

And it's not perfect.

Dress rehearsal never is, and this one couldn't be, not when it's their first time on a real stage with this Frankenstein's monster of a set, not when Gina's calluses are still far from re-formed and Eva comes in late on two verses because she's trying to hold back tears.

I love you, I love you, I love you, she thinks. She tells herself this is directed at the empty space where the crowd will be.

"Babes," says Gina, when the last harmony has rung out under the clear sky.

They don't talk about how they're going to say good night, walk off. They've done it before. It'll *happen*.

"We're going to be amazing," Gina says.

"Absolutely." Celeste turns, hands on her hips, to Eva and Steph. Expectant.

"Gina's always right," Steph says, raising their hands, protesting innocence.

Gina snorts. "Liar. *Flatterer*."

"Eva?" Celeste prompts.

"Yeah," Eva decides. "I think so."

It can't be anything else at this point. The music is in her blood again, not dormant, not malignant, but welcomed. Thriving and jubilant, and Eva knows, at the heart of this concert, all the town needs from them while they're onstage is some joy. All the fans need from them is some joy. Eva can do that now.

EVA

They're all quiet at dinner, resting their voices. There'd been talk of an all-crew, all-musicians joint dinner, a kind of preconcert party, but ultimately it was another thing to organize and attend, and everybody was too exhausted for that.

Eva volunteers to deal with the dishes. Celeste stays behind to help, while Gina disappears outside to talk to Georgia, and Steph goes to check on their grandma.

When Eva and Celeste head upstairs, Eva hesitates in the hallway. It's the last night before the show. Despite their arguments earlier in the week, she can't imagine spending it without Celeste.

"Together?" Eva asks.

Celeste's eyes brighten, and they walk together into the guest room.

Maybe it's all in Eva's head. Maybe she imagined—but Celeste's been there, this whole week, leaning against her in the car, bringing her tea, her eyes full of shy, nervous delight when Eva thanks her in words or touches. Eva likes to think Celeste wouldn't do that for someone she was planning on leaving, not again. And Celeste apologized, didn't she? She wanted to be friends, at the very least.

Once they've set Gina's suitcase outside Steph's room, there's a wordless exchange that results in Celeste taking the first shower, which was Eva's goal. There's somebody else she needs to talk to tonight. She thinks about creeping downstairs—about doing this anywhere but here, about setting up temporary shop in the kitchen, under the piano in the basement, any tucked-away corner—but she stays propped against the now-familiar pillows.

She opens her direct messages with Kay.

> **celestial-vision**: Hey . . . came to a conclusion today that's kind of abrupt but also kind of been building for a while, and I wanted you to know first

Eva takes a breath, then another. Is she doing this? She doesn't have to. Maybe she should—and maybe she should have a month ago, a year ago—but she doesn't *have* to.

She's doing this.

> **celestial-vision**: I'm leaving fandom. Well, not fandom entirely, but this one

> **kaystar**: OMG. Did something happen???

> **kaystar**: <3 <3 <3

Kay is almost always online when Eva really needs her to be. Even if it's only for a minute. Sometimes that minute of sympathy makes all the difference.

> **celestial-vision**: Yes? No? I don't know

> **celestial-vision**: Nothing happened, like, in fandom. I'm not getting secret anon hate that you don't know about

celestial-vision: Please don't take this the wrong way, but I think I need a break from being in a celebrity fandom

Eva's not certain what's going to happen after tomorrow's concert, but she's pretty sure the band isn't going to ghost each other again. She doesn't need to be a fan online to show the others her support. The Cosmic Queers section of Tumblr isn't the place for her anymore. She knows she was stealing, almost, invading a space that was never meant for her, not really.

She's ready to bow out now.

kaystar: I'll be really, really sad to see you go, but I get that. It can be kind of exhausting sometimes

celestial-vision: So—I haven't made a new blog yet, and I probably won't get a chance to until next week. But I'll message you once that's set up?

Leaving fandom doesn't mean leaving friends. That's Eva's hope, anyway. She's tired of leaving friends when she closes the chapter they first appeared in.

kaystar: oh thank god

kaystar: I was kind of worried you were leaving-leaving and I'd never get to talk to you again

kaystar: But I promise we NEVER have to talk about MO again, if you don't want to

celestial-vision: Thanks. I'll let you know <3

Eva hears the water shut off and begins to type faster. She's got one more item of business to take care of before Celeste reappears.

celestial-vision:

I'm not sure this needs an announcement, but it didn't seem right to disappear without saying goodbye. I've really enjoyed my time here with all of you—pushing songs to #1, reblogging every angle of Gina's red carpet pics—but I've also realized it's time for me to go. I've been broken up with before, so believe me when I say: it's not you. It's definitely, entirely me. I'm grateful for how this little business corner of the fandom has welcomed me over the past year or so. I can't emphasize enough how fun it's been—how much you reminded me it was okay to have fun! And love things! And love music and girls and MO! This isn't an "I'm in college and too old for this" thing. This isn't "I'm better than pop music." This isn't "I'm better than bandoms." But it's not the right place for me anymore.

Love, thanks—and adieu.

'Til the moon crashes into the sea.

She deletes her account right as Celeste opens the bathroom door.

"Hey," says Celeste. "You okay? You look . . ."

"I deleted my Tumblr," Eva says, looking her in the eye.

"I didn't know you still had a Tumblr." Celeste adjusts the pillows before slipping beneath the covers. She didn't blow-dry her hair, and the damp strands cling together against the pillow.

"I changed the username from the one you knew, but yeah."

"Oh." Celeste clears her throat. "Was it . . . was it like . . . a hate account? Which I wouldn't blame you for, you deserve—"

"What the fuck, *no*. It was—the opposite, okay? It was—I was—this no-drama, OT4, industry analysis *fan* blog."

She wants to look down. She's still embarrassed at how hard she clung, when everybody else walked away. But Celeste's smile isn't pitying, isn't condescending.

"Of course it was. God, *Eva*, come here."

Celeste tugs Eva toward her, or maybe Eva falls into her, or both. Either way, her face is buried in Celeste's shoulder, and Celeste's arms are wrapped tightly around her.

"None of us deserve you, you know," Celeste says. She presses a kiss to the top of Eva's head.

"That's not true," Eva mumbles. She turns her head slightly, so it's her ear, not her forehead, pressed against Celeste. "I missed— literally everything that was going on with all of you that last summer."

"We could agree that we all sucked then," Celeste concedes. One of her hands moves up to rest on Eva's neck, her thumb stroking back and forth, catching now and then on Eva's hair.

Eva languishes in the feeling for a minute: the way she can feel Celeste's rib cage moving against her as she breathes, the way Celeste doesn't let go.

Celeste clears her throat. "Maybe that's a cop-out, though. Like, it was all of us, so we can just dismiss it and move on. That's not what I really think."

"Yeah. But I also don't—I don't want to get caught up being like, we were all shitty all the time to each other then. I don't want to brush off every good thing because of one shitty night, even if that shitty night had been building for a long time."

"So we won't," says Celeste. "Were they good to you, in fandom?"

"To former pop star Eva Bell, or to me like my blog?"

"Oh—both."

"They were really good to the girl who decided to go to college. As for the blog—most of them were great." Eva's startled by her own smile. "Sometimes they got mad if they thought I was ignoring myself—like, not being supportive enough of their college girl."

"I love them," Celeste says decisively. "I mean, not really if they were mean about it, but that's how it should be. You should stan yourself. And you should be around people who tell you that."

"Some of them—the ones who got mad—thought I wasn't in it for the OT4."

"That is . . . so wrong. You were our champion. And that shouldn't have fallen just to you. I should have been in there with you."

"You've been here this week. You wanted this show, the four of us."

"I do," says Celeste. She pauses, then adds, "Thank you. For . . . what you were doing online. It means a lot that you would do that, even though we weren't talking."

"You broke my heart," Eva says.

She's never said that out loud before, and she couldn't bear to say it last night. Somehow, it finally feels like she's ready to name it. She told her parents that she and Celeste had broken up. She told Lydia that she had an ex, that the relationship had ended badly. Her heart never came into play.

"I know. If it helps, I broke mine, too?" Celeste offers.

"Not really. But—I know why you did it. We're okay," says Eva. She means it. "I'm going to take a shower, so we can go to bed." She eases away from Celeste.

"Eva . . ." Celeste is frowning.

"We should sleep. I really—I'm really glad we talked tonight. And we can keep talking tomorrow. But I want to have slept before the concert, and I know you do, too."

Eva lingers at the bathroom door until Celeste nods.

When Eva crawls back into bed twenty minutes later, Celeste is lying down properly, rolled on her side, facing Eva. "Could we . . . ? If you want," says Celeste.

Eva turns on her side, away from Celeste, but reaches back to pull Celeste toward her. Celeste tucks herself against Eva, her nose touching the back of Eva's neck, one hand on Eva's hip. Eva closes her eyes. Celeste is here. Tomorrow, they're going to sing. And after—they'll still be *something*. Eva will go back to L.A., finish her summer class, maybe finish her degree. She just won't have to do it without the others this time.

"Good night, love," Celeste whispers.

STEPH

Steph is with Gina on the balcony again, which is where they've ended up most nights this week. Grandma Marit is fast asleep in her room.

"I kind of hated you guys, by the end," Steph says. They dart a glance at Gina, whose mouth twists into a knowing grimace.

"I'm sorry," Gina says.

Steph tips their head back against the chair. The waxing crescent moon is a bright sliver against the dark sky. It's fitting, Steph thinks: they couldn't have a reunion concert under a new moon. This one's mostly hidden still, but at least it's on its way to full. "I resented you—not *you*, but all of you. The three of you. You were so . . . you were so goddamn giddy about being a girl band, you know? Every time you gushed about how amazing it was to be a queer *woman*, every single time someone mentioned the history of girl groups at a concert or in an interview—and that stuff is good and important, but it wasn't mine. And the band was supposed to be mine, too. But you got to be comfortable with it. You didn't have to worry about what the media would say if you, if I, came out and wrecked it. You just got to have all that joy. That I wasn't a part of, and you didn't even know." Steph swallows. "I mean, I didn't know, for a while. Or I didn't want to know. I knew 'girl band' didn't feel right, but I figured, it felt right to you all, so whatever, I'd go along with it . . ."

"Like you went along with everything," Gina says, her voice soft. "You didn't think we'd really . . . do this."

"No," says Steph. "I didn't. And I'm glad I was wrong. But it didn't give me a lot of room to figure out—why it felt so wrong. And it didn't give me a lot of options once I figured that out."

"We can change the name," Gina says.

"No."

"We can," Gina insists. "If Moonlight Overthrow is too wrapped up in 'girl band,' we can. We've taken a hiatus, we can certainly rebrand. If you want that, don't worry about it. Eva and Celeste will back us."

Steph likes how Gina says "us," not "you." She doesn't make Steph the problem.

"I still like our band name," they say.

Our band. It's theirs, too, not just the girls'. They wish they'd known that from the start. They wish they'd known that from the first meetings after the contracts were signed, when the label decided they wanted to go all out with "the girl band thing"— female producers, songwriting partners, engineers. Max Martin had Britney, Kelly, Katy, Avril, Ariana . . . Taylor. Jack Antonoff had Lana, Lorde, Carly Rae . . . Taylor. Neither of them were getting Moonlight Overthrow.

They wish they'd known that when Moonlight Overthrow won Best New Artist at their first Grammys, and every media outlet fell over themselves proclaiming a new era of girl bands, when the real story was about queer people getting to win for themselves. Steph knew that much at sixteen, even if they didn't know how to tell the others that every time an article focused on their brand as "girl" and ignored the "queer," they breathed just a little too shallow.

They're good with their body now, mostly. Their family's good now, mostly. But this life where Steph doesn't make music any-more? *That* center cannot hold.

At the end of it all, Steph wore the music lightly, surface-level across a skin stretched too tight. Now they let it sink back in, knit-ting itself back together with muscle and bone. Holding Steph up. Letting them move.

Steph swings their legs over the side of the chair, leans their elbows on their knees. "Look. Here's the thing. Sometimes we have to change names, you know? Sometimes the name someone else gave us doesn't fit, or the name we gave ourselves doesn't, and we need a change to be ourselves." They take a breath. "But in this case—I think we just need to make space to grow within that name. And it's—how we define it. It's *ours*."

"And if we change our minds next month, or next year, the label will have to deal," says Gina.

Steph grins. "Exactly."

It's different for Gina, they know. She doesn't *need* this, not like Steph. Or—maybe she does. Gina says she wants it. But if Eva can't be convinced, Gina will still have her acting. She could still go solo. Steph could never do a full show under the spotlight alone. The others might joke about how Steph kept them steady, but Steph couldn't have shouldered the scrutiny without the three of them at their side.

Gina nudges her foot against Steph's leg. "We're going to do this, all right? And if MO doesn't end up being what happens—there's going to be *something* for you, whatever you want it to be, and I'm going to make sure you get it."

"Yeah?"

Almost as soon as they moved to L.A., Steph began thinking of the city, and the music industry, like Oz: something that required tinted glasses to shine. Gina wants to give them a chance to build something real, together.

"That's what friends are for," says Gina. Somebody else would have said that lightly, laughingly, but Gina doesn't hide her sincerity.

Steph looks back up at the moon, small but bold against the clear, dark sky. There's a kind of serenity in looking at it, or maybe surety. It's like looking at a friend. It'll be there.

And when it's not there, it'll come back.

EVA

The Texas sky above them is clear, pale blue and unbroken as far as the eye can see. Eva's eyes don't care to see anything beyond Celeste.

Celeste is watching her, too, head tipped against the high back of the patio seat that's just wide enough for them to share. They were laughing a moment ago, sharing a meme they'd been tagged in, and a small smile lingers on Celeste's face.

She's never going to ask me, Eva realizes.

Eva has been waiting for months now. She wasn't expecting it to be under fireworks at a New Year's Eve party, but she thought, maybe, under confetti right after a concert. Lit by sparklers on the Fourth of July. Don't they shine?

It's Eva who feels bright now, but not the glinting, glittering kind, not the kind where if you just wait a minute, all that's left is smoke. She feels sure, steady as the afternoon heat radiating on the rooftop.

Eva wants this.

She tips her head forward, just a little. She lets her gaze drop to Celeste's lips before looking her straight in the eye. A blush forms, high on Celeste's cheeks.

"Celeste," says Eva, quiet but the furthest thing from hesitant.

"Yes," says Celeste. There's something aglow in her brown eyes, something hopeful and delighted that wasn't there before. She tilts her chin, inviting.

Eva closes the distance between them. She kisses Celeste once, soft and light. Their noses brush when she pulls away. Her lips are tingling, her heartbeat a wild staccato, but somewhere at her center, she's never felt more grounded.

"Eva," says Celeste, and settles a hand on her waist.

"Yes," she says, kissing Celeste again. "Yes, yes, yes."

GINA

Gina wakes up earlier than she has to, not so much by design as by sunlight and half-opened blinds. There's no rush to rehearsal this morning; at this point, some rest will do their voices more good than anything else. When she checks her phone, there are several texts from Georgia waiting, even though it's two hours earlier in California.

Georgia
You're going to do amazing. I'm so sorry I can't be there. Make it up to you when you get back? ;)

I'm trusting that somebody is going to film it all/put together all the videos so I'll be able to watch it at about 3 a.m. tomorrow.

I can't wait.

I'm so excited for you. You've been missing this and wanting this—I hope it's everything you need it to be.

> Have fun with MO & co <3 <3 <3

> If I don't catch you before the show . . .

The final text is a series of emojis: a singer in a red dress, a music note, a studio microphone, a lake, and three kissy-faces.

Gina presses her face into her pillow, even though there's no one around to see her smile. She stays in bed for a while longer, the sun warming the blanket over her legs, rereading Georgia's texts. She knows that by the time she goes onstage tonight, she'll have each one committed to memory.

Thanks, she sends back. Another time.

Gina's heart is racing, like the faster it beats, the sooner she can get to the show. She's going to *perform* again—music, live, one take only.

First, the concert. Then a conversation with Eva. She can go back to L.A. once her music plan is in motion. And as soon as Georgia's film wraps, she's going to take her out for dinner.

As part of the effort to minimize the chaos and expense of the concert, their late morning interviews are conducted at the venue itself. Once they've arrived, there's a lightning-fast round of hair, makeup, and styling. Someone—an underling of Pip's, Gina imagines—has set up an interview space in a meeting room. When Gina sees the four canvas chairs, a lump rises in her throat. She swallows it down, straightens her shoulders, and arranges herself in the far right chair.

"I thought that you and Celeste would be center," Steph says, hovering in front of Gina.

"I wasn't before," Gina says.

Celeste gently pushes Steph toward the seat next to Gina. Steph stumbles, catching themself on the chair and sitting, more by way of gravity than choice. "This isn't my seat," they say.

"It's your city," Celeste points out. She settles herself in the far left chair, leaving the other middle seat for Eva.

"I liked the couches better," Eva says.

Gina shares a smirk with Steph. Those couch interviews were essentially dedicated Eva-Celeste cuddle time, which meant they were band cuddle time, because Gina wasn't about to let them out themselves through soft, possessive touches before they seriously considered whether they wanted to go public as a couple. Gina never minded; fans always liked it that she'd let Steph wrap an arm around her waist, or that she'd rest her head on Celeste's shoulder, when Celeste's lap or hands were otherwise occupied.

"Everyone found a seat, I see," Pip says, her eyes surveying the lineup in a single sweep. "Here's how it's going to go: five radio stations, only a couple of minutes each. Those will be filmed for their social media sites, so smiles, eye contact, you know the drill."

Gina nods; Steph flashes a thumbs-up.

"Next will be three TV journalists, then three entertainment websites to wrap it up. I'll be watching the clock and cutting people off," Pip says as someone positions a fifth chair, offset from their row. "You've got to get to sound check, and the vocal coaches want you for a mini rehearsal late this afternoon."

The first radio host approaches. She's short, with white-blond hair and a bob that reminds Gina of Anna Wintour. When she mentions she's from a local radio station, Gina reaches out to squeeze Steph's hand. Steph squeezes back.

"Good morning, Moonlight Overthrow!" she says, once she's received the go-ahead from her producer.

Gina's breath catches in her throat.

"Hello to you, too," she says. She gives the interviewer a little wave across the three feet of space separating them.

"I was actually working in Milwaukee when you girls—"

Gina coughs pointedly.

The radio host's eyes widen, and she blinks rapidly as she corrects herself, "When you all put that first EP on Spotify, but I wish I'd moved earlier and had a chance to interview you back then."

"Well," says Steph, "we're all here now." They indicate the five of them.

"We're very glad to be in Duluth for such an important cause," Celeste says.

The host leans in eagerly. "Can you tell us how that came about?"

Gina glances at Steph.

"As these things usually happen, I think. I got a call about the possibility of it, so I called the rest of them," says Steph.

"And you were all on board, just like that, after almost two years?" the interviewer asks.

Gina doesn't permit herself to look toward Eva. She keeps her eyes and smile fixed on Steph.

"The timing worked well with everyone's schedule," Celeste says. Her tone is upbeat, but there's an underlying caution Gina knows the interviewer won't pick up on. The fans, perhaps, once the video is released . . .

"Duluth gave so much to us," says Eva. "It seemed only right that we try to give back."

"But you could have done that in other ways," the interviewer presses. "Celeste, for example, you're in the middle of a solo tour right now. You could have added an extra stop here, done a mini concert or something, for those who were affected by the storm."

"Duluth formed *us*. Duluth asked for *us*." Celeste's voice teeters between icy and the friendly gratefulness she's supposed to project at all times.

"Celeste, how are you feeling about sharing the spotlight tonight?"

"Overjoyed." Celeste's smile is razor-sharp, even as she drapes a languid arm over the back of Eva's chair. Gina keeps her own expression bland, but internally she's rolling her eyes. *Subtle, babe.* Beneath the light layer of makeup, Eva's ever-deepening flush is clearly visible.

The remainder of the interviews follow the same path: what made them decide to come together for this show (*love for Duluth*), if they'll be reuniting as a band (Eva, stiff two seats away, always answers this one, her tone a practiced blend of firm and gracious as she spins a line about *focusing on our own projects, thank you*), what it's like being back in Duluth (*wonderful, such a privilege, heartbreaking*).

"Last one," Pip calls out. "Then we'll take a quick break."

The final interviewer begins with the usual style of questions. Gina relaxes into the mind-numbing rhythm of it. She knows when to laugh, when to reject the premise of the question, how to make the topic applicable to Steph as well, instead of only Celeste. The fandom always appreciated that about her: how well she was media trained. To them, it was something to be amused by, something to be proud of—*that's our girl*. For her and the rest of the band, it was survival.

"Tell us what it's like to all be back together again. Old tensions? New jealousies?" The interviewer hitches on a beguiling smile. It's almost cute, the way he thinks they'll turn on each other, now that they're not contractually, professionally required to present a united front. Gina looks forward to giving an exclusive to his main competitor.

"None of that," Celeste says. "I can only speak for myself, of course, but I think we're stronger than ever, now that we've had a chance to grow up a little."

"Oh, I don't know," says Gina slowly, throwing a wink at Celeste when her eyes widen with alarm. "I'm pretty jealous of how hot Steph is. And Eva's college classes—everyone spent years telling me *I* was the smart one, but it just goes to show, what you choose to do on your own matters more than those made-up labels."

Celeste grins. "You're so right, Gi. I would kill for that dress you wore to the *Oscars*. And every lyric Eva's written over the past two years? *Damn*, I want that songwriting skill."

"I can't hear you over the sound of your sold-out arena tour," Eva teases.

It's a real tease, no hidden barbs—Eva's tone is all light, her eyes shining as she smiles at Celeste—so Gina relaxes back into her chair once more. Her job here is done.

"So, that's a—" the interviewer tries, but Celeste cuts him off.

"People tried that line after the band split up. But there's a difference between Moonlight Overthrow and us: Celeste, Eva, Steph, Gina. You're not going to get anything from us other than support for each other, because that's what there is."

They change into more casual clothes for lunch, sound check, and one-on-one time with the vocal coaches before the mini rehearsal together. Gina loves the costumes and the couture that come with the territory she's claimed for herself in the industry, but there's nothing quite like strutting onstage in a tank top, mic pack clipped plainly to her shorts. There's no pretense: she is who she is, take it or leave it, sweat stains and sneakers and all.

When sound check is complete, Celeste stops them before they head offstage. "Let's just take a sec, okay?"

They gather center stage in a loose semicircle, looking out. Celeste leans into Eva, who wraps an arm around her waist. Steph waggles their eyebrows at Gina.

"Here's to one more show together," says Celeste.

"Let's make it the best one yet," says Gina.

"Save the emotions for after, please." Eva's voice is unsteady. "I won't be able to get through the show if you start now."

Steph nods, starting to turn away. "They've got to reset for the openers, and I want to work with Alicia on a few of those chest/head voice transitions."

Gina follows Steph off. The next time she's on this stage, it'll be for real.

JULY 2021
CELESTE

Through hair and makeup, Celeste has a waking nightmare that goes something like this: she walks onstage. Concert muscle memory takes over. She starts singing her solo set. Eva never speaks to her again. *Black hole.*

"Wave for the fans," Eva commands, breaking into Celeste's silent horror. She's aiming her phone at Celeste. "Pip thinks a backstage getting-ready moment would be good for social media."

"Liar," says Gina affably as she checks her hair in the mirror. "Pip didn't say that."

Celeste waves, then blows Eva a kiss. The camera, Eva. Same difference. It's only fair, after all: she caught Eva's kiss at dress rehearsal yesterday. A little hint of supernova, already reality.

"Get a room," says Steph.

"You're in it," says Eva, before Celeste can protest.

Celeste's stomach flip-flops. The idea that Eva . . . maybe? . . . still wants her—it does things to her. Butterflies taking over her insides kinds of things. *Ditch the concert and kiss me* things. And Eva is so damn gorgeous right now: her hair teased into half an updo so it won't be in her way when she's playing the piano; a thin, loose blue dress that shows off her arms and calves. She could be a country queen if she weren't so completely pop (and so completely queer).

Once Alix has dismissed them from last-minute styling and Alicia has dismissed them from a final vocal warm-up, they sneak into the small backstage area, listening to the last songs from the openers.

"Let's take a selfie," Celeste says. "Not for Insta, just for us."

"I'm in," says Eva at once.

The four of them crowd into the camera frame, faces close together, everybody clutching everybody else.

"Hey," says Pip as Celeste hands her the phone for safekeeping during the show. Pip's voice is too soft for it to be meant for the others to hear. "You've done a great job this week. I'm proud of you, and I'm proud to work for you. People in my job, we don't always get to say that."

"Thanks," says Celeste. "We couldn't have done this without you, you know."

"Oh, I know."

Celeste laughs. "And I think . . . maybe . . . things might be a little easier for you, after this. Or harder, but better. I'm not sure yet. Different, definitely."

"So I assumed." Pip tilts her head. "Who are your albums about, Celeste?"

"Eva Bell," she says. "And tonight she's going to know it, and . . . hopefully someday, everybody else will, too."

"That's my girl," says Pip.

Celeste rejoins the group as the last opener walks offstage to cheers and applause. Crew members scurry around, getting Moonlight Overthrow's instruments and microphones into place.

Pip, waiting in the wings, gives them an abrupt nod.

It's time.

Impulsively, Celeste reaches for Eva's hand. Eva takes it, then reaches out for Steph, who's already holding hands with Gina. Together, they walk onstage.

There's still a little time before sunset, and the crowd is a golden wave spread out before them, signs and flags and a small ocean of shrieks. Celeste grins, takes two deep breaths, and lets go of Eva. She hums their starting note, her eyes searching down the line until she's made eye contact with all of them. Contrary to Eva's fears, they start—and stay—on key. As planned, they switch out "L.A." for "Duluth" during the bridge, prompting yet more screams as the audience realizes the change.

"Hello, Duluth," Celeste says, one song down. She takes her mic out of the stand but doesn't move, not yet. She waits for the applause to diminish even a fraction before continuing. "I'm so happy to be here. Thank you for welcoming us into your city tonight, after this tragedy. We're hoping to give you guys a good show, okay? You all deserve that. Give yourselves a round of applause."

Beside her, Eva, Gina, and Steph clap, pointing and waving out at the audience.

"All right," says Celeste. "Enough chitchat. It's been a while since some of us have been here, so I'm going to introduce everyone. There's Steph" (screams), "Gina" (screams), "and Eva" (screams). Celeste feels like screaming right along with them. She grins at the crowd. "I'm Celeste, and we're Moonlight Overthrow."

JULY 2021
STEPH

Steph waves at the crowd with both hands, then jogs to their drum set. Four songs down. It's time to set the fucking world on fire.

Steph counts them in, Eva's first verse hits the open air, and the energy of the crowd, already so much higher than Steph dared to dream, explodes. As it should, Steph thinks, as they pound out the beat. "Burning" is hot as hell, and Eva's sashaying to the front of the stage, adding in a half-remembered dance move here and there from the years-ago choreography. A not-insignificant fraction of the crowd pauses in their singing to shriek as Eva rolls her hips. Steph whistles into their mic before launching into backing vocals.

After another song, Steph takes their time walking toward the girls, reveling in their slacks, their suspenders, the open collar of their button-down against the back of their neck. They've never gotten to wear even the idea of a suit at a concert before. Somewhere, Kayla is probably fainting at the masculine cut.

"I know Celeste's already covered this," Steph says, stopping next to Gina. "But I'm gonna say it again—gonna say it all night: we're so happy to be here. And you know, I've been here the last couple of years. You let me come home, and I can't thank you enough for that."

As was the norm at their old shows, this audience is filled with pride flags. Tonight, though, most people are also clutching small, identical homemade signs, the words SING WITH DULUTH encased in a blue heart. It's not anything Pip coordinated, which means the fans did it themselves.

"WE LOVE YOU, STEPH," someone screams.

"I love you, too," says Steph, in the general direction of the scream. "If you're here with somebody, now might be a good time to hold their hand. Or introduce yourself to your neighbor, if you're comfortable. This is 'Standstill.'"

Duluth sings with them. Gina runs a hand along Steph's suspenders as she passes. For the first time onstage since—ever, really—Steph feels like they belong. All of them, exactly as they are.

EVA

They're meant to be reconvening at center stage for "Before," but Celeste lays a hand on her arm, gently stopping her.

"Eva," Celeste says. She speaks into her ear, not the mic, like it doesn't matter that thousands of people are watching them, that they're halfway through a set. "Just so you know—it's for you. This song."

"What?"

"I wrote it for *you*."

You can't just say something like that in the middle of the show, Eva thinks, reeling. *You can't say something like that and walk away*. The song—for *her*?

Steph and Gina are already in position, making heart shapes with their fingers at people holding signs, thanking sponsors, stalling for them. Eva tucks herself into Steph to avoid looking at Celeste. She can't decide how she feels right now, and she doesn't have time to dissect every possibility: the show must go on.

Only . . . Celeste wrote it for her. Celeste wrote it for Eva, not expecting Eva to have to sing it, not even expecting Eva to ever hear it. She still wrote it. She still put it on her album.

Maybe just because it's a good song. But maybe because she really means it.

"This next song is not a Moonlight Overthrow song," Gina says, "but we hope you'll forgive us for performing it anyway."

Eva's song. Celeste's song, for Eva.

Celeste didn't text. She didn't call, she didn't invite Eva to parties or concerts or long walks on the beach. But she missed her all the same. She wrote a song. Maybe—Eva's heart catches—more than one.

Eva clears her throat and steps out of Steph's shadow. "I'm a big fan of it, and I'm excited to sing it tonight."

She means it. When she glances at Celeste, Celeste mouths *thank you*.

"This is 'Before,'" Celeste says, adjusting her grip on her guitar. "And this song wouldn't exist without Moonlight Overthrow."

Eva doesn't sing near Celeste. But Celeste keeps moving, so she does too, and by the second verse, she can't tell which one of them is orbiting the other, only that she can't look away.

At the end, over the surge of screams, Celeste says, "You know, I'm not the only one who's been making music lately."

That's supposed to be Eva's cue to introduce "Yours Tonight," a song she wrote and then sold to someone else. Except there's a sure, sudden feeling that she needs to sing a different song of hers this night.

Eva begins to walk toward the piano, and the others follow her, as planned. There's no way to warn them she's about to go way off-script. "Steph did some thank-yous earlier tonight, so I'm going to copy them," she says, instead of talking about the "Yours Tonight" performer. "Thank you to Steph's family, for hosting the three of us. To my parents, who promised they'd love me even if I never got on another stage again, and then, this week, that they would love me even if I sucked tonight." She lets herself smile. "Thank you to Lydia, for always having my back in L.A. . . ." Her heart skips a bit. She should say the next one, too. For honesty's sake. "And to Kay. You're a star."

Gina's smile is easy and wide for the crowd, but across the

piano, her stare is intense. Steph just looks bemused. As Eva sits down, she checks herself: Is she really going to do this?

She could play the chords the band is expecting, notes that will be familiar to anyone who listens to pop radio, and the four of them will give the crowd an exclusive cover.

She could. But she won't. She wants *this* song.

"This is a brand-new song I've been writing for the past couple weeks. Nobody else has heard it yet. How do you feel about being my test audience?"

As it happens, the audience seems to feel pretty good about the prospect.

Onstage, Gina's jaw drops. Steph starts clapping. Celeste grins, both hands clasped over her heart.

Eva lets her smile stretch so wide it's almost painful. She *missed* this. How could she have forced herself to go without for all this time? How could she have thought she'd be content with songwriting credits, not when she could have this, too?

"This is a very rough draft, so if anything official ever happens with this, no promises that it'll be the same. But I started writing this song the night of the storm, before I knew the storm was happening. It feels right to share it with you all tonight." Gina and Steph are half turned toward the crowd, mics down at their sides like this was the plan all along, but Celeste's eyes never leave her. Eva looks back at the audience. "This song is called 'After Today.' And it goes like this."

Her fingers press down on the keys.

All of a sudden, it's quiet, far quieter than any performance she's done in a long, long time. No one is singing along, because no one can: no one knows the lyrics but her.

She lets her eyelids flutter closed. Her brain filters out the ambient noise, until the keys and her voice are the only sounds that exist in the world. To her left, the audience is watching, listening to every new note; straight ahead, unless she's moved, is Celeste. Right here, strong in her chest and light in her fingertips, is the song.

JULY 2021
EVA

The remainder of the set passes in a blur, a medley of *Supernova*, *Bright*, and *Lunar*, of laughing with the audience and laughing with Celeste. At the end—the first end, the false end—Eva knows she's supposed to say something before they briefly disappear ahead of the encore, but she can only bring herself to wave.

"Thank you, we love you!" Celeste takes Eva's hand and pulls her backstage as the applause crashes and crashes behind them.

"It can't be over," says Eva. Someone hands her a water bottle, and she drinks gratefully.

"We've got one more song," says Celeste.

Eva shakes her head. Even though Celeste is technically right, it doesn't *feel* right. One more song—it's not enough.

"C'mon, let's do this," says Gina.

They run out again. Eva sits down at the piano. She lets her eyes linger on the crowd, on her band, on the lights reflecting off the piano. She plays the opening chords of "This Afternoon."

Night has fallen. The stage lights obscure the stars, but she knows they'll be there on the way home. Celeste and Steph open the song together, their voices twining together, perfectly balanced. Gina does a runway walk the length of the stage as she leads the pre-chorus:

"Others have midnights and middle of the nights
you and I have two p.m. and more laughter than fights."

Eva slips in and out of the song, verses and harmonies as they'd planned, her fingers moving relentlessly across the piano keys. She reaches the bridge, which is all her, vocally and instrumentally. Heart and soul.

She turns her head toward the crowd.

"I'll love you in starlight but right now it's daybreak
I'll love you at sunset and the times in-between
but right now it's this afternoon, you and me."

When the song is over, Gina grabs Eva's hands and twirls her off the bench into the group hug, a tottering circle center stage.

"It can't be over," says Eva, her voice breaking. Tears run down her cheeks, but she doesn't brush them away. "We're not done."

"We're not done forever," Celeste promises. "Just for tonight."

"No," says Eva. "No—we haven't done 'Hallelujah.'"

Their cover of "Hallelujah" was their most popular song from their Spotify EP, the song that caught the attention of someone who knew someone who knew someone at Capitol Records. It didn't make it onto their first album—or the second, or the third—but they sang it at the start of every show as a support act, and every show their first headliner tour.

"We haven't rehearsed," says Gina.

"I don't care, I can still do it," says Eva.

"We need to get offstage," says Steph.

"No," says Eva. "Please."

She can't explain the feeling, but they *can't* leave yet. It's not time. It's "Hallelujah," and if there was ever a concert to sing it at, it's this one.

"I'm in," says Celeste.

Gina glances between them. She shrugs, but there's already a smile betraying her. "I should have known we were never going to stick to the plan."

The crowd murmurs, confused.

"You're right," says Steph. "I don't know what's going to happen when we get to the fourth verse, but you're right. We have to do this."

Eva whoops and pivots toward the crowd, running up to the front of the stage. "That was supposed to be our last song," she says into her mic. "But we're having too much fun, and we changed our minds."

The other three fan out next to her.

"This has been . . . tonight has been so amazing," Eva says, "I can't even begin to say, and I hope it's felt the same way for all of you. And since this is—the four of us, back in Duluth, back where we started, there's one more song we really need to sing. I've been thinking a lot about ending things the right way, and it wouldn't have felt right to end with any other song."

She can tell, by the scattered but building shrieks, that some of the audience has figured it out—the longtime MO fans, the Cosmic Queers, the hometown cheerleaders who were rooting for them at the start.

"One last time . . . thank you for having us, Duluth. We're not always here, but we always love you. This is 'Hallelujah.'"

Gina starts them off, her voice low and rich, with a solemnity that was compelling when she was thirteen and is no less so now. On the second line, Celeste joins her; the fourth, Steph; and by the time Eva releases that first jagged *hallelujah*, it's all of them: a perfect four-part harmony.

The first lines of the second verse are hers alone. The notes feel ripped from her throat, only not just her throat, her lungs and her stomach and every bit of stardust that makes up her being, like she's been holding back these notes for almost two years, and longer still, almost as far back as you can go, and they won't wait any longer.

She thinks, fleetingly, about the roof she'd first kissed Celeste on: four years ago, Austin, Texas. The heat of the patio seat beneath her thighs. Eva looks at Celeste. Their eyes lock, and Celeste inhales, preparing to join in with the harmony.

Back at the beginning—before the beginning, really, when she'd first heard the song, for real, not in a movie soundtrack but in sixth-grade choir—she misheard the third line of the second verse. Gina corrected her, and she always sang lyrics Leonard Cohen himself would recognize during shows.

Eva prepares to sing the version she first imagined, and she doesn't care if the fans spend the next week comparing cell phone recordings of the song, reassuring each other that, *yes, Eva actually did that*. In fact, she hopes they do.

Eva angles her body closer toward Celeste, takes a breath, and actually does it.

Not her beauty *and* the moonlight, but her beauty *in* the moonlight.

And Eva, as always, is overthrown.

JULY 2021
CELESTE

The converted "green room" is packed: the openers and their guests, the crew, Celeste's mom and her sisters, not to mention Steph's entire family and a half-dozen new friends they'd made after coming back to Duluth, Gina's parents and a handful of cousins, *Eva's* parents . . .

Celeste can't take so much as half a step without being congratulated, hugged, asked for a picture. Which is fine, okay, except for the fact that a very large part of her wants to whisk Eva away to a deserted room with a door that locks and not emerge until . . . until *something*.

Grandma Marit waves her over to where she's sitting in one of those convertible walkers. "That was the best concert I've ever been to, and I've been to a few in my time."

"You don't have to say that," says Celeste. "But thank you."

"I'm too old to lie about art. You take care of your girl now, you hear me?"

"My—Eva? We're not . . ." Celeste shakes her head rather than finish the sentence.

"Yes, Eva. You can't fool me." Grandma Marit wags a finger.

Celeste's brain spirals into a movie montage of every interaction she's had, or seen Eva having, with Steph's grandma this past week.

"Did you think—this whole week—? Eva's not my girlfriend," Celeste says.

"It's bad manners to argue," Grandma Marit says, winking. "If you'll excuse me, I need to go hug my grandchild again."

Before Celeste can even begin to process that—and god, does she need to process that—her own mom pulls her close. "Don't cry, honey, you were perfect."

Celeste brushes a hand across her cheeks; her fingertips come away wet. It's a good thing her makeup is waterproof.

"I'm so proud of you," her mom continues.

"I want them back," Celeste confesses.

It's so loud back here, she's not worried about being overheard. And if she were—if the others did hear—so what? It's not anything she's planning on keeping a secret.

"You have to ask," her mom says, right into her ear.

Celeste nods. She knows.

Her mom steps back, turning to greet a man Celeste can't see properly, and for a wild second she thinks the man is her father, here as a surprise, but of course it's not him. It's Eva's dad.

Celeste hasn't seen him since their last concert, when she spent every second backstage avoiding him and Eva's mom while trying to maintain the polite farce that she wasn't *trying* to avoid them, it was just that she'd broken their daughter's heart, and surely that was a betrayal of their warmth and generosity as well. She was planning on using the same strategy here—conveniently, accidentally never speaking to them all night, because, look, if there's anything worse than breaking someone's child's heart, surely it's breaking a heart and then wanting it *back*.

"Celeste," says Will. "It's good to see you."

Will is tall, six-two or six-three, and his round, still almost boyish face has a nearly perpetual expression of pleasant seriousness, like he can rationally suggest and placidly disagree his way through anything. Or, if not anything, at least through tense entertainment contract negotiations.

"Hi," she says, and then, belatedly, "You too."

"Angela's around here somewhere." Will waves a hand. "I'm sure she'd love to see you."

I'm sure she'd like to stab me with one of my VMAs, Celeste thinks, but she smiles and nods anyway.

"They put all the families together, you know," Celeste's mom says.

Celeste did know this, actually. She assumed that Gina's and Steph's families would act as a buffer zone.

Celeste nods again. She can whip out a fifteen-second fan interaction after a twelve-hour flight. She can waltz through meet-and-greets when she's dead tired and all she wants to do is inhale a full meal and crawl into bed. She can dazzle an entire after-party while heartbroken. But she doesn't know what to say now. She doesn't know what to do with her face. Is she supposed to look knowing, sorry, distant, polite—who does he want her to be?

The noise from a dozen other conversations is buzzing in her ear, and she blurts, "I taped that motto up. In New York. It's—a Post-it. Begin—"

"—as you mean to go on," says Will. "I'm glad you found it useful."

Celeste opens her mouth, ready to say she did, but abruptly, she stops. Will is still smiling at her, but beneath the twinkle in his eye is steel. Or maybe, more accurately, that twinkle is whatever fire stars are made of, and it's not afraid to burn in the interests of his daughter.

"I took it down, actually. After a while." She swallows. "I realized . . . maybe sometimes you *don't* begin the right way, and you have to let yourself go on a different way. Or maybe what you thought was the beginning wasn't the beginning at all, so—you had it right, then wrong, or . . ."

"It's okay, Celeste. You did wonderfully tonight." He reaches out, pulling her into a half hug.

"Thank you," says Celeste. She means for all of it.

GINA

Gina had very politely, very firmly vetoed the idea of an after-party, or at least anything more formal than the crush of their families backstage after the concert. The community is still grieving, and Gina thinks it would be too presumptive to treat the concert as anything akin to the rainbow sent to Noah, queer double meaning fully intended.

After about an hour, she hugs her parents one last time and finds Steph. "Ready?"

Gina takes Steph's hand, so as not to lose them as they wind their way through the crowd toward Celeste and Eva, who, naturally but unhelpfully, are already standing close together, talking with two of the tech crew.

"We're thinking of heading back," says Gina.

"Yeah, we should probably clear out." Eva glances toward the door of the meeting room, toward the hall that leads to the darkened stage and the field that is now empty of all but the workers cleaning up.

Celeste hesitates. "I know Pip wanted to go over some stuff with me . . ."

"We'll wait up," Steph says.

"I could stay?" Eva, of course.

"Leave Celeste to her business," Gina says, keeping her voice light and even. She needs Eva alone.

"You guys go, get comfy, relax. Hopefully this won't take long." Celeste sets off across the room, a determined look on her face.

Gina needs to move, fast. "Shall we?"

They hitch a ride with Mrs. Miles, and once they're back in Steph's kitchen, Gina says, "Meet downstairs in ten?"

She wants to wash her makeup off and change into more casual clothing, and she and Steph decided this is a conversation best had in neutral territory: thus, no bedrooms.

By the time she gets downstairs, Eva is already sprawled on one couch, in a blue dress that could be a cotton knockoff of her concert outfit. Gina sits next to her, while Steph plops onto the other one.

"Thoughts, Eva?" Gina says.

Eva tilts her head back against the couch, addressing the ceiling as she says, "It was amazing, and I loved it, and I hated that I loved it, and I could do it three nights a week for the rest of my life."

"Good," says Gina. "We're in agreement then."

Eva sits up straight. "What?"

"I want us to re-form Moonlight Overthrow," Gina says, looking Eva directly in the eye.

She expects Steph to jump in, but Steph watches them quietly. Next to her, Eva is still.

After a moment, Eva says, "You're serious."

"Yes," says Gina. "I know things didn't end well last time." Eva snorts; Gina inclines her head in acknowledgment. "But we've all had time away, now, to explore other areas, and to figure out what we really want."

"You can't just . . . want it back." Eva frowns now, looking down at the carpet.

"Isn't it better to admit I've changed my mind, than to pretend I haven't?" Gina says. She lets her body settle, soft, into the couch cushions. "As it turns out . . . I don't want to be Gina Wright without you. I'm not Beyoncé. I'm not Camila."

Eva doesn't look up. Steph doesn't chime in.

"Didn't you . . . have fun this week?" Gina asks. She laces together her trembling fingers.

"I did," Eva says, smiling again. "So much fun. With *you*."

The relief is so thick, Gina feels smothered in it.

"That's what I'm saying. Us, again."

"Can I ask you something?" Eva fiddles with the hem of her dress.

"Anything, babe."

"Why do you want to re-form the band?"

Gina stares for a moment. Isn't it obvious? Didn't she say already?

"I miss singing. I miss performing live. But mostly—I miss you. A lot. Stuff happens on set and I wish I could text you, and then I remember I can't, and it's the *absolute worst*."

Eva nods. "What did you give up for this plan?"

"What?" Gina lurches fully upright again. Eva raises her eyebrows. "What did—how did you know?"

"You're not the smart one anymore," Eva says, teasing.

Gina swallows. "*Bayahibe Rose*."

"You did *not*," Steph says suddenly.

"I did. That's how badly I want this, all right? I need you back."

"You have us. I promise. You don't have to bribe us with the band," says Eva. "I *want* you to text me from every set. Every Broadway rehearsal."

She isn't supposed to know I want that, Gina thinks. But that's the thing about old friends: they know all your first dreams. They know which ones you would never give up.

Eva runs a hand through her hair. "I'm not in the business of telling people what they want, but like . . . I don't think the thing you really want is the band. And I know it's not what I really want."

"But you . . . you did want the band," says Gina. She needs Eva; Eva wants the band. She was supposed to be the easy one to convince, OT4 champion extraordinaire. Instead, Gina feels like a stage light just fell on her head.

"Isn't it better to admit I've changed my mind, than pretend I haven't?" Eva echoes. She bites her lip. "Will you hate me if I say no?"

Gina doesn't hesitate. "No. Never."

The tension in Eva's shoulders loosens. "So don't be Gina Wright without us. But . . . be Gina Wright. Bug Celeste to let you feature on a song on her next album."

"Call your agent and ask if they've booked someone for *Bayahibe Rose*," Steph adds, their tone firm, exactly the older sibling voice Gina has missed for so long.

"I wanted to find a way—"

"You don't need to, Gi," says Steph.

Gina tucks her legs beneath her. She just needs to *think*.

Eva grabs a notebook from the coffee table and holds it out. "It's not a custom-embossed padfolio, but maybe this can help."

"Didn't you want me to be done planning us?" Gina says, shaking her head but accepting the notebook instinctively. "I need us to be friends, and creating together. Because even when it was shitty and exhausting, you reminded me that I was a real person, and we laughed about dumb stuff—and did spontaneous things that were objectively bad ideas but somehow still perfect—"

"Like sing 'Hallelujah' without practicing," Steph says.

"Like that," says Gina, her voice breaking.

Eva pushes a pen into her hand. "Why do we need the band to do any of that? We're here. Check, done. So now what?"

Gina twists the pen between her fingers.

"Did you do everything you want to? All the things you said you'd do once you left the band, did you finish that?" Steph asks.

"You know I haven't." She tries to laugh. "And it *doesn't matter*."

"I think it does," Steph says. "And . . . I know I didn't say this when we were talking last night, but I'm kind of wondering how long it would take for you to resent us again—to feel stifled."

"But I know better now. I have different priorities." Gina can't believe they're arguing about this. It was all so perfect. So neatly arranged.

Eva and Steph exchange glances. Gina ignores them, flipping the notebook open to a clean page. Her planning made Moonlight Overthrow a success the first time—why should the second time be any different?

Moonlight Overthrow: the rush of performance, the late nights, the road trip games, the constant jet lag, the thrilling strategy behind every move, the schedule she had no hand in making, never being without her best friends, always being the only Black one in the room.

Her pen slows. She draws a line separating the top half of the page from the bottom.

"Remember," says Eva, "no Moonlight Overthrow—but *we're* still there. The four of us, 'til the moon crashes into the sea."

Gina thinks of when she told Kayla, just last month, that she wasn't going to renew her management contract. She wants music. Fashion. A live audience. Four takes to nail a complex character. Some time—a big chunk of it, consecutive weeks—where she doesn't have to be someone else's Gina Wright and can instead figure out who she is when she's the one making choices. She wants her friends. If she gets to keep them no matter what—if she trusts Eva and Steph when they say their friendship is not dependent on any one career choice—

A reunion is what she's been saying to herself for months, to Steph this week, and to Eva tonight. Gina suddenly feels trapped beneath the weight of every word.

Isn't there another way? she thinks. And of course there is.

She's been so focused on the endgame, she forgot how much

the means matter. She forgot that there's almost always more than one way to win, and that deciding there's only one path usually leads to failure, not success. Steph and Eva are right. She doesn't want to do another three years of relentless Moonlight. She is so, so far overdue for some overthrow. The weight lifts—not from her shoulders, but her chest. She can breathe deeply again. She could hold a note for a long time.

She can make the music she wants—and know they'll support her. Film a sequel—and message them between every take. Disappear for a year—and have them join her on a private beach. She still has her foundation, her allies. Her friends. The sky is such a low limit to have.

Gina feels like crying out of sheer relief. They know her and love her and want her—no contract necessary.

"You make . . . really excellent points. But so far we've only talked about me. I don't get why—don't you guys want to re-form the band?"

Steph kneads the couch cushion beneath their palms. "Look, do you remember when—"

The door to the basement opens.

"Anybody home?" Celeste calls.

EVA

The conversation freezes when Celeste comes downstairs, wearing cotton pajama shorts and a Minnesota Pride T-shirt. She looks at Eva, clearly waiting for someone to say why they aren't already fifteen minutes into a movie, why they aren't doing fan service on Instagram, why they're all just sitting here. When no one speaks up, Celeste settles next to Steph on the other couch and starts telling them about some drama with her opener.

Eva's head is still reeling. *Gina*, asking if she wants the band back. The unlikeliest thing after weeks of unlikely things. She feels like she did that afternoon when Steph asked her to be part of the charity concert. She said yes for Duluth . . . and for herself.

Love, and let go.

She didn't really think it would happen like that. Somehow, it has. No, not somehow: because this whole week hasn't been about the band. It's been about them: Celeste, Gina, Steph, Eva. She's always needed them more than she ever needed Moonlight Overthrow. She can make her own music. It's hard to be your own friend group.

"Um," Celeste says, when no one reacts to the end of her story. *Oops.* "I feel like I'm missing something?"

"No," says Eva. She lets herself grin. "We're all right here."

Steph rolls their eyes. "You missed the bit where we decided *not* to re-form the band, so I hope you're on board with that."

Celeste immediately looks at Eva. She nods.

When Eva was dancing to all their old songs tonight, it *almost* felt like it was still two years ago, three years ago, and she was still on top of the world with Celeste, and nothing ever went wrong. But that's not who she is anymore, and she doesn't want the same things as she used to.

"I could—I mean, I'm still on contract for a third album, but—"

"Stop," Eva says, but gently. "Nobody wants it. At least, not the full thing."

"The full . . . ," Celeste echoes.

"I don't actually like touring," Steph says, their tone a confession even though it's not exactly new information. "I know it's exhausting for everyone, but it's—*really* hard on me. And as amazing as tonight was, as perfect as the show just was, it also reminded me how much I can't do that, for months at a time. And we'd need to—and you'd *want* to."

"But I thought you wanted music again," Gina says.

"I do. But I want to focus on producing right now. Track maker, not topliner for a while."

Of course. Now that Steph's said it, it seems so obvious.

Celeste nods, a speculative look in her eyes. "You think we could meet up this winter? Do a song or two?"

"That would be . . . yeah." Steph ducks their head. "I'm there."

Gina turns to Eva. "You were right, about me and *Bayahibe Rose* and—*us*. Us, not MO." Out of the corner of her eye, Eva sees Celeste glancing between them, confused. "But you said you loved it. You said you could play shows for the rest of your life."

Celeste inhales sharply.

It's not that Celeste was right, that night in the hotel. If Eva had gone solo then, it would have been out of spite, pressure from Kayla, heartbreak. It would have been about other people's choices. Up until this last week—up until tonight—even *thinking* about going solo felt like a betrayal of her slightly younger self.

I get to choose, too, she reminds herself. *I get to want. I get to change.* And maybe a relationship isn't a zero-sum game that Eva loses by changing her mind. Maybe it's okay if Celeste *was* right—at least a little.

"Sometimes they get it wrong," Eva says, shrugging.

"What?" says Celeste, still focused completely on Eva, like nothing else in the room even exists.

"The singers. Like, cool spot in the Top Ten, but you got the song wrong."

"You know how to fix that," Gina says, slowly, as if she's afraid to say it.

"Yeah." Eva leans back into the couch, letting a smirk tug at her lips. "I do. And I'm going to. I want to keep singing. I want to go solo. My words, my voice—for me."

"Oh my god!" Steph basically launches themself from the other couch and wraps Eva in a tight hug.

"I'm so, *so* happy for you," says Gina, burrowing into the embrace.

Eva squeezes back. Who knew she could be so happy *not* to reunite the band? But she is, a happiness as deep as any ocean. Across from them, Celeste has one hand half covering her smiling mouth, her brown eyes glistening with tears.

"Hey," says Eva. "Could we get a minute?"

Gina and Steph glance at Celeste.

"Yeah, babe," says Gina. "We'll talk more tomorrow, before everyone's flights."

"Good night, kids." Steph throws a wink over their shoulder as they head for the stairs.

"C'mere," says Eva, once the basement door has shut again.

Celeste folds herself into the spot just vacated by Gina and reaches out for Eva's hand. "I know you didn't do this for me. I just—need you to know that I know that."

Eva brushes a thumb along Celeste's palm. "I know."

"Eva?"

She turns her head. Celeste is biting her lip, hope and uncertainty flickering in her eyes. Eva can see the blush forming on Celeste's cheeks as she looks and looks without speaking.

"For the record," Celeste begins, her voice low, "I'm sorry. And I still . . ."

Eva's glad Celeste doesn't jump right into *love you*. There's been too much time, too much hurt and distance, to fall back into each other exactly the same way.

"I'm sorry, too," Eva whispers. She clears her throat and makes her choice. "What time is it?"

"What?"

"The time."

Celeste cranes her neck to look at the wall clock. "Past midnight. Why?"

"It's afternoon somewhere," says Eva. Her stomach clenches.

"Ye-es, that's how time zones . . . oh," says Celeste. Eva can see the moment she understands, her eyes widening, her smile stretching. "*Oh.* Good afternoon, love."

Celeste tilts her chin, just so, the way she used to when she wanted to be kissed.

Eva kisses her.

It doesn't feel instantly familiar, but it's not like a first kiss, either. It's a gray in-between space, a dawn with someone who will be there to become familiar with again when day hits.

Eva brings a hand up to Celeste's cheek, subtly adjusting the angle of their kiss, and Celeste closes her eyes as she allows Eva to guide her. The world narrows to Celeste's lips against Eva's, her hand on Eva's thigh, every touch magnified by each day of longing between then and now.

Much too soon, Celeste leans back. "Does this mean—can we try us? Together?"

"Yes. *Yes.*"

They shift, until Celeste is tucked into Eva, where Eva can drop kisses into Celeste's brown-and-blue hair.

"We're gonna do it right this time. Separate, okay?" Celeste says.

"Hmm?"

"Like . . . the two of us, and the band, it was all mixed together. It was both, one. So no matter what's happening with our solo careers, or your songwriting, or your degree—the success of any of that needs to be separate from what's happening with *us*."

"*Yes*," says Eva. "Agreed."

"And we're gonna have to talk about shit. The stuff we think the other person doesn't want to hear."

"I know. Not just in Voice Memo songs, either."

"Maybe sometimes," says Celeste, giggling now.

"Maybe sometimes," Eva agrees.

She's in no hurry to move. Celeste's body is a soft, sturdy weight above her. "Hallelujah" is still vibrating beneath her skin. She could stay like this all night and be content, but—she remembers touring.

"Okay," she says. She tips her head sideways, letting her cheek press against Celeste's hair. "You have to perform again on Saturday. You should probably go to bed."

"In a little bit."

"You sure?"

Celeste twists around to face her properly. "You said it yourself, love. It's afternoon somewhere."

Celeste kisses her again.

It's every sun-dappled afternoon and every star-strewn midnight, and yes. All the times in-between.

JULY 2021

lesbianbayyy:

I'm going to do a full write-up of the concert in a bit but HOLY SHIT hands down best night of my life, and the thing I've been thinking about is that I can't even decide which one of them I was happiest to see??? (Guys. I saw them. All four. Performing. Together.) I change my mind approximately every .25 seconds. I MEAN:

Gina: MY QUEEN. She's been stunning on red carpets but you could just tell she was dying to sing again and there she was! And her voice was soooo fucking gorgeous, as usual, SO BEAUTIFUL.

Steph: Totally disappeared, and then they came back like WHOA and obviously are so confident and comfortable in themself, in a way that makes it really obvious how much they were NOT that last tour especially, and my heart broke in retrospect but was put back together by all the love the girls showed them onstage, and all the love they gave back in return.

Like I absolutely want Steph to keep doing what is right for them and if that means not performing, I accept that, but . . . they were SO AMAZING last night, maybe they'll show up for a couple Jingle Ball performances or something?? (Also, can we talk about their suit. o h m y g o d.)

Celeste: It's not that I think Celeste has really been lonely onstage, except for maybe those very first couple of solo performances, I know I'm totally projecting when I see pics from her shows now and go "aww my baby all alone." I LOVE her solo stuff, okay? But. Hot damn, she loved being with the three of them last night. She was ALL SMILES during the show, watching the others, checking in to make sure they were okay and having fun and all of that. And you know she was loving every minute, cheering them on during their verses, jamming out with Eva, the whole thing.

Eva: My darling, my love. I think it's special for her, or it was special watching her be there because . . . if she wants to go to college and write for other people, GO FOR IT, GIRL. She could retire to an island for the rest of her life writing no. 1s. But the point of this post is baby is BACK. She was glowing and honestly she seemed just as surprised and grateful as any of us that this was actually happening. I was SOBBING during "After Today." I am desperately praying she doesn't sell that to anybody else, that song is HERS.

#WTF IS MY LIFE #part 2 #I can't believe I have to work on Saturday this is homophobic #I need way more time to recover #and answer all these asks lol

maybeitsmoonlight:

LET'S TALK ABOUT EVA.

SHE MADE THEM SING HALLELUJAH.

I know some of y'all think that was a stunt and they were going to sing it all along but WATCH how long they stood on stage after This Afternoon, look at Eva's body language, and even though they were SOOOO GOOD, it was not as well rehearsed as the others.

Basically: EVA CAME THROUGH FOR US.

She knows what we want and she DELIVERS.

Girl gave us a beautiful new song, and then she gave us Hallelujah.

#EvaBell2024

ginestebest:

If you're like me, the second question on your mind this morning (after "Is there going to be a reunion?") is "Who hurt Eva?" "After Today" is so heartbreakingly lovely, strong and sad and quietly powerful and ultimately hopeful.

I firmly believe in her imaginative abilities, but the heartfelt emotion in that song—this song that she wrote and supposedly hadn't shared with anybody else yet—makes me think she really, deeply meant it.

#eva bell #duluth benefit concert #after today

moonlit-babe:

IN.

IN.

HER BEAUTY IN THE MOONLIGHT.

<u>Please</u> <u>enjoy</u> <u>all</u> <u>these</u> <u>receipts</u> <u>of my babe</u> <u>Eva</u> <u>changing</u> <u>the lyrics.</u>

Sometimes with lyric changes (especially pronoun switches for ~maybe closeted artists) it's not *all* that clear what they meant to be singing, but Eva is Empress of Enunciation. Plus look at how she tilts her chin up right before, and that little smirk? Yeah, she knew what she was about to do. It was planned, it was deliberate, she was proud as fuck to sing it.

We've known from the start that "Hallelujah" was important to them, without a ton of specifics on why. For Celeste, we assumed most of the significance is because she's Jewish, but the party line was basically "we fell in love with the song and also the moon is a queer icon" (truth). Still, "and" to "in" is such a specific change: small but infinitely impactful . . .

I don't know what girl Eva loves in the moonlight, but she wanted her to know last night.

#wild speculation tag #eva bell #duluth benefit concert #hallelujah #lyric changes

---

kaystar:

There are . . . kind of a lot of asks in my inbox right now.

This is what Eva said last night: "And to Kay. You're a star."

I totally admit, my fangirl headcanon is that Eva is talking about me. DUH. Everybody named Lydia is doing the exact same thing, go yell at them. (Even though we know she's talking about her college friend.) (Don't go yell at them. Let them have their fun.)

Here are some true facts: There's a lot of Eva's life we don't know about. There could be—and clearly is—somebody named Kay we know nothing about. Good for them. I bet Eva is thoughtful, generous, no drama, OT4 'til the moon crashes into the sea. I bet she bakes a mean banana cake. I bet she remembers the names of your cats and your nickname for your crush (pause for a shout-out to my Cute Library Girl).

I, personally, have never met Eva. I have never met any member of MO or their staff or friends or families, to unknown but surely large degrees of separation. (Obviously, guys. You know 85% of my friends are online only.)

The other thing is . . . do you even hear yourselves? We like to pretend we're so much better than other bandoms/celebrity fandoms in general, less toxic, fewer stalkers. And maybe we are! But the asks I've been getting suggest maybe this pedestal we've placed ourselves on is all gilt and no gold. You ever notice how Eva's real, non-famous friends don't show her off on their social media? They don't gossip about her dating life. Eva deserves better than that, and they know it (everybody deserves this, by the way). And I know you know it, because you haaaate on celebs' non-famous friends who clearly mooch off them. Why is it so different now, when you think I might have ~insider info? If you thought I was the kind of person who would, after somehow miraculously becoming friends with Eva, share private info about her to Tumblr . . . why are you following me? You shouldn't be. That person would be an *asshole*. It's frankly insulting—to both of us.

Much love to Eva and to the many, many wonderful Cosmic Queers in this fandom. The rest of you—stop asking me shit.

#seriously

JULY 2021
STEPH

Despite the late night, Steph rises early on Friday. There's a conversation they need to have before the next time they talk with the girls, for the not-band meeting.

As expected, Steph's mom and grandma are already sitting at the kitchen table when Steph enters the room, both of them drinking from steaming mugs. Over the past year and a half, Steph has spent a lot of early mornings at the table with them. In the space of a week, though, they've fallen out of the habit, and now, walking to the coffeepot, they feel unmoored. Apart. They're supposed to be in that tableau, but they've missed their entrance cue.

The three of them have the same oval face shape, straight nose, and hidden cheekbones. Steph got that a lot growing up: *you look so much like your mom, you look so much like your grandma*. It wasn't that they couldn't see the family resemblance. It wasn't even that Steph wished they looked more like their dad. Steph wasn't sure how they felt about so obviously being the next one in the matrilineal line, the next one of those Nielsen-Miles girls. It'd be an honor, if that didn't also feel like having to take on their womanhood as well.

"We thought you'd still be sleeping," Steph's mom says as Steph pours coffee into a UMD mug.

"Need to talk to you," they say. "Before everybody else gets up."

"You really were wonderful last night." Their mom pushes out a chair so Steph can sit down.

"You're my mom. You have to say that," says Steph.

"I have a dozen music publications who'll back me up." She waves her cell phone at Steph, where, yes, they can see a Twitter feed that seems to be full of complimentary adjectives.

"When are you going?" their grandma asks.

Steph freezes. *How could she know?*

Steph's mom, though, pats her own mom's hand. "They aren't a band anymore, remember, Mom? This was just a one-time show, for Duluth."

"Oh, yes," says Grandma Marit, her brow furrowing. "But when . . ."

"That's actually what I want to talk to you both about," says Steph, before the conversation can be too derailed. "We all talked last night, after the show. And . . . we're not going to get back together as a group. But I do want to do music again, some of it with them."

"Sweetheart." Their mom says it more like an exhale than an actual word.

Steph stares into their coffee cup. "I want to, but it'd mean a lot of time not here. Some recording in L.A., and probably New York. I mostly want to produce, but I also want to start collaborating on songs, if I can. Singing, I mean. Maybe a few guest performances at festivals and stuff."

"Festivals!" Steph's mom says, in a tone they hope is more "excitement" than "disapproving disbelief."

Matt and Meghan's offer was one thing, but ultimately the work of the household—and Steph's decision about music—rests on Steph's mom.

"But if that's not going to work for us, as a family . . ." Steph swallows. They take a breath. "Then I'll tell them no. And I won't call the label."

"You can't do that," says their mom.

Steph doesn't reply.

"Steph, look at me," their mom says. Steph jerks their gaze away from the coffee's dark brown depths. "You miss it, don't you? You miss music, your girls—"

"Yes, but—"

"There's no 'but.' You miss it, and you have another chance at it."

"It's not that simple," Steph begins.

"Yes, it is."

"I wouldn't be able to *be here*."

"And we'll miss you. But that's okay," she says.

"Are you *sure*?" Steph says.

They need their mom to be sure.

Grandma Marit stands up. "This is a conversation you need to have with your mother. I'll be in the living room, if you want to talk later."

"Thanks, Grandma," Steph says, squeezing her hand as she passes, but they're distracted, too focused on whatever their mom is about to say.

At the doorway, Grandma Marit pauses and turns around. "If you'll permit your grandma to say just one thing: I will miss you every day, but we will all take good care of each other. I love you more than you can know. Don't you dare stay for me."

She leaves before Steph can swallow the lump in their throat. Shaking, they look back at their mom.

"Listen to me," their mom says. "You were in a bad way at the end of the last tour. You needed to come home, and we wanted you to come home, and yes, I'll admit, it was easier with you here. You have been such, *such* a big help to us all, and I'm so proud of you for that." Steph looks down, embarrassed, but their mom presses on. "I'm proud of you for stepping away when you needed to, and for stepping up to help your siblings. But we're all on steady ground now. You shouldn't feel obligated to stay. The world is so big—"

I know, Steph thinks. They've seen a lot of it, more than most do in a lifetime.

"—and you're so young, and have so much to offer it. What kind of mom would I be, if I let you stop following your dreams at age twenty? It's okay to regroup sometimes, and we were all glad to have you here. And now it's time for you to do music again."

Steph starts to cry. "What if—what if it's *not*?" they force themself to say.

"What if it *is*?" their mom counters.

"It wasn't real," Steph says, but for the first time, that feels like a lie.

Maybe not a lie. Just not true. Those years were real, and that's why it hurts: they lost those years, they were lost in those years. What doesn't seem real is that they could find their way back, not without losing the rest of it: Meghan and Mari and Matt, the drawer of sports bras upstairs.

But their phone has blown up over the past week with messages from other non-binary singers and producers. Invitations to join them in the studio, or just hang out when Steph next visits California.

"You're ready," Steph's mom says.

"Pushing the baby bird out of the nest?" Steph tries for a smile, lifting one shoulder and rubbing their damp cheek against their T-shirt.

She stills, creases deepening around her eyes. "Did I do the right thing, signing for you? Should I have made you wait?"

Behind every child star is a parent. Maybe that parent was indulgent. Maybe they were naive. Maybe they were pushing it just as much, if not more, than the kid. But somewhere, there was a parent who said yes and signed, just like Steph's mom did.

"No. I don't think so," says Steph. "You couldn't have . . . and I didn't . . . we couldn't have predicted what it was going to be. If I had known it was really going to happen, I would have wanted it more."

"You don't have to try to make me feel better, honey."

Steph wonders if, all this time—since the end, at least—their mom has been feeling guilty. Did Steph overlook that, just as much as Eva had missed the deterioration of the band that last summer?

"You can't predict the future. You thought you were . . . making my dreams come true."

It sounds cheesy, but it's also the truth: that's exactly what it felt like, those fleeting moments when Steph let the others' excitement and certainty fizz through them. Like a fairy tale, and their mom's signature was the stamp on the visa into the Otherworld.

"That doesn't mean it was the right thing to do."

"You were working from limited information."

Steph's mom nods. "Then we both were—all of us were. And now you know what it's going to be like, and you know *you*. And if you try it again and what you start doing now isn't for you, either, at least you tried again, with full information. You can always come home."

"I thought the saying was you can never go home again," Steph says.

"You came home," she says. "You tell me."

Steph swallows. "Okay."

"Okay what?"

"I'm going to do music again."

Steph's mom pulls them into a tight hug, kissing the top of their head. It's a long time before Steph lets go.

The four of them settle in the basement again, balancing plates of toast and fruit on their laps.

"Basement to the Billboard Awards in one album, babe, I swear," Gina says, pointing at Eva.

"Parks to *Pitchfork*?" Steph suggests, their tone sly. MO's albums were too pop to merit a review, but the site has a soft spot for former group members' solo endeavors.

Eva raises her middle finger, but lazily. Celeste is tucked against her on the couch, their bodies pressed together shoulder to knee. They keep stealing glances at each other, cheeks flushed.

"I was thinking, last night," Eva says, glancing at each of them. "And I think . . . we all have things we want, on our own, right now. And I feel pretty confident that our group chat is about to get a lot more active."

"It'd better," says Steph.

"I just want to say—when I said no last night, it wasn't a *never*. It's not a conversation we can't ever have again."

Steph's heart skips. Some bands don't tour. Or Steph could stay at the drums for every song, let Eva dance. Maybe, one day, that would work for them. But later, once they've had a chance to try out the rest of what they think they want.

"We could pencil in another conversation," says Steph. They look at Celeste. "After your next tour."

"After your Tony Award," says Celeste, nudging Gina with an outstretched foot.

"Your college graduation," says Gina, grinning at Eva.

"Maybe it'll be no again, from all of us," says Eva. "But it never hurts to ask."

"Speaking of . . ." Steph steels themself. They need one more favor. "I'd love to work with you all again. Producing, writing, any of it. And if and when I lead my own stuff, I'd love to collaborate sometimes on that, too. I'm wondering"—they glance at Eva— "I'm *asking* if you think any of that could be done here. The Cities would be okay if we had to, but I'd really like to be *here*, especially if I end up touring at all."

"Definitely," says Celeste.

"Never mind *your* reasons, the air quality is so much better here," Gina teases.

"Duluth can be our Montreux," says Eva. Queen may have had Switzerland, but Minnesota will suit them just fine.

"We are the champions," Steph says, singsong, and the conversation devolves into lyric references until Pip arrives and Celeste has to leave to catch her flight.

AUGUST 2021
EVA

Eva's been to four of Celeste's concerts since Duluth, flying out on weekends to wherever Celeste is once she's finished her homework for her summer class. She's starting to recognize the security guards at Burbank again.

Celeste will come visit her in L.A. once the tour's over, but for now, it's Eva's turn to travel. After they spent the entirety of their first relationship living in each other's pockets, Eva's glad for the slower start mandated by the twin constraints of tour and class.

Plus, her non-college life in L.A. has become busier. She and Gina occasionally team up to bring Georgia to clubs and parties, reveling in the "Girls' Night Out" headlines and sending Steph pics that the tabloids will never get. Steph replies with Snapchats about the progress the road crews are making to repave the damage wrought by the storm, and the charter boats that are back in sailing shape.

And Olivia is producing "After Today."

It's been nice to have a summer with Great Translated Novels *and* a contract.

The first time Eva went to Celeste's show, in Albuquerque, she watched—danced, screamed, sang along—from the VIP section, right next to one of Celeste's sisters. Celeste didn't make the crowd say "Hi, Eva," but she covered "Burning."

Celeste onstage was splendid, spectacular, luminescent with joy.

Eva let herself love Celeste's solo work in a way she hadn't before, not really, even back when she was fangirling with the best of them online. There had always been a part of her that couldn't and wouldn't separate Celeste Rogers, solo artist supreme, from Celeste Rogers, ex-girlfriend, ex-bandmate, ex-friend. Gone now is the bitter taste Celeste's words used to leave in her mouth.

While Celeste was meeting with fans, Eva flipped through her pictures of Celeste from sound check, looking for one to post to Instagram. The one she settled on was of Celeste adjusting her grip on her guitar, a blue-tinted strand of hair falling into her face. Eva captioned it, *A star before the show*.

Celeste liked the photo, but her real reply came more privately, in the form of a thirty-second Voice Memo, sent to Eva two days after she'd flown back to California. *You don't have to finish this for me*, Celeste said in the recording, *but I'm always open to a collaboration*. Eva's favorite part of the song snippet goes like this: *first loves don't last, but here we are again / I'll put you first, love*.

Eva retaliated—lovingly—with snippets of her own. Sure, the chorus ended with *back when we were in love at the top of the charts*, but it was the final iteration, the twist that all good poems had, that really counted: *now that we're back in love at the top of the charts*.

She's not sure they'll be ready to be publicly together by the time Celeste's third album is due, but that's okay. Songs can keep.

Eva also doesn't know what the fandom made of the Instagram photo or her obvious attendance at the show. She didn't let herself read the comments. The day after the concert, she and Kay talked about single-origin spices and the summer's breakout memoir. Their first conversation after the Duluth show, on the other hand, had been a little awkward. Kay had promised to take the secret to the grave. Eva had thanked her for the truly magnificent post. Both of them were careful to avoid writing anything too clear, to guard against the ramifications of a hack or a nosy roommate or, god forbid, a future fight. Kay had replied with about a million exclamation points, and that was that.

Eva and Lydia have talked about it all, though, over lots of frozen yogurt. Eva can't wait for Celeste and Lydia to meet, eras colliding into a star-strewn galaxy where Eva can have everyone she loves together.

The third time, in Phoenix, Eva watched from the wings. Celeste covered "This Afternoon." Eva's fingers itched to be on the piano. Afterward, Celeste and Eva went out to a park, close enough to the hotel to be convenient, but far enough away that stalkers wouldn't be pre-positioned. The park's pond was no Great Lake, but Eva took a picture of the moon's rippled reflection on the water anyway. These comments, she let herself read: according to the chatter on her Insta the next day, Cosmic Queers thought she was sending a message.

Maybe she was. Her notebook is littered with new verses for her and for Celeste. Most of the songs will just be hers, but some narratives demand a partner.

Eva thinks *Eponymous* has a nice ring for her solo debut.

On the fifth visit, next to her in the wings, Celeste's PA flashes her a thumbs-up, then thumbs-down. "Need anything before you go on?"

Eva shakes her head and adjusts her right earpiece. Steph squeezes her other hand once, while Gina cradles her bass. Dallas has no idea what's about to happen. When it comes to OT4, bet on Eva Bell. As long as you know that OT4 doesn't always mean Moonlight Overthrow.

Above a swell of applause, Celeste calls out, "I've been saying this a lot this summer . . . but this concert comes with a twist, too." The crowd screams. Eva's heartbeat accelerates. "I know you all collect gifsets of me being like 'this has been the best concert' and 'I've never been so excited for a show' and all that, and you think I say that to everyone and I'm lying to you. Real talk tonight, okay? This has been an amazing tour for me, and it couldn't have happened without you—both right here, singing along tonight, and also months ago, when a lot of you bought your tickets. And I'm not dissing any previous audience when I say that tonight is the best, because it took every previous show, every previous fan, for me to get to tonight."

Eva blinks rapidly, torn between wanting to cry and wanting to grin and run out there and tackle Celeste onto the stage floor.

"No tears until after," Gina whispers in her ear.

Eva clears her throat and sticks out her tongue.

"But let's cut to the chase," Celeste says to her crowd. "You came to the show tonight because you want to hear some songs, right?" (Cheers.) "Yeah. So I'm going to invite some special guests out right now, some really special friends of mine." Later, probably, Eva will laugh at Celeste's phrasing, but right now, Eva draws a deep breath. "I'm honored they've agreed to sing with me. The last time we were onstage together, it was to mourn and to heal and to comfort. Tonight, we're going to celebrate."

That's their cue. Flanked by Steph and Gina, Eva strides onstage, her hand already up and waving as the crowd screams. The next minute is a blur: pacing down the B-stage, greeting the audience, hearing all their names, over and over. It's been a long time since Eva's stood in front of a crowd this size, and it feels—amazing. She blinks away tears as she summons the first note in her mind.

The stage lights are glaring down on them; in front of Eva, Celeste's eyes are bright.

In the moment before she sings, a hundred futures flash before her eyes. It is, maybe, a little like the opposite of dying. Albums all by herself, with Celeste, with Moonlight Overthrow. Walking across a stage in California not to receive an award, but a diploma. Eva and Celeste on the shores of Lake Superior, doing anything, doing nothing.

Eva glances up. It's an outdoor arena, and although the stage and city lights obscure the stars, she thinks she catches sight of one, twinkling high above, surrounded by millions she can't see but are there all the same. Maybe she's just imagining its shine, but she wishes on it anyway.

She looks back at Celeste. Celeste won't come in on the guitar until after Eva's sung the first line. Eva lifts her chin and, smiling, starts to tap out the beat against her thigh.

The song Eva begins to sing is, of course, "Girl Says Yes."

AUTHOR'S NOTE

When asked by *Vogue* what advice she'd give to someone wanting to become a singer, Taylor Swift said, "Get a good lawyer." Moonlight Overthrow has a good lawyer. I am not a lawyer, but I know enough about the music industry to tell you that I have best-case-scenario-ed, simplified, and otherwise glossed over many contractual elements and other business considerations. Forgive me: Sometimes sunset clauses would have been in the way of a good sunset. For further reading on legal matters, I highly recommend *All You Need to Know About the Music Business: 10th Edition* by Donald Passman. Cheers also to the podcast *Switched on Pop* for musical analysis. It's been the joy of a lifetime to write this industry wrong—and so relatively welcoming to queer artists and their fans.

ACKNOWLEDGMENTS

Writing a novel is a bit like being a solo singer: It took many teams of people before my name could end up on the cover.

To Claire: On June 11, 2017, I told you I wanted to write this book, and you said I should do it, but maybe in the morning. Thank you for your careful eye on multiple drafts, for so many metaphors that helped me through edits, for untangling characterization threads with me at all hours of the day, and generally for enduring while this was my primary conversational topic, for years. For music movie nights and endless Taylor Swift references. For championing Steph. For dreaming all the biggest dreams I'm sometimes too shy to name.

To Maria: Given our origin story, it seems narratively, cosmically correct that we would end up here. Thank you for your boundless enthusiasm and love for my band, for prescient line edits, for the first fic (and the only one I can ever read) and first commissioned fanart. Thank you for correcting my space facts, even though they didn't make it to the final version. Like your girls in the original epilogue, they're always in my heart.

To my agent, Jessica Errera: I'm a big heart-eyes emoji every time I think of the excitement you have shown for MO from the start. I am so grateful that you saw the potential in this book and in me—for your deep passion for these characters and your commitment to my career. Thank you especially for guiding me through this story's tension troubles and staying levelheaded and practical in the face of my many anxieties. You have been a stellar, stalwart partner through this entire process. Let's do it again.

To my editor, Rachel Diebel: It's such an honor to be your first solo project! I'm so thankful for your insight into and care for the story I was trying to tell, for your humor as we tackled the word count and my obsession with logistics, and for not letting me get away with an ending that didn't match my characters' growth. It's been an absolute joy to work with you, and I've learned so much.

And to Jess and Rachel together: Every step of this book's journey—the timing, the people—has felt like fate. We are the dream team. Eveste couldn't ask for better shippers.

To so many others at Feiwel & Friends and the Jane Rotrosen Agency who helped turn this story from a complicated Scrivener document into a real book, including but not limited to: Jean Feiwel, Valerie Shea, Celeste Cass, and Mandy Veloso. Special thanks to the cover illustrator, Jenn Woodall, and designer, Trisha Previte, for giving me such a starry book. And thank you to my authenticity readers for their invaluable insights.

To my family: I grew up surrounded by people who love both music and reading, and this book couldn't exist without that foundation. To my parents, thank you for all your love and support. To my brother, thank you for encouraging me to take my ambition seriously. I want to especially thank the Steve Miller Band, who performed at Summerfest in 1982, my parents' second date. As the story goes, the band played its encore, and then Steve Miller said, "We've played every song we know, so we're just gonna start over." And they did. Hallelujah.

To the 21ders: For your wisdom, support, generosity, and humor. It's a privilege to debut with you all.

To fandom (all kinds): For helping me find my way back into music, and showing me how joyous it can be to love pop songs—and girls—and all these happy endings we create together.

'Til the moon crashes into the sea.